OUTSIDE DAYS

Very Best Wishes from

Max Hastings

December 1991

OUTSIDE DAYS

MAX HASTINGS

Line drawings by
William Geldart

MICHAEL JOSEPH
LONDON

MICHAEL JOSEPH LTD
Published by the Penguin Group
27 Wrights Lane, London W8 5TZ, England
Viking Penguin Inc., 40 West 23rd Street, New York, New York 10010, USA
Penguin Books Australia Ltd, Ringwood, Victoria, Australia
Penguin Books Canada Ltd, 2801 John Street, Markham, Ontario, Canada L3R 1B4
Penguin Books (NZ) Ltd, 182–190 Wairau Road, Auckland 10, New Zealand

Penguin Books Ltd, Registered Offices: Harmondsworth, Middlesex, England

First published October 1989
Second impression December 1989
Third impression February 1990

Copyright © Romadata 1989
Illustrations © William Geldart 1989

Set in Monophoto Plantin Light
Printed and bound in Great Britain by
Richard Clay Ltd, Bungay, Suffolk

A CIP catalogue record for this book is available from the British Library

ISBN 0 7181 3330 7

The illustration for Chapter 10,
Running away to the river bank,
is attributed to E. H. Shepard

To everybody who has put up with my
company over the years on the hill or
the river, in the sun or the rain – above
all my wife
TRICIA

CONTENTS

INTRODUCTION

I HAVE A WEAKNESS for Victorian sporting memoirs with titles like *Wild Sport and Some Stories, The Moor and the Loch, With Gun and Rod in the High Himalayas*. In a bookshop in Simla a few years ago, I came across a classic specimen of the genre, dedicated 'To Johnnie, my wife, the best pal a sportsman ever had'. I have always cherished a fancy to continue this minor literary tradition, though conscious that my own wife would think poorly of being classified as a 'pal'. My sensible publishers questioned whether anybody seeing the title *Outside Days* in a bookshop would have the faintest idea what the phrase means. I said it would strike an immediate chord for anyone with a love of field sports. Nobody else would be likely to get past the first few pages. It is a title which conveys – I hope with the appropriate hint of self-mockery – the notion that I am continuing the indulgent tradition of Victorian sportsmen, who believed that if it was worth putting up a rod or taking out a gun, then it was worth writing a book about the experience afterwards.

I met a racehorse trainer out shooting the other day, who asked what I did for a living. He professed surprise on discovering that I was a writer, indeed mostly a journalist. 'Not many people like you shoot, do they, or get asked to places like this?', he asked innocently. Lest this sounds as if I am patronizing his ignorance of my trade, I should add that, in my turn, I was asking him questions about whether he had produced any winners lately, oblivious of the fact that he stood fifth or sixth in the flat trainers' table. And he was perfectly justified in suggesting that not many writers shoot or fish or hunt, (although I remember meeting the present editor of *Horse and Hound* for the first time in the midst of a firefight in Cambodia and he talked about fox-hunting all day in a ditch).

In some measure, it is because few people who work in newspapers or television follow or sympathize with field sports, that those of us who do feel a responsibility to contribute what we can towards making the general public a little better informed about them. When opportunities arise, I write newspaper articles about country pursuits. And, like most writers, I also love putting pen to paper for its own sake. Writing about fishing and shooting days gives me almost as much pleasure as taking out a rod or gun. Many of the pieces I have written for country magazines have been designed to preserve, for my own memory, favourite moments on the hill or the river. My father, himself a writer, used to try to enthuse me as a teenager about 'the challenge of a blank sheet of paper'. I understand today, as I did not then, exactly what he meant.

This is a book about pleasures – rural pleasures, which mean much to me. It is not a book of instruction, and anybody who has ever seen me shoot or fish or ride a horse will acknowledge the importance of that disclaimer. Many sporting books are written by experts. Instead, I am writing as a mere enthusiast. 'Novelty and ignorance must always be reciprocal,' wrote Dr Johnson on his tour of the Hebrides, 'I cannot but be conscious that my thoughts on national manners are the thoughts of one who has seen but little.' Likewise there are many vastly more experienced grouse shooters, salmon fishers, stalkers who can write with greater knowledge than myself, when I am still relatively young and relatively green. This is, then, a collection of articles and essays about aspects of the countryside, field sports and my own dalliance with them.

I am, I think, a pretty typical field sportsman of my generation, in being only a part-time countryman. Although I have lived in the country for long spells, including a couple of years in Kilkenny, much of my working life is still spent in cities. From my modern office in the London docklands, I watch ducks and cormorants fly by. But the window will not open, to enable me to hear them. This sort of frustration is common to most of us, who spend much of our lives cut off from nature, and thus cherish it all the more passionately when we can escape into the wilderness. Dr Johnson, in the Hebrides again: 'Of these islands, it must be confessed that they have not many allurements but to the mere lover of naked nature.' Like so many of us in this urban age, I am a lover of 'naked nature'.

If I cannot claim a depth of knowledge, I have been lucky enough to sample a fair variety of sport, at home and abroad. Some of these experiences, like shooting duck in India or tiger-fishing on Lake Kariba, were by-days in the midst of assignments as a foreign correspondent. Others I owe to family or friends. I grew up in the south of England, knowing something about shooting and fishing, but next to nothing about horses. My wife, a Leicestershire girl, points out that I still know nothing about horses. Since we married, however, I have learned a little more about people who do know something about horses, and understand how disturbing overreaches are, even if I seldom suffer from them myself. I have only hunted a handful of times, but my wife has done so all her life. I have never dared to test our marriage to the limit of offering her a choice between a romantic weekend with me in Paris and one of the Quorn's good days.

Her story, anyway, is that I lead a selfish life and spend too much time working out how next to enjoy myself. Somewhere on the charge sheet, it is suggested that I can seldom find time to go and watch a horsy event with her, while I usually seem able to fit in a Monday shooting day, if one is on offer. She asks why I can't wait until I am sixty to fish salmon in Alaska or join another party on the Spey. I answer that I rather doubt whether anybody will still be asking me to anything by the time I am sixty. If I am run over by the proverbial bus, I want to be sure that I have not wasted a minute beforehand. When I was earning my shilling as an author and living in the country, I sometimes shot three days a week. I then came home, went to sleep for an hour and worked until after midnight to salvage my bank balance and conscience. Now that I sit behind a London office desk every day, it is difficult to fit the work around the sport in quite the same fashion. But I don't do badly.

Each sporting season seems to bring more pleasures than the last: the company and the settings are irresistible. I am even getting to the stage at which I don't mind so much whether I catch a fish or shoot dozens of pheasants, if the sun is shining and all is well with the world. One day last season on which I had shot next to nothing, I was back gun at the last drive. One by one, three cock pheasants came climbing back along the edge of the wood against the sunset, amid a barrage of gunfire from the line. Somehow, I managed to make each in turn crumple. The last one called for a long retrieve for my old dog. After five minutes, she came trotting back across the plough with the bird, pleased as punch and her master. Then, I didn't mind if I didn't shoot another pheasant all season. I was perfectly content with the fulfilment of that winter moment beneath the fading blue sky.

I feel exceptionally lucky about my lot in life: at home, in my work, on the moor or the loch. I cannot claim that it was alway so. When I was eighteen or nineteen, I was racked with self-pity that I had been brought up to love field sports, but never seemed likely to have the money or the opportunities to consummate my passion. Come to that, it seemed likely that, within a few years, socialism would triumph in Britain, and traditional country pastimes would be abolished.

Today, almost miraculously, the prospects for the future of both capitalism and field sports have been transformed. They seem brighter than any of us could have dared to hope a decade ago. My colleague Perry Worsthorne, cautioned us all in a *Sunday Telegraph* editorial after the 1987 general election against what he called 'bourgeois triumphalism'. Yet personally, having been teased by my contemporaries for years as a conservative, a follower of field sports, a young fogey, I am not in the least opposed to a little bourgeois triumphalism now that our side looks like winning against the odds. I shall discuss some of the difficulties of sustaining field sports against political pressures in the concluding chapter. I remain, however, an unashamed optimist.

Most of the pieces that follow are adapted from articles that have appeared in *The Daily Telegraph*, *The Field*, *Country Life*, *The Shooting Times*, *Country Times* and other publications. I hope readers will accept the collection in the spirit that I intend it: as a modest celebration of field sports, from a follower rather than a master of any of them. My mother has often lamented the frightful damage my father did to my overdraft from an early age to the present day by encouraging me in expensive rural passions. I have to say that I do not regret a penny (not even the bill for that week in Norway in which we never glimpsed a salmon). The countryside has given everything back to me in generous and happy measure.

MAX HASTINGS
Guilsborough Lodge,
Northamptonshire

GREAT EXPECTATIONS

ONE DAY, SEVERAL seasons ago, one of the four guns in our little shoot was away and sent the sons of two friends to take his pegs. At the first drive, half a dozen pheasants flew over one of these London guests, a pleasant young man of twenty-four or so, and were roundly missed.

Afterwards, our keeper had a discreet little moan about marksmanship. He and I seldom disagree, but we did on this occasion. I said that I could never get cross about anybody's shooting, unless he was dangerous. These two guests had told me how few days they ever got and they were touchingly pleased to have this one. More than that, I remembered so vividly how poorly I shot myself at their age. To explain: nowadays I sometimes shoot badly. In those days, I did so with frightful consistency.

Unless one is lucky enough to be born the son of a great estate owner, it is a painful and frustrating business growing up with a passion for shooting. Among the landless, until we are past thirty, few of us either have the money to pay for our own sport or enough well-placed friends to invite us to share theirs.

My father, Macdonald Hastings, was an enthusiastic syndicate shooter. More than that, he was the author of several books on the sport and had ghost-written a well-known textbook by the gunsmith Robert Churchill, *Churchill on Game-shooting*. I grew up in a house full of guns, books about guns and sporting equipment of every kind.

My father sometimes took me to stand behind him at the marvellous Iliffe shoot at Yattendon in Berkshire, although, characteristically of childhood, my clearest recollection is of an autumn partridge day when I grew bored and stuck a row of empty cartridge cases on my fingers. One of them proved to contain a bee. There are other childish memories: of the misery of being sent to walk through a field of kale among a line of beaters who, unlike me, were wearing waterproof leggings; of the odd day decoying pigeons in the stubble with a 20-bore, my first gun; of a pioneering trip to Scotland, which I adored, where I shot my first grouse at fourteen – it was ten years before I had the chance to shoot another.

My early teenage enthusiasm, though, was founded upon the frail foundation of not more than a dozen days a year when I went out with a gun, perhaps three of them with my father. He did not rent any Scottish sport to which he could take a boy, confining himself instead to grouse and salmon parties with male chums. Occasionally, we shared target practice on the lawn with a .22. I never went to a shooting school then. Since I don't believe many of us improve at anything unless we are coached, perhaps it is not surprising that my principal recollection is of how badly I shot. How many cartridges did I fire for each bird I brought down? Seven, eight, nine? Something like that. I never seemed to get any better and the knowledge depressed me. Then, when I was sixteen and my father was a little over fifty, he lost his own interest in killing things and gave up shooting.

His enthusiasm for spectating and writing about sport persisted, but his access to it was gone. Perhaps once a year, a kindly local farmer invited me to join a walking-up day. However the equation then was much as it will always remain: if you are seen to shoot badly, it is unlikely that anybody will be in a rush to ask you again. People are most commonly asked to shoot because they themselves own good shoots; for the pleasure of their wit, marksmanship or celebrity; or in pursuit of commercial advantage. Until one is old enough to have made friends and a way in the world, invitations are likely to be few, unless one can reciprocate them.

The nearest I came to serious sport was leafing through the pages of *Shooting Times* which I had sent to me at school every week. There was a local farm where I enjoyed a licence to walk the hedges, and did so enthusiastically for seven or eight years, shooting a pheasant or two more often than not. I lacked a dog, though, and dogless shooting is ineffectual and frustrating because of the difficulties of picking up anything one brings down. Many evenings I sat in my father's library, leafing through the tales of great Victorian sportsmen, gloomily resigned by my early twenties to the feeling that none of the real sport would ever be for me. At twenty-three, I took half a gun I could ill afford in a Hampshire syndicate composed of men much older than myself. I shot too badly to enjoy it and found the social side hard-going. At twenty-four, things improved enormously when, with a little group of friends, I took a dogging moor in Sutherland, of which more later. A passion was born that has never since deserted me, for both Sutherland and shooting over pointers. Yet, even through the years of repeat visits that followed, down south in the winter I found few invitations and still missed legions of pheasants when I did go out. I made a note in my gamebook, just short of my thirtieth birthday, about the absurdity of being so fond of shooting, yet having so few opportunities to do it, and using them so poorly when I did so.

It was not until I was ten years older and made a conscious resolution to do something about my marksmanship that the perspective began to change. I put myself in the hands of the splendid Michael Rose at the West London shooting school.

Session by session, Michael began to move me step by painful step, from being a very poor shot, to becoming an adequate one. Now, this is where the sad part comes in. Very early on, Michael made me empty my mind of all the old ideas on which I had been reared – of my father's Churchill-inspired teaching of 'the theory of automatic allowance'. This sometimes worked for men shooting with Churchill's short 25-inch barrelled guns, he said, but not for a man shooting with normal 28- or 30-inch barrels, as I was.

From the moment that I began to seek to lead the bird in the conventional manner, my aim improved and so too, dramatically, did my enjoyment of the sport. As I approached an age at which I was lucky enough not only to be able to pay for good shooting, but to receive a generous share of invitations, I found that I could do something like justice to driven pheasants, even if I was still an indifferent performer at grouse. I could not help feeling some sense of betrayal, looking back upon my father's lifelong commitment to Churchill and his methods. I once cherished the idea of revising the book for a modern edition. Today, I feel that it would be dishonest to do so. The technique did nothing for me.

I felt a little better about it, however, when I came across a fifty-year-old gamebook of my father's, from a period of a year or two when he noted down his record of cartridges to kills. He was averaging around four or five to one, which scarcely spoke well for the influence of Churchill on his own shooting.

Now that my children are of an age to shoot, I try to give them more chances than I had. That is to say, it remains in their own hands whether or not they want to do it, for I am against driving a child in any direction. But if they do, then at our shoot one of them can share my peg. We extend the same invitation to any guests who want to bring sons. I don't think it does much damage to the pheasant population and it seems a safer practice than encouraging boys to wander off with the beating line, where they cannot be supervised. At the end of every October, we have a boys' shoot. This used to take place in January, until we discovered that the birds on those frosty and windy days were too testing for young shots. Nowadays, we find that a walk around the outsides at the beginning of the season pleases our sons and usefully shakes up the pheasants.

In sport, as with everything else, when we are young we think that we can avoid making all the mistakes our parents made. As we get a little older, we understand that we can simply make a different set. Today, I see my son sulking a little after missing half a dozen walked-up grouse and I tell him from the heart that I know exactly how he feels, because that is how I felt when I was his age, except that I never had six grouse on the trot to shoot at. A few boys are natural shots as teenagers. Most, like the Hastingses *père et fils*, are not. For myself, I care only that he should master his sport with a decade less pain and frustration than I went through.

PATERNAL BLESSINGS

MANY COUNTRY PEOPLE – indeed, experts on any subject –
find it irritating that most of those who make a living by
pontificating in newspapers or on television are less knowledge-
able than themselves. I have seen this myself, when interview-
ing war veterans for military history books. There comes a
moment in their reminiscences of bombers over Germany,
tanks in Normandy, destroyers in the Arctic, when suddenly
they ask themselves why they are telling *me* the story, rather
than making money out of it themselves.

The answer, of course, is that the only difference between
us is that I possess a certain facility with words, which
confers an unjust advantage when it comes to telling a tale.
And thus it is that the majority of those who make television

films about nature and the countryside, garage their unblemished Range Rovers in places like Chiswick or East
Cheam. They – or perhaps we – leech off the knowledge of
real countrymen, who live hard lives in remote places. The
most barbed exclamation of abuse that is thrown at me by my
wife, a forthright farmer's daughter, goes something like this:
'Oh, you're so urban! Why don't you take that Shogun of
yours back to London where it belongs?' This sally is usually
prompted by my committing some crime, such as wandering
around the garden without bothering to put on gumboots and
then walking through the house in my shoes, which she says
no properly-educated countryman would do. Other mis-
demeanours in the same category include showing signs of
impatience with local acquaintances who intercept me rushing
somewhere and want to dally for a chat; buying unsuitably
urban bedding plants for the garden; discussing in a public
place the shortcomings of a horse somebody is trying to sell;
or suggesting a nameboard at the end of the drive to prevent
those looking for the house from forever getting lost.

Most of these sins my wife attributes to my hybrid upbring-
ing, and I am not sure that she is wrong. My father was one
of the most successful of the first television generation of
country commentators and writers, but he, too, spent much
of his own life in London and never owned more than nine
suburban acres. He possessed an intensely romantic view of
the countryside, based upon far wider reading than most
countrymen aspire to, but only a slender basis of personal
experience. Yet he made a long succession of splendid television films about Britain's rivers and canals, wildlife and
birds, farmers and field sportsmen. In the fifties and sixties, he
played a significant part in explaining to the urban public
some of the realities of rural life, at a time when most people
in Britain were growing ever more remote from these.

He wrote a series of detective thrillers set against rural
backgrounds. His fictional hero was the elderly chairman of a
big insurance company, Montague Cork. Today, the books
still give me much pleasure, but they are incurably dated.
Such women as appear in them are housekeepers, secretaries
or remote goddesses to be worshipped rather than invited to

bed and the books are thickly populated with recent war veterans, evil foreigners and mad squires. Even so, I find Father's picture in *Cork in Bottle* of the remoteness and primitiveness of some Norfolk coastal villages even in post-war times convincing, if melodramatic.

My own enthusiasm for Sutherland was first fired by *Cork on the Water*, a salmon fishing tale that he wrote with the Helmsdale partly in mind. He conveyed splendidly his affection for country places, even if his country characters were often stereotypes.

For a while in the fifties, he edited and part-owned (at ruinous cost to his overdraft) a magazine called *Country Fair*, to which he attracted marvellous contributors, who wrote about rural life in a rather more down-to-earth fashion than some country publications contrive to do today. A. G. Street, who was co-editor and a warm personal friend, was the real article – a Wiltshire farmer who turned to authorship only in middle age. Street's books, mostly written in the thirties, are at last being republished in the eighties, and very well they read, too.

I think Father was regarded by most of his rural acquaintances as a charming eccentric, rather than one of themselves. Like most children, I grew up regarding his behaviour as perfectly normal, until I had lived apart from him for long enough to gain a sense of perspective.

Shooting on the Berkshire Downs in the early fifties, Father liked to end the day with a little target practice using some of the large selection of German automatic weapons he had looted in the war. The garden seat at my mother's house still bears the scars of the time I emptied one of his Lugers into it at the age of twelve, supposing that this was a perfectly reasonable Sunday afternoon amusement. There was the time, too, when Father became bored by shooting with modern shotguns and turned out with a selection of muzzle-loading flintlocks and percussion-capped weapons. These left him wreathed in smoke after every shot and did not do much damage to the partridges. They satisfied his enthusiasm, though, in much the same way as the extravagant firework displays he laid on for himself from time to time.

I believed for a long while that father had devoted most of his sporting life to double-gun shoots on grand estates. It was only when I began to take an interest in his past that I learned how little of his childhood or youth had been spent in the countryside. He came to game-shooting only when he rented a very rough shoot in Sussex in the late thirties. I have pictures of him in those days, wearing unsuitable clothes and clutching a .22 rifle in a dangerous manner. It was only when he acquired a girlfriend with a more highly-developed sense of country standards that he cleaned up both his appearance and his shooting.

He possessed to a high degree one of the most important attributes of eccentricity – an absolute lack of self-consciousness or self-knowledge. He was never impeded by seeing his actions as others might regard them. One day in the early sixties, he took me out from school to go with him to a country house near Haslemere where he planned to do some filming. Before the war, he knew a cottage on the estate where lived a seventeenth-century executioner – reputed, indeed, to be the regicide of 1649. As an act of bravado, this character had set in the lintel above his front door a wooden representation of a headsmans' axe. There, at least, it had been in 1939.

Lunch with the new and unknown owners of the estate in 1962 proved a trifle sticky, or so it seemed to me as a teenager. They knew nothing about any headsman's axe, but, after coffee, we all trooped solemnly down to the cottage and were admitted by a bemused cowman's wife. We inspected the lintel behind the front door. Not only was there no axe, but the wall was newly plastered.

Father was momentarily disconcerted, but quickly recovered. Drawing a penknife from his pocket, he chipped away an inch or two of plaster to get at the wood beneath. Still detecting no signs of the axe, he levered away some more plaster, ignoring the increasingly intense hand-wringing going on behind him on the part of the cowman's wife. Several square inches later, he concluded that more serious measures were required, and telephoned to Haslemere for professional aid. An hour or two later, most of the wall had been hacked away by the plasterers, or rather deplasterers, when an aged yokel stopped to watch, and asked what was going on: 'You looking for that axe thing? Why, that was taken away to the museum these twenty years ago . . .' At that moment, the cowman entered and began an extended and impassioned oration with the words: 'I may not know much about my rights, but I do know . . .'

As we drove away, Father was the only man in that corner of Sussex oblivious to the trail of havoc he had left behind. Hesitantly, I hinted at this: 'No, no, of course it's all right boy, you don't understand', he said dismissively, 'I shall send the man's wife some flowers tomorrow . . .' Dear Father.

I have somewhere at home the angular stainless steel lock handle with which he was presented by the British Waterways Board, for his contribution to public understanding of the national treasure we possess in the canal system. I also inherited a collection of impedimenta for brief and vanished enthusiasms that would put Toad's boat-house to shame: rabbit nets and ferret lines, powder horns and line driers, falcons' hoods, spurs with rowels that my wife claims would cause any self-respecting animal-lover to summon the R S P C A, and horsewhips in profusion.

The last-mentioned items, it must be said, were a trifle fraudulent. Although father always claimed that Hunting, Shooting and Fishing were his pastimes, I doubt whether he rode to hounds more than a couple of dozen times in his life, the most recent *circa* 1950. But affectations of this sort were dear to him. Having formed a picture of himself in his own mind, he was determined to stick with it through thick and thin. Unlike many urban countrymen, however, he did not seek after a sanitised image of rural England: 'Death and sex are the principal business of the countryside,' he declared with relish and, although a naturally gentle man, his supply of instruments of death would have made Nancy Mitford's Uncle Matthew envious. He sought to persuade me that the most efficient means of dispatching a wounded bird was to crush its skull in one's teeth. If I was asked for an abiding image of Father, he would be set in the shooting field, a pheasant's head between his jaws. Great as was my affection for him, it never extended to emulating this example.

Although we had some bad-tempered quarrels when I was a teenager, in Father's later life we found ourselves in accord about almost everything. I admired his essays about the countryside. 'If there are three things that foreigners give us credit for,' he wrote, in characteristically romantic mood, '. . . these are the lushness of our grass, the beauty of our children and the mettle of our horses. Why then, when all three are brought together, do we who speak Shakespeare's tongue call the occasion a gymkhana?'

He adored the works of Sir Arthur Bryant, above all the lyrical passages that described the eighteenth-century Agricultural Revolution; and of course Dickens and Surtees. Wessex was his favourite region of England, though he also loved Cumberland and Northumberland. I shall say something later of the passion for Scotland that he passed on to me.

It is remarkable how, for most of us, childhood sensations of enthusiasm or dismay persist for the rest of our lives: I can never stand Surrey, because I was unhappy at school there. However, Father's devotion to Hampshire and Berkshire remains with me, even now the best parts of those counties have become suburbia, the chalk streams corrupted by an excess of tame trout.

It is seven years since father died, and relatively few people remember his books or television programmes. He never made much money out of them, because he shot the films in that innocent period before presenters commanded star salaries and he wrote the books he wanted to, rather than the ones that would sell. I have them all on the shelf beside me now. One of the pleasures of coming from a family of writers – I am the third generation – is that, long after they are gone, one can summon up a vivid image of the people they were, by reading their books. Father may not have been a true rustic, any more than I am. But he imbued me with a passion for England and the English countryside that I have cherished all my life. If he did something of the same for a wider public, then I do not think his contribution was negligible.

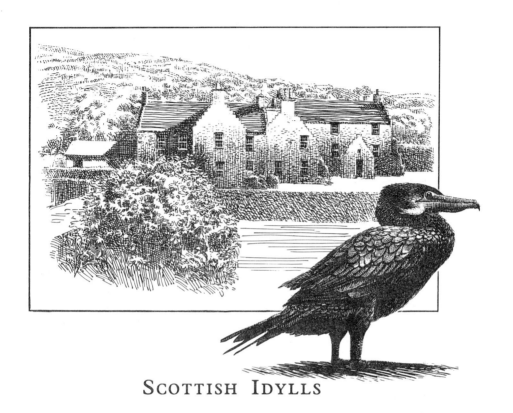

SCOTTISH IDYLLS

IN MY TEENS, I formed a romantic enthusiasm for Scotland, based upon a single holiday visit to work on a farm in Invernesshire, where I also spent a few days on the hill and shot the odd grouse. My feelings were reinforced by a taste for Scottish history and the novels of John Buchan. In the spring of 1970, I made up my mind that if I was going to pursue my distant love affair with the Highlands, it was no good waiting for invitations.

I rang up that estimable institution Messrs Strutt & Parker, and asked them to send me particulars of Scottish lodges to let, at less than extortionate rents. Five or six sets of particulars dropped through the letter box in the next few weeks. From these, I chose one, more or less at random: the House of Tongue, in Sutherland, on the northern coast of furthest Britain.

I knew nothing of Tongue, and little more of Sutherland, except that my father loved it. I arranged to take it for a fortnight in September.

Now, when September came, to my great embarrassment I was sitting among a throng of other newspaper correspondents in the Inter-Continental Hotel in Amman, watching a Jordanian civil war get underway. Hour by hour, the situation was deteriorating. The threat of being beseiged for weeks hung over us. After some ruthless chicanery towards both my newspapers and the airline industry that does not matter here, I escaped from Amman one morning on a plane that subsequently proved to be the last civil flight out of Jordan for days.

On the way from Heathrow, I stopped for ten minutes at my London flat to change clothes and collect guns and rods. I arrived out of breath on the platform at Euston, just in time to meet my father and a cluster of friends whom I had invited to join the party – and share the cost. We clambered on board the Royal Highlander, bound for Inverness.

Father had a gift for imbuing with magic journeys to places that he cherished. As we rattled north in the dining car, in those long-lost days when night sleepers served dinner, he reminisced delightfully about Scotland in general and Sutherland in particular, through half a dozen of those little miniature whisky bottles. None of the rest of us was over thirty, or knew Scotland well. We were enchanted. We woke in the morning to look out upon those wonderful final miles past Newtonmore, Aviemore and Carrbridge, until at last we rolled into Inverness and sat down to porridge and kippers at the Station Hotel. We had arranged to hire two Land Rovers from a local garage. Once loaded, we set off northwards.

Father possessed a limitless stock of local anecdotage – of the days when James Robertson Justice kept his beautiful house and falcons on the Dornoch Firth, of old acquaintances such as Eric Linklater, and of Glen Grant, the butcher at Dornoch whom father insisted was the finest of his kind in the Highlands. He made us divert thirty unregretted miles to view Grant's carcasses and buy a cargo of beef.

It was afternoon before we rounded the hill above the Kyle of Tongue and looked down upon a view that I still think the best in Scotland: the ruined tower on the hill across the estuary, the estate farm buildings nestling among the corn stooks, the sea reaching out to the cluster of islands offshore. We drove down through the village towards the sea, searching for a glimpse of the house we had come to find. At last, we drew up alongside a large, solid, Victorian edifice that seemed the only place in Tongue large enough to be ours. My heart sank. Had I brought a dozen friends more than 600 miles north to spend a fortnight in this? I walked up to the front door and knocked. A face appeared. No, this was not the House of Tongue, but the youth hostel. What we were looking for was around the corner.

Still uncertain, we turned beyond the point, and drove a few hundred yards along the seaside, until we came to a high, grey stone wall with a flagpole on the corner. We turned again, along a drive to a long creeper-clad, seventeenth-century house, fronted with flagstones as old as time, encircled by perfectly kept lawns, sheltered from the sea by the garden wall. It is a figure of speech to declare that one's heart leapt, but mine did so then. I thought, as I have thought ever since, that this was the most beautiful house in Britain: not grand, not imposing, but simply perfectly set amid its surroundings. We ran through the garden, gazing at the borders, still blooming with the sort of flowers that were finished in England in August. I climbed the ladder to stand upon the wall, looking down at the Kyle of Tongue, the boat moored at the end of the little stone pier and the essential ingredients of *moules marinières* clinging to the rocks above the tide line among the kelp. The only sounds were the cries of the sea birds.

The house itself was furnished not in the stark pine of most rented lodges, but in the generous chintzes and tartans of a Scottish country home. 'You're very lucky, boy,' said my father wryly. He was captivated, as I was.

In the days that followed, we fished the little river Borgie and walked miles over the hills. We took the boat out across the Kyle and had barbecues on the sands of Rabbit Island, where we sat marooned until the tide rose again to float our transport. A study of the old gamebooks in the house revealed how the island got its name. Right up to World War II, successive Dukes of Sutherland killed rabbits in their hundreds there. In the boat-house also hung a rack of harpoons, testimony to bloodier ducal pastimes.

We went after mackerel from the tiny, lonely, perfect little harbour at Skerray. I have always enjoyed sea fishing, but we felt embarrassed about what to do with the catch. After one day pitching and rolling off the cliffs with our long lines of feathered hooks, we took home over a hundred fish. We ate mackerel for breakfast and mackerel pâté for dinner for three days, then, rather shamefacedly, tipped the balance off the end of our little pier.

We decoyed rock pigeons among the stooks along the seashore, crouching in the gorse alongside as the birds fluttered down. A dozen pigeons was a good afternoon's bag, but they gave us something to do when the weather was too wet to go to the hill.

Having a passion for fireworks, I had ordered a vast box and we set them off to fine reflective effect above the waters of the Kyle.

In a true Piccadilly Highlanders' gesture, one night we arranged for a piper to drive over from the Strath of Kildonan to play for us. He stood on the end of the garden wall while we danced incompetent reels on the flagstones in the darkness outside the front door. The idea provoked fits of giggles among friends who heard about it afterwards. We thought it was wonderful.

We lived almost entirely off the food of the country: grouse, salmon, trout, kippers, porridge, the odd load of lobsters or crabs from Skerray. When we were not catching salmon, we swapped grouse for fish with more successful visitors to the river. Vegetables came from the garden. One of the finest in the Highlands, it was tended by Hughie, a quiet young man never seen without his Scottish Nationalist badge. He had done a spell with the Yorkshire police as a motorway patrol driver, but resigned and returned to the far north in presbyterian disgust at the inadequate sentences meted out to offending motorists by southern magistrates. We liked

Hughie, who sometimes came to the hill with us to carry the gamebag, and talk about the shortcomings of English management of Scotland, without apparent personal ill-will towards our own Englishness.

The great sweep of hills, the moonscape views of glittering lochs from the summits, the silence and the sea reaching away towards arctic nothingness combine to make the north of Scotland an intensely emotional place. Passions run strongly. Tears and laughter, happiness and melancholy, come easily. Later, when I grew to know Sutherland in winter as well as in summer, it became easy to understand the compulsive drinking and seasonal gloom of so many of the inhabitants. The shadow of the Highland Clearances hangs heavy over the region, above all in Strathnaver, where the most brutal evictions took place. We all read John Prebble's powerful book on the clearances. Two of our guests were still arguing about it over tea at the Station Hotel in Inverness on the way home. Their neighbour at the next table listened for a while, leaned over and scribbled 'John Prebble' in the flyleaf before he left. One of many things I love about Scotland is that it is such a small place.

Very quickly, one moulds oneself into the isolation of the hills. For us at Tongue, even a drive to the tiny station at Lairg to pick up a new arrival, or to shop forty miles along the coast at Thurso, created an unwelcome culture shock, encountering people and cars in relative quantity again. The joy of single-track roads with passing places is that they create a formidable deterrent to the casual tourist, who likes to keep hold of a lifeline to civilization.

Over the years that followed our first visit, the friends who came with us to Tongue pursued a fine range of enthusiasms: there were the sketchers, the gatherers of wild flowers, the shooters – of whom more anon – the walkers, the fishers. I have always enjoyed drifting across a loch with a fellow fisher and a boatman, trailing a leash of flies in pursuit of small trout. I find the stew-bred fish of southern English lakes and rivers almost inedible, but the delicate pink flesh of a wild Scottish loch trout is unbeatable at the breakfast table. It seems a crime that some lochs are even now being stocked with alien rainbows, matching our English follies.

Today, my family and friends look back on our boating expeditions of twenty years ago and blanch at the memory of what we got away with. Trips to the further offshore islands, most often the deserted village on Eilan Na Ron – Seal Island – in a heavy old steel ship's lifeboat powered by an untrustworthy Seagull outboard, usually involved a breakdown somewhere when a wave swamped the motor or the propeller struck a rock. Then everybody rowed frantically to hold the boat in the swirling currents or to avoid beaching ourselves on the shifting sandbanks. I enjoyed every moment of it. Others have since confided that they were just plain terrified.

I fell in love with my wife at Tongue, not least because she combined an ability to cook better than our paid cook, look more feminine and beautiful than any other guest at the dinner table, and keep up with them all on the hill the next day. Her enthusiasm for joining the party diminished somewhat after we were married, because she began to have a sight of the bills I was paying for each summer holiday, which she knew was wildly extravagant for our slender income. But we took our small son up there four years later, and I cut holes in the bottom of a rucksack for his legs so that I could take him to the hill on my shoulders. I am suitably grateful that he is now old enough to do his walking for himself.

It is two decades since we went to Tongue for the first time and, in the intervening years, I have stayed in a good few Scottish houses and lodges. Many have had better shooting or fishing. Some have had wonderful cooks. Others have gathered delightful company. But nowhere has matched the grip that the House of Tongue gained upon my imagination. It was my first love in Scotland; and the memory of first loves is inimitable.

POINTING AND SETTING

IN THE SUMMER of 1971, for the princely sum of £450, with two friends I rented for the season a 25,000 acre moor in Sutherland, a few miles from Tongue, together with the right to shoot 125 brace of grouse. None of us, on that first sunny September morning beside a loch, had ever seen pointers work before. Three guns, assorted wives and loved ones, together with the keeper's rather corpulent teenage son carrying the gamebag, crossed a rickety little bridge across the river and stood curious and expectant. The keeper loosed the first pointer, a wonderfully slim, tense, black and white dog named Sue. She began to lope to and fro across a 200 yard front, nose down in the heather, the shooting party straggling companionably behind.

After some fifteen minutes, Sue froze, tail rigidly horizontal, head and body bent into the wind. The keeper directed us to line out on either side of her. Inch by inch, he coaxed her forward, her companion, Seamus, pointing behind. Suddenly, there was an explosion from the heather in front of us, and a dozen grouse were in the air. Novices, we were slow to get our guns up, but the ragged volley that ensued brought down three or four birds.

We picked up amid the usual outbreak of excited chatter and recriminations that follow the long seconds of silence on point. We stroked the grouse, marvelling – as I still do – at the softness and delicacy of their plumage, compared with the cheerful vulgarity of the pheasant's. Then we marched on across the hill, collecting a bird here, a brace there, until by tea-time we clumped wearily but utterly contentedly back to the Land Rover with twelve brace in the bag. Three weeks later, we finished up with ninety. Ever since that day, I have been a passionate devotee of dogging grouse. To me, the combination of those long, lonely walks high in the heather, the sense of exploration for birds, the magic of watching the pointers go about their business, come as close to perfection as any form of sport.

We shot that moor, the same little group of us, for five seasons. I have killed grouse there on odd days many times since. In later years, though, the stock of birds was much diminished and we no longer had the time, as we did in those salad days, to spend three weeks at a time on the hill, learning every ripple in the heather.

We came to know all the idiosyncrasies of each other's shooting. Being of an impatient disposition, I usually got my gun up first. One of our companions, on the other hand, seemed to take a while even to notice that grouse were in the air. We waited, bemused, while he thought about them for long seconds, but then his gun went to his shoulder and, again and again, at extreme ranges, birds came down.

The dogs, too, had their little ways. Sue would run herself ragged in the search for grouse, a mass of canine nervous energy. Her accomplice, Seamus, was a big brown brute of a German pointer, who performed well in his day, but would never drop to shot. Rather, he would bolt forward and scoff a dead grouse down to the claws in a few seconds unless one ran faster and beat him to it. Seamus was also uncommonly hard to restrain on the leash until a Highland farmer friend, shooting with us one day, drove his enormous boot swiftly between the dog's hind legs when he pulled once too often. Thereafter, Seamus recognised that he had met his match. Both these dogs were marvels at pointing their birds far enough out to keep them on the ground, even if the wind was against them. In later years, I have shot over less expert pointers and setters who have ruined a morning's shooting by overrunning the coveys with dreary consistency. Nothing is more frustrating when grouse are scarce, and there may be another mile to walk before the next point.

Yet a large part of the thrill of those long marches in Sutherland, to extremities of the moor that the keeper said had not been visited for years, lay in the sense of hunting for grouse. More recently, I found myself walking behind pointers on an Invernesshire moor stiff with birds, which we were shooting for a week before it was driven. I did not enjoy the experience half so much, with a point every few yards. The suspense, the uncertainty was gone. I preferred the sort of days we enjoyed for several of our later seasons in Sutherland, walking with a wonderful retired keeper. I don't think he will mind my mentioning his name – Alec Macdonald.

Alec is over eighty, but still covers the ground like a teenager. His dogs are wizards. They are more slightly built than our old friends Sue and Seamus, but they work the hill brilliantly. A day with Alec and his pointers, seldom shooting more than six or seven brace, is my idea of what Scottish sport is all about. On our best day ever in Sutherland, we shot only sixteen brace. We were never reduced to the desperate nineteenth-century expedience of Mr Scott of Annegrove, who one day found himself so overladen with grouse that he tied strings around his trousers at the ankle and dropped birds down his waistband as he shot his way home. But there were many afternoons when the gamebag seemed inordinately heavy, after ten miles across country and a thousand feet uphill.

In our first seasons almost two decades ago, we suffered grievously from the absence of retrievers. There is no bird like a grouse for falling dead into a deep drain or tucking itself, wounded, into thick heather, where even a good labrador can walk over it. Dogless, we depended on long eyesight searches or coaxing the pointers into marking fallen birds, which they seldom cared much for.

Then there were the grouse that fell into lochs. More than once, one of us waded into waist-deep water to pick out a bird. There was a notable occasion when our fishing party came back to the house in the evening clutching three brace of trout and a grouse they had netted. It splashed stone dead beside their boat, after flying strongly for half a mile from the point of shot. How often all of us have lost birds that succeed in breasting a Scottish horizon, of which there are so many, before falling. Once out of sight, grouse are very hard to pick. I have never shared the view that walked-up or dogged grouse always present easy shots, as contemptuous critics claim. Of course there are shameful days when one finds that one has murdered cheepers, reflex having caused one to shoot too quickly to check. But mounting a gun at an away bird, there is often no opportunity for a corrective swing onto the target. I make a terrible mess of those shots.

We loved the occasional day on the high tops, puffing and panting up onto the rocky scree almost 2,000 feet up from the sea, in search of ptarmigan. We seldom met them and, when we did, we were usually caught unawares, unloaded or wrong-footed or in thick mist. We saw a few golden plover, and had some marvellous encounters with deer at close quarters, a sight that made the day more than any shot. We gazed down from the ridge upon the R A F's jets, streaking disconcertingly below us on training flights.

Sometimes we used a boat across Loch Loyal, to ferry us to and from the beat. There was an evening when one of those sudden Highland gales blew up while we were on passage home. We were very frightened that our craft would founder, overloaded as it was with people and pointers, while waves dashed over the prow. We feared for the loss of our precious guns. Then the keeper announced a more pressing concern – he could not swim. Somehow, we came safe home.

I tell my wife that it was on one of those blue days among the tummocks below Ben Stumanadh that I discovered how deeply I felt for her. The pointer had been moving forward in fits and starts for several hundred yards, pursuing grouse that we could not see, but which were obviously running in front of us. Suddenly, we heard a whirr of wings and I spun towards the sound, to see a good covey getting up behind, at my then fiancée's feet. The grouse were an easy shot, if I took her with them. True love is watching a spread of birds vanish over the horizon unshot at. That was my story, anyway.

The quality of those pointing and setting dogs varies enormously. Some cover great swathes of ground, never overrun their birds even in poor conditions. Others are worse than useless. It is better to walk-up grouse with no dogs at all, than to go to the hill with pointers or setters too lazy to cover their ground or too wild to stand steady. The steadiest ones of all, of course, pose a special problem: if they are ranging widely on a thinly-stocked moor, they can drop onto a point out of sight and take half an hour or more to find again.

We discovered over the years that we needed at least three or four dogs, to be sure of fielding a team every day. In that big, wild country, it was essential to run two in rotation, twenty minutes at a time. Even then at the end of a long day, unless they were properly fit, their pads became raw and sore. There was always at least one dog unfit to shoot, and often two. When I see a serious dog handler setting off for the moor with six or seven dogs, I know that this is by no means an affectation.

Nowadays, I feel more relaxed about grouse shooting. I have learned to appreciate that, if it is raining or there are no grouse or one is shooting badly, there will always be tomorrow, and, after tomorrow, next season. In those first years, however, each day of dogging commanded passionate concentration. Every miss was a misery; every hit an ecstasy; the scenery and the dogs and the birds and my companions, fragments of heaven. I cherish the memory. Dogging in good company and bright sunshine will always be my first choice for a day on the hill.

'WIND HIM IN, THEN!'

MOST BOYS ARE thrilled by the chance to catch a salmon, but few, I think, develop a deep passion for salmon fishing until they are in their late twenties at least. Teenagers find shooting more rewarding. Even with modern carbon fibre rods, it can be hard work casting a long line all day across water that shows no sign of life. Few boys can work up the conviction, essential to every cast of the day for a successful salmon fisher, that *this* will be the one that hooks a fish. Now that I am over forty, I achieve almost the same eager expectation as I watch my line drift across the stream at six pm as I did when I started at nine am. But, I cannot say that I felt like this at sixteen, because I had never caught a salmon.

In those days, after an hour or two's floppy casting, my

spirit sagged and I searched for an excuse to pack it in, the very next time I cracked a fly off. I fished once on Testwood Pool, then a wonderful stretch of water near Southampton where my father caught his share of fish in the fifties. But I came home with nothing more than a handful of foul-hooked grey mullet. On the Borgie in Sutherland, a difficult little spate river, the combination of my own ignorance and the shortage of fish ensured that I never did any good. For every novice salmon fisher, much depends upon having the luck to be properly taught by a good ghillie – shown not only how to cast, but also how to identify the likeliest places in a pool. I wasted countless hours on the Borgie, fishing in a fashion that I know with hindsight never gave me a chance of success. If I was starting all over again today, I would go and spend a week at one of the excellent fishing schools run by the likes of Arthur Oglesby or Hugh Falkus. This would have saved me a lot of wasted time and maybe even some money.

I was thirty-two, an adequate fly-fisherman with plenty of trout behind me, before I caught my first salmon. We were living in Ireland, beside the River Nore in County Kilkenny. One of our neighbours a few miles downstream was a delightful, raffish character named Freddy Teignmouth – Lord Teignmouth to *Who's Who*. A short, slight figure who won a D S C commanding torpedo boats in the war and then spent an improbable fifteen years designing clothes for Hardy Amies, Fred had recently retired to the family's rather ugly Victorian pile in Kilkenny to devote himself to shooting and fishing. He was a master of both, a superbly elegant and economical shot. I have seen a line of guns clap him to the echo for bringing down an impossibly high pheasant. He was a fine fisherman with both fly and spinning rod and I watched him for many hours as he cast across the pools of his beloved Nore.

One March afternoon, with the river high, Fred thought there was a chance and invited me over. He settled me on the bank with one of my father's old cane spinning rods, a Hardy Super-Silex reel, and a large Devon. Then he retired up the hill to the house to watch a rugger international. I had been throwing the bait for about twenty minutes when a fish took.

For a few seconds, I was sure I was foul-hooked. Then, as the taut line was slowly towed across the current, I understood that there was a salmon on the end. I knew it was critical to maintain tension on the fish. I wound in until I encountered strong resistance. The rod was bent into a bow. Terrified to tighten further lest I make a mistake, I stood on the bank and wondered what on earth to do next. The nylon line seemed so frail; the dead weight on the end so great. Somehow, I must hang onto the fish, which seemed perfectly content to hold its ground in the current all afternoon. It was a stand-off. I simply settled down to wait for Freddy.

It must have been half an hour before I glimpsed him stepping lightly towards the river bank, the invariable cigarette-holder in hand, some Cowardesque period line on his lips: 'What a gas!' Fred took one look and said, 'What are you waiting for? Wind him in, then!' What, just like that? Fred showed his impatience, and told me to get on with it. Ten minutes later, he netted a fifteen pounder for me.

Like every novice salmon fisher, I was fascinated by the beauty of the fish that Fred wanted to treat so nonchalantly. I felt like taking it to bed with me. Instead, of course, we simply ate it. I yearned more than ever to get properly to grips with fishing for salmon with a fly. It was marvellous to have caught a fish. But I cannot say that either then or now I find playing salmon on spinning tackle a very satisfying experience.

The following April, I was invited to the Helmsdale. I had fished there briefly in the hot summer of 1976, when the water was so low as to be virtually impossible. In the spring of 1978, however, I reached Sutherland to find the river in perfect condition, and full of fish. The rest of the party were highly experienced and equipped with carbon rods. When I began to cast with one of my father's limp old cane rods, I suffered a good deal of mirth from the others at the expense of both my tackle and my technique. Indeed, looking back on it, I was casting so badly that I cannot think how fish could have been foolish enough to take my fly. But they were, they were. The first day was blank. On the second I had two fish; on the third three; on the fourth two.

The Helmsdale remains for me, as for a host of other salmon-fishers, the perfect Highland river. It possesses an intimacy that is lacking in its greater brethren, the Spey and Tay. The beauty of the strath; the charm and skill of the ghillies; the flow of the long pools and steep cascades, are matchless.

I had never been coached as I was now, with the precision of those ghillies: 'Right, there's your line out. Now, next cast two yards further, just short of the rock, and if he's there he'll have you.' He did, too. If I am ever asked how I shall spend my time in the next world, if I am allowed there, the answer must be playing Helmsdale salmon on a cane rod with a Hardy Perfect reel. To do it twice in a day was extravagant, thrice was riches. I never lost a fish that week. Nowadays, having lost my share, I realize that no man can be a fisher until he has seen the rod straighten a good many times, just as no one can be a horseman until he has done plenty of falling off.

One of my worse vices is an excess of exhilaration. I made myself increasingly unpopular with hosts and fellow guests that week for a variety of reasons, but not least because of those evening returns to the lodge, bursting with delight about my fish. I was, by some distance, the most incompetent caster in the party; yet I caught most fish. Not a few times since, I have been on the reverse end of that equation. I accept it as part of salmon fishing, but none of us likes it much. As that Helmsdale week went on and my catch mounted, so too did the tension in the lodge. My departure on Sunday was unregretted. I learned a painful social lesson, as well as a few fishing ones.

Each of the Helmsdale's six beats is divided into an upper and lower stretch, separated by several miles. Thus, if the top of the river is fishing better than the lower, or vice versa, every day on every beat a rod has a chance. That week, the river was stiff with fish from the dam to the estuary. The one that gave me most pleasure came at the very end of Wednesday. The ghillies were heading for home. I had two salmon on the bank and resolved to fish the beat through again alone. I cast painstakingly down through every pool until, after a couple of hours, I reached the last one, Sykes' Corner. Half-way down it, I hooked a fish and gaffed it (to my host's mild irritation) after a fine fight. Here at last was one all my own, without a ghillie at my elbow. Salmon fishing had cast its spell upon me, and it has never receded.

Looking back today, I know how lucky I was to savour that wonderful spell of success relatively early in my salmon fishing career. This served to encourage and sustain me through other expeditions that were not rewarded in the years that followed. Blank weeks are never fun, however sporting we try to be about them. They are easier to endure, however, when one cherishes the memory of past victories.

A year or two after that splendid spring week on the Helmsdale, I found myself staying in a stalking lodge, Glen-kinglass in Argyll. After a long, dry spell, the rain came down and the river was in spate. For two days, we made a marvellous killing of salmon and sea trout. I remember sacrilegiously telling the stalker, as he watched me play my second fish in ten minutes, that I would give him all the stags in Scotland for the thrill of a tussle with a good salmon.

In the past ten years, I have had good days and bad days on Tweed and Naver, Thurso and Spey. I cast an adequate line (unless there is a strong wind) and I have thrown away sentiment and armed myself with carbon fibre rods. I have read most of the good books on salmon (I find Arthur Oglesby's the most helpful in practical terms), and spend hours shadow fishing in the sitting room at home, trying to work out how much better I shall do it next time I take a rod out. Working through my gamebook I find that, on average, I have caught a salmon for every 1.4 days of fishing (not counting Alaska, which is something else again).

In my heart I suspect that, with salmon-fishing, I have still failed to make the breakthrough into consistent competence. I remember the hourly cry of the Upper Hendersyde ghillie on Tweed a few years ago: 'You must throw a longer line! You won't catch many fish here until you can throw a longer line than that!' And, indeed, I had to be content going home after two days with a single grilse. All too often, my fly lands on the water with the cast in a fatal curve behind it. Sometimes,

I catch fish. But I fancy a good fisher would take far more salmon out of the pools I cover. That is the curse of having spent hours watching a maestro like Freddy Teignmouth do it: I know what perfection on the water looks like, and how far I am from attaining it.

THE ART OF THE POSSIBLE

NOT SO MANY schoolboys now practise rifle shooting, I think, as did in the days of National Service, or even when cadet forces were compulsory. Perhaps partly because my own school was in Surrey, all of us were familiar with Bisley – that mecca of target shooters. Judging from my own childrens' knowledge, those huge Brookwood ranges have now diminished in celebrity and popularity. At school, I shot occasionally and got my marksman's badge, in common with most members of the cadet force who could be bothered to try. I did just enough target shooting to develop a modest enthusiasm for it, which persisted into my twenties. On the odd weekend summer afternoon, I used to drive over to Bisley. Among the gorse and stockbrokers' Tudor in that

depressing belt of tank tracks between Camberley and Aldershot, I lost myself for a couple of hours in the world of
Victorian rifle clubs and slouch hats, magpies and elbow
pads, Fultons, the famous Bisley gunsmiths, and hand-loaded
ammunition.

Full-bore rifle shooting as practised at English clubs, you
may say, bears as much relation to the rural beauty of field
sports as does a go-kart track to the Cheltenham Gold Cup.
In the higher realms of target shooting, the rifle becomes an
angular assembly of sculptured wood and machinery, with
none of the grace of a stalking Rigby or Mannlicher. On the
range, each round of ammunition is treated with the care of
crystal glass. Every shot demands the kind of exactitude
deployed in higher mathematics. Yet, in the days when I had
little access to game shooting, an afternoon at Bisley seemed
fun. Membership of one of the rifle clubs cost only a few
pounds a year. I never competed or even troubled to hand in
a scorecard, but simply bought some ammunition and shot.

The place is worth a visit, merely as an historical curiosity.
The village of clubhouses around the ranges still has an air of
an imperial cantonment that dates back to the days of its
youth, when Aldershot seemed but a short step from the
North-West Frontier. The verandas, with their deep basket
chairs, give the place the look of Simla rather than Surrey.
The faded pine panelling round the walls is carved with the
names of long-forgotten club presidents and captains, and the
air is redolent with a bracing of scent of stale gun oil and
four-by-two. In Victorian and Edwardian times, the place was
a social centre of slightly upmarket Pooterism, of militia and
Territorial officers who congregated in jolly marquees for
summer meetings and evolved clothes and rituals for the
ranges that did not change much for a century.

Throughout the summer, each of the rifle clubs booked
targets at various ranges every weekend; for example, one day
at 200 yards and 500, the next at 300 and 600. Unless one chose
a particularly crowded match day or special occasion, there was
seldom a long wait before spreading one's groundsheet behind
a numbered peg, setting ammunition and score pad beside it
and preparing to take the first two unscored sighting shots.

On the basis of equipment alone, I don't think I ever looked like a very serious rifleman. I began shooting with an old .303 Lee-Enfield given to me by a notably eccentric friend of my father, the great firearms expert Hugh Pollard. Hugh, who possessed a vast range of weapons in his house, mostly loaded and mostly unregistered, handed me the Lee-Enfield with such carelessness one afternoon that I knew it must be from that part of his armoury that appeared on no firearms certificate. As his own past history included a spell as a Black and Tan and a prominent role smuggling Franco into Spain to start the Civil War, he acquired enough guns over the years to be able to part lightly with one or two of them. I shot with his rifle until I exchanged it one day at Fultons for a Mk IV Lee-Enfield, rebarrelled in 7.62mm.

Most range shooters have a telescope mounted beside them to mark their shots without losing their firing position, but I made do well enough with a pair of field glasses. The flags fluttering across the ranges gave notice of the wind. Most competitors arranged themselves beside large, custom-fitted wooden boxes, stuffed with compartments for scorebooks, cleaning rags, gunsmithing tools and, of course, individual slots for each round of ammunition. The shooters lying beside me on the firing point could tell at a glance that I was no competitor, with my ammunition lying loose in the box. Above all, at longer ranges, meticulous attention to these things makes a difference of inches.

A Bisley shoot began with two unscored sighting shots. Then followed the ten scoring shots that gave a 'possible' of fifty. Between shots, the target was hauled down behind the butts to be replaced by a marking frame. The markers in the butts put up a frame with a black square positioned to show whether the last shot was an outer, worth two points, a magpie, worth three, an inner, worth four, or a bull, worth five. Then they rehoisted the target with a tag indicating the exact point of impact of the last shot. A pleasant ritual, it always seemed. In 1987, two decades later, I was allowed to try the army's new range scoring system, which instantly projects the point of impact of each shot onto a television screen beside the shooter. It is all done acoustically. There is

no need for a paper target at all, except to give the rifleman
something to aim at. In a year or two, the army said, riflemen
will practise at holograms. It all made me yearn for the good
old magpies in the butts.

The gulf in target rifle shooting lies between those who can
cross the great divide, and score consistently forty-six or
forty-seven out of the possible. I and the friends I sometimes
took with me to Bisley could lie down on the firing point, fire
off ten rounds of cheap ammunition without undue care or
special equipment, and make several bulls. We could routinely
manage forty-two or even a little better and go away feeling
pleased about it. But shooting at Bisley to win – and that,
after all, is what the whole business is about – involves a
capacity for taking pains, for obsessive concentration upon
every shot from first to last, of which few casual riflemen are
capable. Successful target shooters are very careful men.

'You're getting your ammunition wet!' cried a friendly
marksman lying next to me at the firing point one day when a
few drops of rain were falling on us as we shot. He was
alarmed by the spectacle of my rounds lying unprotected
beside me on the groundsheet. He knew that a little moisture
could make a difference of an inch or two at the target. He
was a serious rifle shot, so he believed this was important.

The men one met on the ranges were a mixed collection.
There were a good many middle-aged, obviously ex-Army
officers who lived among the Surrey hills and drove over
every Sunday to shoot quietly and without fuss, turning in
consistently solid score cards and having tea together afterwards in the clubhouse. They must be diminishing in numbers, now. Then there were the eagle-eyed adolescents, either
practising in the holidays for the school eight, or keeping an
eye in after leaving it. But the group that always seemed most
conspicuous was that which gets least look-in at game shooting
– bank clerks and small businessmen, computer programmers
and quiet fellows who lived near Woking and worked in the
City. They came to Bisley in slouch hats with strings of
badges, shoulder bags groaning with equipment, rifles beautifully tended through the winter – and passionate enthusiasm.
I was always a little coy about sharing a target with them and

letting them see my scores. At the end of a shoot they passed over their cards to be countersigned for a score of forty-four or forty-five, nursing quiet resentment towards themselves because the last shot but one was a freak magpie instead of a bull. They were the ones who were always in the club gun-room afterwards, holding heated debates about the best methods of handloading ammunition. Bisley is a great leveller of shooting ambitions – there isn't much scope for imagining an extra pheasant or two in the bag when it all ends up as neat arithmetic.

Although the place possessed a strong and friendly social life of its own – and there was nowhere like it for finding willing help and advice if one was in trouble with one's shooting, Bisley always seemed to me to lack the joyful atmosphere of a rough game shoot, the perfect setting of the riverbank. That tearing crackle of rifle and automatic fire doesn't make for repose – mine, anyway. But it was fun taking a friend down for a gentle private competition. There was a fascination about using a superbly accurate tool, knowing that if your own hand and eye did their parts, the weapon would carry out one's will to perfection. For over a century, the rifle has been one of the highest refinements of the industrial revolution. To use it well is a satisfying business.

But one day, as with many people who flirt with target-shooting, I felt that I had done enough. I went into Fultons to sell my Lee-Enfield. I meant to emerge afterwards empty-handed. But life being what it is, I came out with a new stalking rifle. If you shoot, you shoot.

Not Exactly Halford

SPRING IS THE time of telephone calls to Hampshire. Is it warm enough? Are they hatching? Is it worth driving down for an evening? In other words: has the splendid season of the mayfly yet come?

In defence of my own enthusiasm for 'duffers' fortnight', I should assert that I no longer kill most of the fish I take. Few of us would dispute that the skills required to tempt a trout to a mayfly do not approach those of cajoling him from beneath his basking bank with a small Wickham's in August. But one of the joys of trouting at different times in different places is the variety of moods the experience evokes. The mayfly provides an afternoon of intense activity and excitement – the pleasure of watching a host of insects fluttering about their business above the water or drifting on the current; the ferocity of that slashing rise; the energy of the hooked fish's run, which seldom bears much relationship to his size.

One of my own favourite techniques would not, I fear, find favour with Halford or Skues. Having identified a fish under the opposite bank, I cast deliberately into the nettles a yard beyond. One sometimes then discovers that the fly is snagged, and lost. But, more often, a light tug causes it to drop softly from the overhanging foliage onto the water. Then – whoompf! The average trout of discriminating tastes seems to find a morsel presented in this fashion as difficult to resist as the fragments of smoked salmon my children linger beside the kitchen table to claim on dinner-party nights.

I wish I could claim, however, that I have ever enjoyed the opportunity to test myself and my mayfly – or any kind of fly – against the traditional wild trout of the southern chalk streams. Instead, like most English fishermen these days, I get almost all my sport among tame trout from the farms. These fish, I think, are seen to most advantage at a distance, rippling beneath the surface of the stream, rising ten yards out. At closer proximity, as they come to the net, the graceless shapes of their heads and tails, become apparent, as does the pallid colouring of many of the rainbows. Worst of all is to see them before one on the table. The grey flesh tastes exactly as its appearance would suggest – of fish pellets and diluted sewage. Oh, that those summer Scottish brown trout, pink with shrimp, could be transported successfully into the summer streams of Hampshire!

In the same fashion that one of the joys of shooting grouse is the beauty of the quarry, so the pleasure of fishing is much influenced by the refinements of the fish. My father encouraged me to start fly-fishing for dace on the carriers of the Wey near my school in Surrey. I smashed a couple of his cane rods without doing much harm to the dace. One of my problems, I think, was that I did not want to succeed in catching those little fish nearly as much as one must to prosper as an angler. A few years later, I put in a lot of agreeable hours on a friend's lake near Guildford, hooking his not very discriminating rainbows. If they were in a taking mood, they were not hard to catch, especially with a nymph.

Like those fish and the fly, however, I found that I could take lake fishing or leave it. In common with many anglers, my enthusiasm became refined, even impassioned, only when I began to practise on Scottish lochs. Fickle, wild brown trout are such a joy to pursue, such a delight to eat.

In Sutherland, we have generally found ourselves fishing in places where there are a lot of fish that are not very big. I am strongly persuaded by those experts who say that our conservation policy towards Scottish trout fisheries ranges between disastrous and non-existent. We strip out the good fish and return the small ones. Even the most distant lochs have become relatively accessible. Some criminals now stock good wild trout lochs with tame rainbows. The Americans are far in advance of our approach to improving fish stocks. Few people north or south of the border yet seem to appreciate how flawed is our attitude to the lochs, which are going rapidly downhill.

One year at Knoydart in Argyll, we spent some happy days fishing a little loch beside Loch Bromisaig, perhaps a hundred yards width of steel-blue water. It stands at the top of a sheer 300-foot hill, which deters all but fit and eager fishermen. That loch held some serious trout, and some beautiful trout. From the first moment we saw it, we recognized that its inhabitants were worth giving of our utmost for. One afternoon up there, as we fished the shallows I spotted a good-sized fish persistently rising in the middle. I made up my mind I had to catch it, if this was the last fish in Scotland. It was feeding at the extremity of my undistinguished casting range. Yard by yard, I worked a line out, with a fair amount of muddling and tangling behind. At last, I provoked a casual, mildly interested rise, an inch or two short. I changed flies, and cast again, and again. The family packed up and clambered down the hill for tea, bored with watching me flog the water.

In the end, it took ninety minutes and maybe six changes of fly before that fish took hold of some variation of Zulu. It then towed me around the loch in exhilarating fashion, before I netted a perfectly shaped three-pounder. Now, to me that fish was worth all the tame rainbows in Surrey and Sussex put together. Catching it was a perfect experience, high amid some of the most marvellous scenery in Scotland. Eating it was pretty good, too. Today, I would probably put it back in the water. There seems a powerful case for introducing a catch-and-release policy for big wild trout.

I have less experience of trouting in Ireland than in Scotland, but I spent a marvellous day a few years ago on Lough Deravaragh in West Meath, casting an artificial mayfly on a six-foot CC De France rod inherited from my father, on an afternoon when everybody else was dapping. I know that dapping is a skilled and killing means of catching trout and salmon, but I lack the patience.

I threw my dry fly until it tempted one three-pounder, and rowed myself in when I had landed a second. On a cane brook rod, those fish felt like tunny. When I came home to Kilkenny, an Irish neighbour who was a passionate fisher asked how I had got on. In my innocence, I thought I had simply experienced an everyday tale of Deravaragh fishing folk. 'Good God, man!' he exploded, 'you might fish another ten years before you catch two three-pounders on that lough. You've had the luck of the devil.'

There again, the magic of the setting, amid the flat, wide Irish horizon; those big wild fish; the hours of rowing alone in the water with a little rod, came together perfectly. How can one compare the Deravaragh sensation with that of dangling a repulsive red buzzer on a fast-sinking line from a motorised boat on a reservoir where the quarry will be a bloated, ill-coloured rainbow with their tails chewed?

All right, so that last phrase is exaggerated. But the sentiment is not, I hope, mere fishing snobbery. I enjoy fishing a reservoir from time to time. But I would honestly rather go home empty-handed after a day plying a dry fly, than catch monsters with a deep-sunk lure dressed like a saloon-bar slut.

A while ago, I was reading the passage in John Colquhoun's classic *The Moor and the Loch* in which describes how he and his sons caught huge ferox trout by very deep trolling in Sutherland lochs in Victorian times. It may well be that the same results could be achieved today, by employing the same methods. But what a dreary fellow he would be, who could be bothered to equip himself with paravanes and lead-cored lines like a minesweeper and spend a day trawling the deep, when he might be guiding a tiny fly dancing on the surface between the ripples!

Trout-fishing, like all sport, is about physical endeavour, chance and beauty. I have a dream, based upon youthful immersion in the works of John Buchan, that perfection is to be experienced in Border streams that I have never fished, and where acidified reality would almost certainly disappoint today. On a trout-fisher's scale of one to ten, a Scottish loch on a June evening deserves at least eight; a Hampshire chalk stream seven. Hampshire would achieve a full 'possible', if I was fortunate enough to fish its bright waters on one of the few remaining stretches where wild trout hold sway. But, then again, maybe I am better where I am. The wild fish would be too many for my casting.

IRELAND IN THE ROUGH

ROUGH SHOOTING, TO most of us, conjures up visions of
walking hedges through the stubble, pottering across the
fields, taking in the odd little spinney.

My own definition of the term changed dramatically when
we lived in Ireland for two years. No man, it seems to me, can
call himself a proper rough shooter until he has fought his
way through hectares of Kilkenny brambles; stumbled through
a Waterford bog; engaged Tipperary gorse stretching to the
horizon; and fallen over a few stone walls, to land with the dog
on top of him. I have never shared the view that high, fast
driven birds present the most difficult challenge to a pheasant
shooter. On a driven day, one stands ready and poised on a
peg, taking birds at reasonably constant and predictable

angles. If you miss a pheasant, two or three more will be along shortly.

On an afternoon's shooting in Kilkenny, one often fired only a dozen cartridges, spread over three hours and five miles walking. The difficulty of maintaining constant vigilance was matched by the certainty that, when a pheasant got up, I would be trapped in a twist of barbed wire with one leg in a five yard hedge, the quarry glimpsed for a few seconds on the other side of a bramble bush. I used to come home gashed and cut about on every exposed skin surface, with the dog exhausted and the gun full of mud. But, heavens, it was fun!

Those accustomed to the manicured fields of the English countryside have little notion of the vast tracts of untamed wilderness that still dominate Ireland. One can walk for hours without crossing a cultivated area, the only company being a few cattle scratching a living out of the scrub.

The shooting, by English standards, is a free-for-all. There are just a handful of organized driven game shoots in the country. Irish law stipulates that hen pheasants may be shot only on ground where they are reared and if a special licence has been granted. In the west, especially, a knock on a farm door and a bottle of whiskey is usually all that is needed to walk a man's land and hustle out a woodcock.

In the east of Ireland, when we were living there, most of the shooting centred upon the activities of local gun clubs. Members banded together and contributed perhaps fifty pounds a year each to the cost of rearing a few hundred pheasants. Threatening signboards were posted on trees over an area of fifty or a hundred square miles, warning intruders that these were the preserves of Thomastown or Inistogue or Bennetsbridge gun club. After that, for the members it was every man for himself: there was freedom to wander across miles of wilderness, attempting to track down those tame pheasants (and a few wild ones), which could prove as elusive as great bustards in Kensington.

At that time I had a splendid, but very wild, labrador named Stokeley. This beast could be relied upon to find pheasants. However, to flush them out within gunshot – ah, that was another matter. We endured agonies together. On my side, there could be an hour's stumble across country until I saw a pheasant get up a hundred yards away; on Stokeley's, there was a look of pained reproach for my failure to make the gun go off when he had done his stuff.

Many regular rough shooters feel a certain disdain for driven game men, because they know that their own sport is much less forgiving. They may only have half a dozen chances in a day. There is no opportunity to get a rhythm going as there is with a procession of overhead pheasants. It is very easy to miss. I much respected the marksmanship of an English neighbour in Kilkenny named John Cripps who possessed not only an uncanny nose for hunting out pheasants, but could hit them even under the most unpromising circumstances. Having retired to Ireland, Cripps had devoted his middle age to making himself almost a professional rough shooter. He was very good at it – too good, claimed some who protested that he was no respecter of boundaries. But then nobody is, much, in Ireland.

I felt a raw amateur when I went out with Cripps and saw his gamebag swell while mine still hung limp. Why was it, I used to ask myself, that whenever the dog put a bird out of a hedge, there seemed a much better than fifty-fifty chance that it emerged on the opposite side to myself?

There were also plenty of good days, however, when I shot two or three pheasants, or decoyed in the stubble a dozen pigeons (with which Kilkenny was wonderfully well-endowed) or shot a couple of woodcock on their evening flight line down the Arrigle valley. Even for a wanderer like me, with a great affection for wildernesses, the sense of remoteness could sometimes become oppressive when the cloud base was low and the drizzle blanketed the sky. Rural silence in Britain is seldom absolute – almost invariably marred by farm machinery, aircraft or distant traffic. But, in southern Ireland, curlews and rainfall make most of the noise.

Then there was Mount Brandon, a substantial heather-clad hill that is permanent home to a couple of coveys of grouse. Having shot grouse in England, Scotland and Wales, I was doggedly determined to complete the geographical pattern by killing a brace in Ireland. Day after August day I walked that hill. Occasionally, I roused the grouse in the distance, but I never got within shot of them.

At lunch at the Beefsteak club in London one day, I was sitting next to Hugh Fraser, the Tory MP. He listened to my tale of the Mount Brandon grouse, and asked, 'Have you tried kiting them?' No, I never had, nor had I heard of the technique, which, Hugh said, was commonplace in the Highlands in his childhood.

I went home and looked it up in a Victorian sporting encyclopedia. Back in Kilkenny, the next time I had a tolerant friend staying, I persuaded him to accompany myself, the dog and a children's hawk kite to the moor. We walked that ground for an hour in a light breeze, the kite deployed to keep the birds sitting tight in the fashion I had often seen the eagle do in Sutherland. I became increasingly impatient, however, of what I perceived as the incompetence of the kite pilot, whose craft kept making unscheduled descents. After one of these, a considerable row broke out between the two of us, as to whether my concept was flawed or his execution was unsatisfactory. It was at this moment that the dog flushed a large covey, twenty yards away. My gun was unloaded. I never did shoot an Irish grouse.

One of the most delightful of a host of splendid characters I came to know in Ireland was Kilkenny's resident stuffer (taxidermist sounds much too pompous) Vin Drohan. Vin lived alone in a little cabin on a steep bank above the Nore, with a tame owl that winked beadily at visitors and a host of liver and white spaniels. From him I bought a puppy that was born on my birthday and christened her Francie Fitzpatrick, after the most delightfully named of all Somerville and Ross's heroines. She has been appropriately uncontrollable all her life.

Vin's cabin was always wall to wall with cock pheasants. Because the birds are so much less common in Ireland than in England, every Irish sportsman wants to have one mounted. I had Vin stuffing snipe and woodcock for me. Once in Kerry, we strangled a wounded woodcock with great delicacy to ensure that it reached home in prime condition. It stands over our fireplace still. We did not descend, though, to the more disturbing habits of some of our neighbours who liked to keep green the memory of favourite dogs. There was usually a dead Pomeranian or suchlike in Vin's deep freeze.

Irish life has a way of encouraging sporting recklessness. We did all manner of things one would be ashamed of in England. There was a day when a group of us was travelling between likely woods in an old minibus with the side door open. For no particular reason, we began taking passing potshots at pigeons as we drove. Eventually when we came to a crossroads, a very irate Fred Teignmouth (the aforementioned salmon fisher) jumped out of the car behind and shouted, '*Do* stop behaving like a gang of Black and Tans!' All right, so this was after lunch. But I can't say that even in the remotest wilds of Sutherland have I felt moved to do anything quite like that within British shores.

Nor was I always always the aggressor. I was shot twice in Ireland – the first time by a Frenchman pursuing woodcock, the second by an Englishman who should have known better shooting snipe. I took a couple of pellets in the face and most of the charge against the back of my jacket. I fell on my knees with sheer shock, and at first my attacker was most alarmed. He cheered up, however, when he found that I was not seriously hurt. I hope I am not gratuitously earnest about these things, but I was quite ruffled by the offhandness of his parting at the end of the day – 'Bye, Max. Sorry I winged you, old chap!'

On one of my few Irish pheasant days on a great estate, we reached the third drive a mile or so from the house, to find a groom holding a horse for our host. Clad in waxed jacket and cartridge belt, he swung into the saddle muttering, 'Just going to drive those birds into the wood.' He then enjoyed a brisk gallop around the field in front of the pegs, pulled up, handed the horse back to the groom and took up his gun for the drive. Rum, as my colleague Bill Deedes would say, or perhaps simply very Irish. Then there was the day we shot snipe on the Waterford municipal rubbish dump. But perhaps that sort of rough shooting story should wait a few more years.

Limited Rods

Two English tourists leaning over a bridge in Sutherland watched me play and land a salmon, then wandered down to the river and said something like: 'Ere – can you tell us where you get day tickets to fish 'ere?' I grinned back at their innocence and told them something pompous about their best hope lying in repeated prayer to the Almighty.

Where and when one fishes – and thus, how many fish one catches – are a matter of chance for most of us. I admire men and women with a thousand, or even two thousand, salmon to their own rods. But I hope I am not being churlish in suggesting that the weight of fishermens' baskets depends principally upon where they are able to practise their craft. We should all fancy a beat on the Helmsdale or a September week on

Junction or a run at the Laxford sea trout. In reality, however, unless one is fortunate enough to own a stretch of a great Scottish river, even the happiest fly-fisher's annual pro- gramme is dictated first, by budget; second, by what week on a river you may have inherited access to from Uncle Charlie's cousin Siegfried; third, by luck – for those of us forever on the lookout for new waters upon which to try a cast.

A few years ago, I was fortunate enough to hear of an available September week on the Naver, in my beloved Suth- erland. For a succession of happy seasons, we fished it passion- ately and all the family caught salmon there. Every river increases its claims upon one's affections as one comes to know it better. I had fallen in love with the Helmsdale, a few miles over the hills from Strathnaver. But my enthusiasm shifted as I worked the pools of the Naver and won fish from them. Before the Second World War, those northern rivers seemed to some sportsmen first, very remote, and, second, inferior to their greater brethren, such as the Tay, Tweed and Spey. Better roads, however, together with the decline in catches from bigger rivers, have made the Helmsdale and the Naver seem infinitely enviable to our generation. They may not produce many big salmon. But, give or take a few painful summer droughts, they go on giving fish from April to mid September (how I love that ghillie's phrase, ' . . . this run should "give a fish" ').

There is an intimacy about the pools of the northern rivers, across which even a duffer can cast from bank to bank, that is missing from the great torrents of Perthshire and In- vernesshire. On the Naver, we learnt to know Dal Mallart and Dal Harrald, Syre and the Potato Park, with a familiarity that I could not claim even for pools from which I have taken fish on the Tweed or Spey.

The Naver possesses a unique set of river rules, alternately a source of charm or frustration to those who fish it. First, of the two rods on each beat, one is a so-called 'limited' rod – it may be fished only by a woman or a boy under eighteen. Now, this was a marvellously civilized invention by its orig- inator, half a century ago, for it compels us all not only to favour, but actively to encourage, our wives and children. My own wife and elder son caught their first salmon on the Naver and, to be honest, I doubt that the male chauvinists would have allowed them on the river, but for those whimsical rules. The frustration sets in when fish are taking, but wives and children are not: that is to say, when the family have insisted upon going home for tea; salmon are being caught; a rod lies unfished; and one knows that within an hour or two, an important opportunity will have passed – perhaps not to be repeated all week.

The other Naver rule is that a beat may only be fished for eight-and-a-half hours a day. This may sound a long time, but if – like me – you enjoy casting for an hour before breakfast, get going properly at nine am, stop for lunch and spend an hour asleep afterwards to kill time, then fishing for the day is still all over by six pm. This is depressingly early for a team of fanatics, such as most fishermen are. Yet, on the other hand, many experts believe that Scottish waters today are being seriously overfished. On the Naver and other rivers, it is striking to behold teams of passionate casters gathered on the bank, who relieve each other on the rod without an interval of a second, and drive downstream to be ready to throw a fly on one pool at the very instant the last man in the relay finishes on the previous stretch. If the water is low, or even steady, every fish in the river has seen so many flies of every size and colour after a week that it is scarcely surprising they stage strikes and refuse to touch the most tempting lure.

Great fishermen, such as Neil Graesser, suggest that, in conditions when fish are stale and have seen every kind of bait, one should go and fish the odd eddies and corners of the river that may hold a salmon, away from the recognized pools. I am sure they are right and keep meaning to adopt their principles. Yet I am one of those foolish virgins who can never resist the pull of a pool where fish are showing. How many hours have I wasted on Dal Mallart, high on the Naver, because I cannot believe that among so many red fish throwing themselves about on the surface, there will not be one, just one, willing to joust with my fly?

I remember some delightful days on the Naver catching fish in good company – and good company matters even more when fishing than it does shooting. I also think, though, of the days losing fish. My first serious seasons on Scottish rivers, I was very lucky – I don't think I failed to land a hooked salmon – but then I began to learn the truth of that bland assertion in Stoddart's *Angler's Guide* of 1853: 'On hooking a fish, there remains often much to be done before he is secured. About one third of hooked salmon escape: some, through sheer carelessness or want of experience on the part of the angler, others, by reason of the fish being slightly or insufficiently fastened, and a few owing to uncontrollable circumstances.'

A few years ago on the Naver, I started a spasm of 'uncontrollable circumstances', letting go of salmon, which caused infinite pain. One morning on Beat I, with his third cast my eleven-year-old son hooked a fish. I ran up to the car, grabbed my video camera and filmed him playing and landing a six-pounder (a tape the family will enjoy twenty years from now). Half an hour later in Dal Mallart, I got into a fish of my own and settled back to play it, looking as matter of fact as I could contrive, hailed by my son's 'Well done, Daddy!'. I lost that salmon two minutes later. The same evening, a fish in the marvellous Syre pool broke me with a great leap after four connected minutes.

Then, two mornings running on 'dawn patrols' before breakfast, I hooked salmon and played them to the edge, only to lose them as I struggled to handle rod and net down a sheer bank. I lifted one fish out of the water on the net, only to have him twist free before he fell through the ring. That was the end of any claims from me that netting salmon is merely a mechanical process. The third morning, as I played a good fish at The Jetties, I saw a bailiff's car driving past and signalled him madly to stop and help. He netted the salmon, saw that it was a hen, and obligingly threw it back in the water for me. That is another Naver rule which can be bitterly frustrating, though ecologically unanswerable: September hens are returned to the river, unless they prove very badly hooked. I have become more enthusiastic about this principle today than I was then.

The Naver and the Helmsdale are both delightful rivers to

wade, except in flood when they are unlikely to be much use anyway. Wading to the knee or the thigh to cast a fly gives most of us a sense of oneness with the river that is entirely pleasing. It is waist or chest wading that becomes an alarming business. Last year on the Spey, I caught a fish I saw showing beside the far bank by forging through the water to within an inch of my wader tops, then casting to the very limits of my abilities. The fish was satisfying, but I could have done without the wading. Only masochists want a taste of fear thrown in with their sport, and deep wading in fast water is pretty frightening. Some of us also have a butter-fingered habit of dropping flies, boxes, nylon, rods, reels, scissors in the river at the slightest excuse, although even I have now learned to tie everything loose onto my waistcoat.

It is fishing beneath the heather hills that makes the Sutherland rivers so irresistible. The Tweed or the Spey offer a much richer variety of wildlife. But one lacks the sense of digging deep into the heart of the Highlands; seeing grouse and snipe; watching the weather change with characteristic northern fickleness; feeling a thousand miles from the horrors of civilization.

I suppose we duffers also have to mutter that on the Naver, one has fewer problems with trees on the backcast, although the hills above the upper beats are cursed with conifer forests, foolishly planted after the Second World War. The trees ruined some marvellous grouse beats, and may yet inflict a toll on the river, by acidification. A Tweed ghillie complained to me recently that the water now falls far more quickly than in the past after rain, because so much of the ground above the river has been drained for planting. So it has been, too, on the Naver. Scottish sport will pay a painful price over the next generation for landowners' greed to seize the tax concessions from forestry.

The last year that we went to the Naver was 1987. We arrived to find the river impossibly low. The tenants in the previous week had drawn a blank. We took to the hills in search of grouse and prayed for rain. On Thursday, in buckets, it came. We went to sleep dreaming of the great killing we should share on Friday or Saturday.

On Friday, the flood made the water unfishable. On Saturday, we laboured all day – and there were a couple of good
fishers among us – but moved nothing. We scribbled the
gloomy tidings of a handful of accidental sea trout in the
gamebook on Saturday night and went home. The next week's
party took sixty salmon. The beat we rented has been sold
now. My last memory of that wonderful river is thus one of
defeat. But I still yearn for a return match.

RUNNING AWAY TO THE
RIVERBANK

AMONG ALL THE anniversaries of armadas and revolutions that competed for our attention in 1988, one of the most momentous passed almost unnoticed. Rat, Mole, Toad and Badger were eighty.

For me, as for most twentieth-century middle-class Englishmen, this was an anniversary with infinitely more heart-warming echoes than those of the Armada and the Glorious Revolution put together. Kenneth Grahame's tale embodies every childhood romantic image of the countryside. Its stature as a classic is today unchallenged.

Spare a charitable thought, then, for the blushing shades of the 1908 reviewers on first publication of *The Wind in the Willows*. The man from *The Times*, for instance: 'As a contribution to natural history, the work is negligible.' *TP's Weekly* referred to numerous incidents in the book, '. . . which . . . will win no credence from the very best authorities on biology'. Arthur Ransome compared the latest work from the author of *The Wind in the Willows* unfavourably with those of his past: 'Instead of writing about children for grown-up people, he has written about animals for children . . . If we judge the book by its aim, it is a failure.'

And so on, and so on. What music it is for every aspiring writer to be reminded that here was yet another classic spurned by distinguished publishers (Bodley Head, in this case, before being unenthusiastically accepted by Methuen) and disdained by most critics. The book was slow to gather popular momentum. It was not, perhaps, until its dramatization by A. A. Milne and its illustration by Ernest Shepard in 1930 that it became established as a popular classic. For more than half a century, however, its grip on our imaginations has never receded, through well over one hundred editions and ten million copies. What lover could think of marrying a partner with an aversion to *The Wind in the Willows*? What friendship could survive a declared lack of loyalty to Ratty and Mole? Who, when observing the likes of Mr Derek Hatton and Mr Denis Skinner hoving over the horizon, does not instantly identify stoats and weasels?

Yet, if many literary creators endure unhappy lives, the fate of Kenneth Grahame, only begetter of *The Wind in the Willows*, possesses a particular pathos. The contrast between the rural idyll upon which his fame rests, and the reality of its author – a repressed, confused Victorian living out his latter life as a recluse – is sharp and bitter.

Grahame was born in 1859, son of the sheriff-substitute of Argyll, where he spent his first years. When his mother died, his father dispatched the children to live with their grandmother at Cookham Dean in Berkshire and never set eyes on his brood for the last twenty years of his life, which he drank away on the Continent. Kenneth Grahame's orphaned childhood years at Cookham Dean bred a deep loneliness, but also became one of the happiest periods of his life, in which his passion blossomed for the river – the Thames – and the natural life around it.

He went to school at St Edward's, Oxford, where he proved academically competent, and the 1st XV found him '. . . a useful forward, always upon the ball, lacks weight and strength'. But then, to his great and lasting disappointment, his family proved unable to send him on to the university and he was dispatched instead to a clerkship in the Bank of England.

In his early London life, Grahame seemed to vacillate between being the shy, elusive bachelor and the ardent joiner of society and societies. Out of the Bank's hours, he drilled with the Volunteers, and worked at Toynbee Hall in Stepney until an extraordinary occasion on which a rowdy group of Cockney girls mobbed him while he was giving a talk on literature, smothering him with kisses, '. . . at the same time chanting, to the tune of Men Of Harlech, "What is One Among so Many?"' This episode, he said, considerably increased his affection for the Volunteers. His fear of women persisted.

Grahame very early displayed his enthusiasm for writing, first as a protégé of W. E. Henley on *The National Observer*, alongside Stevenson, Kipling and Yeats, and then on *The Yellow Book*. He was an essayist, in a style that seems mannered in our day, but was much admired in his. He seemed perfectly content to fit in his writing with work at the Bank. He quickly became a recognized literary figure, yet maintained a social distance, a remoteness, that impressed itself upon his contemporaries. 'He seemed,' wrote one of them, C. L. Hinds, in 1895, 'to be a man who had not yet become quite accustomed to the discovery that he was no longer a child.'

Graham Robertson, the artist who later contributed the sole illustration to the first edition of *The Wind in the Willows*, remarked that in London Grahame '. . . looked all wrong . . . that is to say, as wrong as so magnificent a man could look anywhere. As he strode along the pavements, we felt to him as towards a huge St Bernard or Newfoundland dog, a longing to take him away into open country where he could be let off the lead and allowed to range at will.'

Through his years at the Bank and the literary salons of

London, Grahame sustained himself by constant escapes: to the West Country, to Italy, which he adored, to the Thames, where he rented cottages alone or with friends, and learned to know the river below Streatley with an intimacy and passion that he always retained, though it is the stretch between Marlow and Pangbourne that decisively influenced *The Wind in the Willows*.

From an early stage, Grahame's writing reflected his commitment to man's cause in the struggle against the machine. Peter Green, Grahame's biographer – from whose pages many of these glimpses are drawn – suggests that the author's enthusiasm for the country, like that of many contemporary writers, was intensified by the sheer awfulness of the late Victorian urban life. 'You like people,' Grahame once said to Arthur Quiller-Couch, 'they interest you. But I am interested in places.' At weekends at Streatley, Grahame walked for miles along the lonely chalk thread of the Ridgeway and wrote euphorically of '. . . chops, great chunks of cheese, new bread, great swills of beer, pipes, bed and heavenly sleep'. His interest in the bleaker realities of rural life was non-existent. He had created a fantasy vision of an English countryside where no rain fell and neither death nor sex intruded, to which he adhered unyieldingly for the rest of his life.

Although he had achieved a modest success with the publication of his first book, *Pagan Papers*, it was *The Golden Age* in 1895 that made him a literary celebrity. This was a collection of tales of a clutch of orphan children, written for grown-ups, that achieved instant success on both sides of the Atlantic. Its innocence, its scorn for the adult world, its envelopment in comfortable fantasy, delighted a host of admirers. Literary triumph was matched by professional promotion. Three years later, at the exceptionally early age of thirty-nine, Grahame was made Secretary of the Bank of England, a post that he managed to fill in agreeably leisurely fashion for a decade. Yet, from here onwards, though greater fame, considerable riches and his greatest achievement lay ahead, much began to go wrong. First, he married a formidable woman named Elspeth Thompson, the daughter of an inventor, who was to prove a termagant. From the outset, their courtship was bizarre. Grahame's love letters to her survive, composed in private baby-talk that is cringe-making even by the standards of the genre.

He seemed an irresistible lure for eccentricity. One morning a gentleman named Mr Robinson demanded to see Grahame at the Bank, and offered him a manuscript tied with black ribbon at one end, white at the other. The bewildered Secretary took the black end, proving, as Mr Robinson subsequently told the jury, '. . . that Fate demanded his immediate demise'. The visitor extracted a large revolver and took several unsuccessful pot-shots at his host before he was secured and taken away.

The Grahame's physical relationship seems to have given neither much pleasure. Their only son, Alastair, or 'Mouse', as his parents called him – was born with eye defects that made him half-blind. The world perceived the child as sickly and dull, his parents thought him brilliant, and spoilt him disastrously. Yet, Alastair's great contribution to history was as the vessel, the catalyst, for his father's masterpiece. One evening in May 1904, Elspeth asked the maid why her husband was late for dinner: 'He's with Master Mouse, Madam, he's telling him some ditty or other about a Toad . . .'

The development of *The Wind in the Willows* is more readily traced than that of most books. In May 1906, the Grahames moved from London to Cookham Dean, reaching out to recapture the scenes of Kenneth's childhood happiness. In the following year, he began to write letters to Alastair whenever they were apart, which the boy's governess preserved.

'My Darling Mouse,' begins a characteristic example, 'have you heard about the Toad? He was never taken prisoner by brigands at all . . . He went off to a town called Buggleton and went to the Red Lion Hotel and there he found a party that had just motored down from London, and while they were having breakfast he went into the stable yard and found their motor car and went off in it without even saying Poop-Poop! And now he has vanished and everyone is looking for him, including the police. I fear he is a bad, low animal.'

As the less kindly critics remarked on the publication of

The Wind in the Willows – entitled *The Wind in the Reeds* until a late stage – there is no logic about the book's characters, who veer erratically between animal and human behaviour. They sob like children, yet live the lives of leisured country gentlemen. Work plays no part in the riverbankers' existence. The essential ruthlessness of nature has been stripped away. If the book has a theme, it is that of the importance of social order. The overwhelming threat is that of loss of property. Already, as Grahame was writing, his world seemed threatened by the creeping fungus of socialism. The riverbankers' view of life was patriarchal and intensely conservative.

There has been much debate about whether *The Wind in the Willows* is really a book for children or one for adults seeking to recapture childhood. Its lush, lyrical passages seem, to many modern young readers, heavily overwritten. I first read the book when I was eight, adored it and have cherished it as my favourite desert island choice ever since. My own children, I find, can take it or leave it. Yet, what adolescent or adult in sentimental mood can resist it? For it possesses a timeless freshness and sheltered innocence that never fade. Mockers may echo the 1908 verdict of the *Saturday Review of Literature*: 'His rat, toad and mole are very human in their behaviour, and remind us of undergraduates of sporting proclivities,' but most will prefer the judgement, uncommonly sympathetic among his contemporaries, of Arnold Bennett: 'The book is an urbane exercise in irony at the expense of the English character and of mankind. It is entirely successful.'

Yet the author's life shrank steadily from the year of the book's publication until his death. Early in 1908, he retired from the Bank of England, apparently unlamented. His dilatory approach to his responsibilities seems to have exhausted his employers' patience. A paralysing indolence overtook him. His literary output ceased and he withdrew from society with his increasingly domineering wife, adopting a reclusive existence.

In 1920, their son Alastair, whose boorish precocity had made him profoundly unpopular both at Eton and Oxford, was found dead on a railway line. A verdict of accident was returned, but suicide was suspected.

Grahame's latter years were landmarked only by fragmentary re-encounters with *The Wind in the Willows* and its mounting fame. In 1919, a bold professor from London University wrote to ask him who looked after Mole End while its owner was off adventuring with Ratty. Instead of the usual rebuff, Grahame wrote to reply: 'A charmouse ... It is evident that the Rat was comfortably off – indeed, I strongly suspect him of a butler-rat and cook–house-keeper.' In 1930, while Ernest Shepard was preparing his incomparable illustrations, he went to visit Grahame at his last home in Pangbourne. Shepard preserved a record of the conversation: 'He would like, he said, to go with me to show me the riverbank that he knew so well ... "But now I cannot walk so far, and you must find your way alone ... I love these little people, be kind to them."'

Grahame died two years later and was buried at Holywell, Oxford. His cousin, that master of literary swashbuckling, Anthony Hope, wrote the inscription for his gravestone: 'To the beautiful memory of Kenneth Grahame, husband of Elspeth and father of Alastair, who passed The River on 6th July 1932, leaving childhood and literature through him the more blest for all time.'

We should probably erase from his memory, as Grahame surely did, the story of the mole he captured one day at Cookham Dean and put it in a box for Alastair overnight. In the morning, it was gone. The cook admitted its execution, believing it to be a rat. Fantasy inflicts less pain.

SMOKED SALMON FOR BREAKFAST

IT ALWAYS SEEMS a mystery to me, why millions of otherwise sensible people are willing to cram themselves into aircraft to be carried south to the Mediterranean, where they roast expensively on polluted beaches surrounded by hordes of like-minded souls, many of whom should be bribed not to remove their clothes in public. Give me, instead, a wilderness, troubled by as little humanity as possible, where there is still a bracing chill at midsummer.

Iceland is one of those places the world has not yet found out about, where barely a quarter of a million inhabitants tenant the coastal fringes of a great wasteland that is otherwise given over to birds – and what birds! – together with a profusion of wild flowers that cling precariously to a few thousand square miles of grass, glacier and volcanic rock. It would be foolish to pretend that this is any place to become a tourist in winter, when day comes briefly and then vanishes before it is worth turning off the car lights. In summer, however, the midnight sun provides continuous daylight. Icelanders possess all the Nordic charms, and seem to save Nordic melancholy for the dark months. Smoked salmon for breakfast no doubt palls if you stick around long enough. But, for anyone passing through, fish and smoked lamb and marvellous cakes seem a great improvement on all those terrible things Greek and Spanish restaurants do to food. You don't get so ill, either.

My wife and I went to Iceland for the reason that every sportsman goes there – to fish. I think we could have been almost as happy, though, walking or camping amid those endless miles of emptiness and stunning views, with nobody but a few Viking ghosts to complain about trespass.

Reykjavik, the capital where half the population lives, is a pleasant but dull modern city of industrial plants and tidy white wooden houses, resembling a hundred of its counterparts in Scandinavia. Fish, and fish almost alone, support the entire economy, unburdened by expensive luxuries larger nations must finance such as armed forces – unless one counts the fishery protection vessels, used to fight off the wicked British in the cod wars.

On our first day in the country, we drove south fifty miles over the barren hills, to look at the south coast. Weekenders from Reykjavik love to marvel at the exotic plants in the hothouses at Hveragerdi, heated by thermal springs. Those of us from more temperate climes, jaded by garden centres, prefer to admire the sea and the endless fields of ponies, which are second only to sheep as Iceland's main livestock crop. Thousands of the hairy little beasts are exported to Germany and Austria for breaking and riding. My wife, a connoisseur of these things, says their noses are too straight. But they are very tough and full of charm, like their owners. They need to be, when they graze most of the winter in the snow.

The flatlands of the south were a disappointment. But next

morning, as we drove north between the mountains and the deep blue fjords, the landscape captured us. Everybody said we were lucky, to hit the only week of summer when the sun blazed down every day. Much of the year, the mountain tops are shrouded in mist and the rain buckets down. That, though, merely makes the average British hill enthusiast feel at home. Most Icelanders outside Reykjavik own four-wheel drive vehicles, in deference to the local roads' habit of switching unexpectedly from tarmac to pot-holed dirt track. Every car moves in a swirling cloud of grey volcanic dust. Even the locals travel into the inland wastes with caution, proper equipment and a guide. If you get stuck away from the coast, it can be two or three days' walk to a telephone box. That is, if you don't fall into a glacier on the way.

We spent most of the week installed in a simple wood-built lodge up one of the gentlest of the northern valleys, dotted with tiny farms busy with haymaking. We were entertained by one of those generous types who think of everything and of everybody's little passions. After that cossetted trip to Iceland, I redefined my ideas of the thoughtful host. The higher slopes of hospitality are ascended by the man who not only supplies Veuve Cliquot out of the taps, but brings with him vast supplies of Smarties, Crunchies, Aeros and all the other goodies that delight the palates of forty-year-old English schoolboys on fishing expeditions.

The system whereby, in Iceland, fishing rights are owned by the farmer on the adjoining bank, has proved an inspired form of agricultural subsidy over the years. The benefits of fishing have been spread through the rural community. On almost every river, the farmers form a syndicate and let the sporting rights jointly at rents which cost each rod £4,000 to £5,000 a week in 1988. The English dominated Icelandic salmon fishing for years. Today, much of the best water is let to Americans. The Japanese, with their limitless resources, threaten to invade the market. Because it is so expensive, many visitors come to fish for three- or four-day stretches, rather than full weeks. We were in this category ourselves, but we felt no sense of deprivation. The midnight sun makes it possible to cram a great deal into three days.

On our river, the Vatnsdalsa, in early July the weather was unseasonably hot, the water low and most of the rods were spinning. I am not a spinning enthusiast, chiefly because playing a hooked fish on a spinning rod seems so much less exciting than on a fly rod and reel. Thousands of fish were circling at the foot of the big lake at the bottom of the river, indifferent to any kind of bait, waiting only for water to move them upstream. But they seemed irresistibly tempting, their broad backs and fins showing above the still, glassy surface as they swam around and around and around. We wasted a few hours there, before accepting that nothing on earth was going to bring those fish to a fly. The upper reaches of the river, likewise, were almost empty of salmon, and would remain so until rain shifted the vast shoals at the bottom of the valley.

But we also had the sea pool. Here, every day, a new run of fish came in from the estuary. And here, every day, we were able to catch salmon. It was a delightful strip of water, full of eddies and currents running among the rocks that the falling river had exposed. It was an easy cast, even with a trout rod. The Icelandic ghillies, very good company, were politely scornful about the two-handed rod I had brought. Nobody bothered with that sort of kit in Iceland any more, they said. Everybody fished with trout rods, which gave so much better sport. In the same way, nobody used nets – everyone tailed their fish. This, I know, is very much the American view. But, perhaps because I am an indifferent caster, I remain happier with a fourteen-foot rod, and certainly find it easier to play fish on.

We caught no big fish in Iceland that first trip. But even salmon of seven or eight pounds tore off line down to the backing, and ran themselves ragged around the pool before surrendering. I lost one good fish by making a mistake I really should be old enough to have avoided. After playing it almost to the bank, I called to my wife, 'Get the camera!' A few seconds later, the fish jumped. I went home with a photograph of myself holding a straight rod, and a line dangling slack in the current.

That trip dispelled several myths for me. The mosquito and midge problem, about which so much is heard, afflicts only a few rivers, of which ours was not one. In the past, I had heard some people say that Iceland is not beautiful. In reality, we found the setting as exhilarating as Helmsdale or Strathnaver. The trip is worth making merely for the birds. Whimbrels, petrels, terns, ptarmigan, swans, every species of duck are there in profusion. Foxes are among the few local mammals, although a ghillie told us that, a while ago, a solitary polar bear drifted misguidedly ashore on an ice floe from Greenland. What happened to him? 'He was shot,' said our informant laconically.

There is a sense of freshness, of nature newly made, about everything in Iceland. Other wildernesses, such as Alaska, are sullied, at least on their fringes, by a surprising miscellany of rubbish and squalor. Yet here the water, the air, the hills, the grass of the valleys seem wholly unblemished.

One night, our party was entertained to a barbecue on the beach under the midnight sun by a prominent local business-man (who lamented the decline of the Land Rover and the rise of the Japanese jeep as the island's principal means of transport). He also owned the tiny local church. He had arranged for a cellist from the Iceland symphony orchestra to make the four-hour trip from Reykjavik to play Bach for us, accompanied by her husband on the organ. We sat twenty strong in the painted pews, the sun still blazing in the evening light outside, wholly enchanted. The only evidence of night was mist rising over the water, so theatrical that in the early hours of morning it looked as if dry ice had been spread across the countryside for some Wagnerian performance. The lunar landscape, so reminiscent of Sutherland or yes, the Falkland Islands, seemed irresistible.

It can, however, become unspeakably bleak in winter. One day our ghillie pointed to a small farm we were passing, high on a hillside. 'You see that place, so close to the side of the mountain? In Icelandic, it is called "The House in The Shadows", because they do not see the sun at all for three months of the year.' The July weather gave us an uncritical, roseate view of the country. For a resident, chronic drunken-ness is a serious social problem, as it is for most far northern societies. For a tourist, food and lodging are as expensive as one might expect in a place where everything but the lamb and fish has to be imported. If the geology of a country with active volcanoes is fascinating, the frequent small earthquakes can be off-putting.

There is nothing of much architectural or cultural worth to see. Iceland is for those who seek natural beauty and solitude, together with uncomplicated friendliness from the inhabitants. They have not yet been troubled by enough tourists to become either grasping or bitter; they seem genuinely pleased that others want to visit their little country.

We came home perfectly content, glowing with smug sympathy for all those misguided souls who waste their summers on Corfu or in the Algarve. Wind burn always seems so much healthier than sun-tan, and wearing Wellingtons you don't even get sand in your shoes. Oh yes, and another myth we dispelled – that Icelandic fish don't eat well. We took three home in our insulated salmon bag. We had one for dinner last weekend, *en croûte*. Even after three hours in the plane and six months in the freezer, it was delicious.

High Days and By-days

ONE SEPTEMBER DAY in Scotland, we were talking about numbers. That is to say, a little knot of us clustered between butts were discussing how many birds on a shooting day are too many. I said I thought 400 pheasants were enough to give even a ducal sportsman as many bangs as he could reasonably want. Most of us agreed that bags of 1,000 or 2,000 birds bring shooting into disrepute. But then that excellent and immensely experienced shooter, Mr Richard Greenwood (inventor of the waterproof sporting skirt), put his finger on the nub of the matter: 'There is nothing wrong with shooting any number of pheasants,' he said, 'if they are high and sporting. But there is everything wrong with shooting even fifty if they are low and unsporting.'

I get a day occasionally on estates where very big bags are made, and have to confess that I enjoy the excitement of shooting continuously for ten minutes from a peg, with the barrels burning through my gloves, the gun going off as fast as I can load. At the end of the drive, though, I often feel somewhat shamefaced as I look upon dead pheasants scattered all over the place and the poor old dog running from one to the other in confusion at the *embarras de richesse*. It is said that some of the best Welsh high pheasant shoots are now being diminished by the rearing of too many birds. On almost every sporting estate, there comes a point at which quantity becomes the enemy of quality and birds perform less well because there are so many of them. It is a great misfortune for the sport that wild pheasant shoots are diminishing in number and prominence. The dependence of most estates upon reared birds is becoming absolute. This provides one reason for the unqualified enthusiasm most of us feel for grouse shooting – we are dealing solely with wild game.

One of Trollope's heroines remarked: '"What an odd amusement it seems, going out to commit wholesale slaughter. However it is the proper thing, no doubt."

'"Quite the proper thing," said Lord Silverbridge, and that was all.' A hundred years on, we must produce some better arguments.

There is no cold, rational case for declaring that shooting say, 500 pheasants is more reprehensible than shooting say, 50. Either one believes that it is acceptable to kill game birds for sport or one does not. There is no intellectual distinction between deciding to kill 500 in one day or 100 on each of five days. But most of us feel in our bones that all sorts of things that are agreeable in moderation become disagreeable when they are overdone.

I am troubled by the increasing difficulty in finding a market for dead pheasants. In my own mind, one of the principal justifications for shooting, like fishing, is that we eat what we kill. But now, amid the new prosperity of the eighties, unprecedented numbers of pheasants are being reared to meet the demand from a host of newcomers to field sports, and from very rich men for whom big bags have become as much a status symbol as they were for the Edwardians. For myself, I welcome the newcomers. The more of us who can share in field sports the better. But I am fearful about the consequences – not least the political consequences – of the drive for big bags.

Looking back over my own sporting experiences, I am struck by the simple fact, which I believe is common to most of us, that so many of my happiest shooting days have been small ones. One of the best pheasant days I have ever enjoyed took place at an enchanting estate in Oxfordshire – a place of seventeenth-century stone cottages and overgrown hedges ten yards wide. The owner shoots it once a year and invites a few friends to share the day.

We had a hard frost and a bright, clear December sky. The little team of beaters from the estate village began to whack their way along the hedges with a chorus of cries and imprecations that would have horrified the master of a big, silent, Norfolk beating line, but fitted perfectly here, because those concerned were so obviously enjoying themselves.

The first bird fluttered out of the brambles amid a great clatter and began climbing and climbing and climbing. Two of us took a wild punt at it. By some miracle, it threw back its head and fell out of the sky. Our day was made. Yet there were plenty more good things to come.

No drive produced more than a dozen pheasants. But all came over the guns on oxygen. We felt no shame in missing them and infinite delight in bringing them down. At the end of the day, we had barely sixty in the bag. But every shot had been memorable. Every pheasant was a wild one. Each of us went home entirely content.

A lot of small days are made by the walking. On a cold (or worse still, wet and windy) day, it is no fun standing on a peg watching beaters tap out a game strip with nothing in it. But if one is on the move, covering the ground and feeling that every step is doing one good, then the bag becomes unimportant. A friend of ours in Northumberland has rented a few hundred acres of moor from local farmers for many years and a few pounds. Very often, there is nothing on it. But then a good breeding year comes along and it is worth the family's while to walk the hill three or four times before the snow sweeps in and blankets it.

I had a marvellous day up there in August, with a couple of fathers and a team of boys. We walked to and fro across the heather, then through tussock grass and a few fields of grazing and marsh and a couple of spinneys. We all had a shot or two at grouse – I think I hit one – and the total was seven brace. There was a host of hares and rabbits, the odd pigeon, the odd snipe. We saw a surprising number of pheasants, a good omen for November. The sun shone and we had a tremendous picnic at lunch-time. At the end of it all, I felt not a trace of envy of the teams we could hear booming busily over the hills nearby, shooting their 100 or 200 brace of grouse while we were collecting sporting crumbs, so to speak.

Many of us started our sporting careers stalking rabbits in the hedgerows with a shotgun or a .22 rifle. In the days when Richard Adams's best-selling book was a national obession, I thought of having a bumper sticker done – I HAVE SHOT RABBITS ON WATERSHIP DOWN. I have, too.

I still thoroughly enjoy taking a boys' team night rabbit-shooting under the headlights. The marksmanship is usually somewhere between moderate and frightful. But the adventures are tremendous. Two boys stand on the seats and shoot through the sunshine roof of our Shogun, guided by chronically contradictory instructions from the driver and other passengers.

A couple of years ago, my own over-excitement nearly lost the vehicle for us. I was backing up a track in a gorse wilderness in Sutherland in the dark, when the keeper manning the spotlight idly mentioned that we were about to disappear over a sheer precipice, and it might be as well to stop.

We sat on the grass in the moonlight beside the tilted Shogun, waiting for him to fetch a tractor. It was five minutes before I noticed to my horror that the vehicle's list was visibly increasing. We hung desperately to the nearside for fifteen minutes, waiting for that tractor. I was tormented by knowledge of the glee that would follow at the breakfast table if we lost the struggle, from all those who believe I am temperamentally unsuited to driving four-wheel drive vehicles on night shoots. There was indeed much disappointment back at the ranch, when they heard that disaster had been averted, and we had been able to get back to the rabbits.

Much of one's attitude to any day's shooting is founded upon expectations. If you go out in hopes of getting 300 pheasants, you are liable to be disappointed if you come home with 150, after watching clouds of birds fly back over the woods. It is even more galling if the team has shot the 300, but you yourself have drawn a rotten peg and been a spectator all day. I am ashamed to say that I sulked in a most unsporting fashion one Saturday, when I was a guest at a shoot where 80 pheasants were shot in a single drive, of which just five were mine. The wind was unhelpful, but the following week, at the end of a big day with seven guns, I reckoned that I had shot about a third of the bag – no reflection on my shooting, just a very lucky draw. I thought sympathetically about the guns who had obviously been left out of the shooting, just as I was the previous week. Some hosts, I think, could be more observant about numbers that are doomed to be unproductive all day and juggle the positions a little. I suspect, however, that a few guests at our own little shoot would suggest I am not beyond criticism myself in that department!

One of the great charms of taking out a dog is that, even if the day's shooting is indifferent, it can be completely redeemed by the pleasure of guiding a good retrieve; satisfaction is increased if the bird is somebody else's. I wish I had more time now for walking the hedgerows alone with a dog, which I enjoyed so much ten years ago, when we had fewer children and fewer commitments.

On those solitary Saturday mornings, one might glimpse three or four pheasants, of which not more than two flushed within shootable range. If one of them fell down and was picked up, I went home perfectly happy. I felt that glow of virtue, of having worked for my bird, that sometimes eludes me on a day that a Land Rover drops me on my peg, the pheasants fly over in clouds and we are whisked off to the next drive before we even have time to pick up. Small can be beautiful with shooting as with anything else. I sympathize with all those big shooting men who have never stalked a ditch, nor come home empty-handed.

A Few Arguments for Fox-hunting

[IN THE AUTUMN of 1980, the clamour against hunting, which ebbs and flows from season to season, took a turn for the worse. It seemed worth making a modest contribution to the propaganda war. This article was commissioned and published by *The Observer*.]

When Prince Charles celebrated his birthday hunting with the Quorn, Michael Farrin, their huntsman, finished the afternoon knocked cold for five minutes after jumping a hedge to find a farm sprayer in his path on the other side. The previous Monday, one Quorn follower broke her leg in three places and another smashed his jaw. The same Saturday, the hunt was out in torrential rain. Horses and riders splashed home, soaked to the marrow.

Why should anybody in his right mind do it? It is not as if their courage wins much popular acclaim. Fox-hunting suffered a rough press when wide publicity was given to Sir Hugh Arbuthnot's afternoon pursuit of the Jedburgh Hunt's fox to an untidy conclusion outside a factory boiler house, amid the growing campaign led by the urban Left to have hunting banned.

Yet high risk, political controversy and rising costs seem to have bruised fox-hunting scarcely at all. The sport has never been in ruder health. There are unprecedented waiting lists to subscribe to the Quorn and several of the other great Shire packs. With 195 recognized fox-hunts and 41 harrier and fell packs, there is more hunting in Britain today than there was fifty years ago. Around 50,000 people ride to hounds during the season and as many as a million more people participate as car and foot followers.

Modern farming and the spread of plough and wire at the expense of grass and hedges have eroded and restricted even the greatest hunting countries in the past forty years, 'But we can still have a flying twenty minutes,' says Michael Farrin of the Quorn, 'with fifty people abreast going into the first fence. That happened twice last Monday. There are days when we may jump sixty to eighty fences. If you're jumping, say, 2,000 fences in a season, then you're bloody lucky if you can get through the winter without a fall.' 'There is a sting in it,' wrote Lord Stalbridge, half a century ago, 'riding a good horse and jumping the big black fences clean from field to field of perfect turf, that once felt can never be forgotten.' Raymond Carr, the Oxford historian, who is one of the more unlikely but passionate fox hunters, remarks that '. . . the persistence of fox-hunting, its power to defy changing circumstances, is truly astonishing'. At a modern meet, he sees hunt followers assembled '. . . to share a mystique, to escape . . . from an untidy troubled present into a vision of some stable past'.

It is true that there is a great element of theatre about fox-hunting, an unreal quality which makes most hunting people behave quite differently from their more pedestrian selves on two legs. The clothes have something to do with this, although these are founded on practical sense. It is hard for anyone with a sense of history not to bring it to the meet. Foxhunters go out to do what men and women have been doing for almost 200 years amid the same fields and spinneys, against the background of some of the most delightful literature in the English language – Trollope, Surtees, Sassoon, Somerville and Ross – and the memory of the paintings of Ferneley, Alken, Marshall, Stubbs.

Those who have done all their riding on lazy school hacks have no hint of the power of a corned-up Leicestershire hunter. It is the difference between riding a bicycle and driving a Jaguar. Lord Stalbridge: 'The hardest and best-mounted riders in the world behind, and all grass and big fences in front.'

I myself have hunted occasionally as the rankest of novices and never – from Saigon to the Cresta Run – have I known such terror. There is a moment of ignition when hounds start to run and the mad scramble across country begins. Sense, manners and – in my case – all control are lost. Fences and fields rush up in headlong succession. The exhilaration of survival alone seems enough.

I have several times found myself quite unable to stop the animal to which I was attached, and obliged to canter in giddy circles as the only means of checking him. On my first outing with the Kilkenny hunt in Ireland, after every fence the splendid Bunny McCalmont, the Master's wife, glanced behind her to inquire fruitily whether I was still of the party. Ireland is the place for novices: nobody cares what you look like or how poor a spectacle you cut. It is enough that you are willing to have a go.

In Leicestershire, there was an unfortunate day when a low branch knocked my hat off. The hunt had paused. I dismounted and recovered the hat. Somebody kindly offered to hold my horse while I remounted (people are kinder to fools than we deserve in the hunting field). I declined on the grounds that sooner or later I had to learn to mount unaided.

At that moment, of course, the hunt took off again. For two swerving, terrified fields I struggled to get my feet into those irons, until a last lurch married me to the mud. The generous owner of the beast, driving a horse box up the road on his way to a day with the Quorn, had the unnerving experience of seeing his £2,000 hunter cantering briskly towards its stable without any evidence of its recent borrower. Thus it is that in the Shires, you may decently borrow a man's hat, car or wife. But there are not many spare horses to be had save hirelings.

Much is often made of the bad manners of hunts, especially of their fits of rage when attacked by hunt saboteurs. The truth is that, while few horsemen are either as incompetent or as frightened as I am, almost all are keyed to the tautest nerves from the moment they couple the box on a hunting day. Many hunters are as sensitive – and thus ultimately dangerous – as racehorses. The best mannered woman will produce a fearsome burst of language at a man whose horse threatens to kick hers.

Beyond all this, hunting is overwhelmingly a middle-class rather than an upper-class sport. Not that many followers can now call on their own grooms. After every day's hunting, most of the field drive home to spend hours washing their own horses, tack and boots. Before the next meet, they have spent many more hours feeding and exercising these horses and saddle-soaping and polishing that tack and those boots.

A hunting morning is an exacting ritual that has cost almost everybody present more than he or she can sensibly afford. To mount at the meet and discover that a mob of demonstrators, complete with sprays, hooters and sometimes smoke bombs, is seeking deliberately to wreak havoc upon a perfectly legal activity conducted on private property is enough to snap the smoothest of tempers. Michael Farrin has trained himself to raise his cap to the saboteurs and say 'Nice to see you out, again', but he is a professional.

It has always been easier for urban 'antis' to identify with the plight of the fox than for those who have seen a chicken run the morning after he has paid it a visit. We lose an average of six birds a year. The last time, a wooden slat was gnawed off the side of the run to enable the assassin to find his way in. The bloody devastation was heart-breaking. Foxes have got to be controlled somehow. Hunting presents no threat to their survival in the British Isles. In Ireland two years ago, it was the hunting fraternity who led the outcry against the organized slaughter of foxes by local country people when the price of pelts briefly soared to £20 and above. Fox-hunters, like other field sportsmen, are passionately committed to preserving the balance of nature.

The commonest complaint from farmers in some big countries is that the hunt does not draw their covers often enough. It often seems odd that city people who see nothing cruel in keeping large dogs in small council houses should find it barbaric for fifty men and women to risk their necks in pursuit of a fox. And they do risk their necks. The accident rate in the Shires is fearsome, hence the respect that is accorded to those who set the pace. At a Leicestershire dinner party, it is still not uncommon to hear a man being run down for passing bad cheques, beating his children, revoking at bridge, only to be redeemed by that last, entirely forgiving subordinate clause, '. . . but he does *go* well'. Fox-hunting commands some marvellous horsemanship and demands rare courage.

I could not try to put the issue better than the novelist T. H. White: 'I had been puzzled at liking to kill things,' he wrote, 'because I am generally more humane than most people, certainly than the warmongers, the flogging magistrates, the snake killers and most school masters. It is . . . a question of art. When it is difficult to kill the thing, when skill and achievement come into it, I find that the killing is worthwhile . . . this may sound silly to anybody who has not shared the perfection, who has not created a cast or a shot or a run, himself. But it is rock bottom.

'To triumph over difficulties is the essence of sportsmanship. That is what the dear old colonels mean, the colonels whose apparent brain weight would give the common vole a sensation of volatility in his head, when they talk about the "sporting chance".'

Shooting and gassing foxes does not create that 'sporting chance'. Michael Farrin, the Quorn huntsman, again. 'There was something in one of the papers last week that our day when Prince Charles came out was "a good one for the foxes", because we only killed one. People don't understand that we go out to control foxes, not to wipe them out. Where there are few foxes, the last thing we want to do is to kill them all. And we only want to kill the sporting ones. A really brave fox takes a lot of catching. I wouldn't want the hounds to chop him in the cover.'

Although hunting people would not want me to put it quite like this, in an increasingly humdrum world, fox-hunting also preserves a great eccentric tradition in the countryside. In Ireland, the glow of Somerville and Ross survives. I remember the hunting priest who still threatens his farming flock with eternal damnation if they stop the hunt riding across their land. Along the muddy tracks and across the fields behind the Kilkenny hunt, Bunny McCalmont's station-wagon follows, carrying an assortment of drinks that would not disgrace the Shelburne bar, and from which lavish stirrup cups are distributed through the day. I owe Ireland some priceless sporting memories.

One day last season I asked a passionate young Anglo-Irish whip why he was riding a strange horse. 'It was like this,' he explained from the saddle, 'on Friday my horse was coughing so I came out on foot. Hounds started running and Mick Curry shouted, "Jump up behind me!" as he took a wall. I got up, but the horse didn't care for it a bit, and threw Mick away into the hedge where he broke his collarbone. So now you know why I'm riding his horse today.'

The East Midlands – the Shires – are these days far more rural in outlook than any other region in England the same distance from London. Hunting punctuates, highlights, celebrates, dominates the seasons. For the fanatics, spring, summer and autumn are exasperating interruptions in the real business of living. The widowed and the disabled testify that the casualty rate is not a myth. A lame or coughing horse is a disaster, not least because the animal is costing a fortune to feed through the season.

Not a few Masters ruined themselves for their hunts in the nineteenth century. 'The pastry cook is the only tradesman who will still give credit,' a desperate minion reported to Lord Suffield when he was Master of the Quorn and hay for the horses had long since been cut off by his creditors. 'Then for God's sake feed them on pastry!' commanded the frustrated peer. Some of his spiritual descendents still ruin themselves for hunting in the twentieth century.

Most newspapers and city dwellers treat fox-hunting as a sort of idiots' pageant. Yet, beyond horsemanship, hunting a pack of hounds is one of the great countryside arts. The merits of the famous Masters and huntsmen are argued as hotly in the Shires as those of Geoffrey Boycott in Yorkshire or Kevin Keegan in Southampton. But Ronnie Wallace, himself regarded as one of the greatest modern Masters, does not carp at the ignorant: 'People come hunting for so many different reasons – some for riding, some for fresh air, some for gossip, some to see their neighbours.'

Since agriculture has become more intensive, perhaps the greatest peril to fox-hunting is that farmers will simply baulk at the damage done by some reckless hunt followers, thrashing across winter wheat after February rain. One tradition that hunting could do without is that of the London swell riding headlong by the shortest route across country. Mr Grantly Berkeley's habit of taking his hounds through the market gardens of Harrow Vale caused a near riot in the 1820s. A noble guest complained that he had '. . . found the asparagus beds damned heavy-going'. The market gardeners put it more bluntly.

Every hunt spends thousands of pounds and hours a year mending fences which have fallen in its wake. Hunts recognize that it is intolerable for farmers to have several hundred horses following a single line. The Quorn limits its field to 150 on Mondays, 130 on Fridays. If it did not, there would be double or treble the number of followers.

A. G. Street, the farmer and writer, wrote thirty years ago, 'I would no more defend hunting than ploughing, sowing, reaping or any other event in the country calendar.' Yet, today, urban Britain is seeking more and more vigorously to dictate the terms of existence of the countryside, even unto its footpaths and farming methods, in a way that Street could never have imagined. To the Left, fox-hunting principally represents a useful Second Front in the class war: an obviously privileged pastime. Yet the only privilege about hunting is that of risking one's neck, often in the vilest of weather, in the company of fifty or a hundred others of like mind, and some of the finest horses and hounds in the world.

A Taste of Alaska

FOR MOST OF us too young to have known the palmy days of Scottish salmon, fishing within the British Isles means casting painstakingly down a beat all week – if our prayers for water, and for a run, have been answered. To average a fish a day means success. Two is riches. Perhaps once in a decade we find ourselves in on a killing, taking half-a-dozen in a day. Fishing in Britain, to hook a salmon is an achievement; to lose it a tragedy. Thus, in the past twenty years, Iceland's popularity has grown with British fishermen who want to experience the thrill of catching salmon in numbers. But Iceland's fish do not run big, and in recent years its stocks have been declining, while the cost of fishing has escalated.

Alaska, which once seemed the end of the earth, has now

become a relatively economic alternative for anybody who wants the holiday of a lifetime, in matchless scenery, with the virtual certainty of finding fish – salmon in vast shoals, salmon running past the waders, salmon stacked in tiers just beyond the rod tip, salmon beyond the dreams of avarice. 'Alaska,' as an expert remarked sagely and accurately before five of us took off from Heathrow to try it, 'is not about fishing. It's about catching fish.'

After an eight-hour flight and an unpromising overnight stop in Anchorage, a town that looks as if it has been put together with the rubbish left over from the rest of the American continent, we flew 300 miles south to Dillingham, where we were met by the guides from Bristol Bay Lodge. We bumped by van for a few minutes on a dirt road to the edge of a lake, where we had our first encounter with the Beaver floatplanes, which are to Alaskan fishing what the station-wagon is to Scottish riverbanks. Twenty minutes flying time later, we tied up at the pier by the lodge – a cluster of comfortable cabins that hold a maximum of twenty visitors. Our little group was given its own hut with a sitting room and big open fire. The weather, in early July, was like a Scottish September, the fresh mornings softening into warmth by noon on most days. We put in a quick hour on the lake to get our hands in, catching a handful of Arctic char each weighing about two pounds. Then we collapsed to become de-jetlagged.

With thousands of square miles of river and lake water within flying distance, it is up to the fishers to tell the lodge what sort of sport they are looking for. The next morning we made our only significant nonsense of the trip, by asking to go after the big king salmon. We crammed behind a cheerful bush pilot in the Beaver, landing half an hour later on the vast expanse of the River Nushagak, locally known to all as the Nush. A guide invited us to distribute ourselves along the bush-fringed bank and start casting across the current. Within an hour we knew we had made a mistake. By afternoon we were praying that it would not prove week-long. First, although we had hooked five fish between us, we landed none. Meanwhile nearby Americans were hauling in vast kings. We saw a forty-five-pounder netted just below us after a struggle that involved the fisherman in a wild dash from the bank to a boat to follow his monster.

The truth was that the Nush, a half-mile width of heavy brown stream, was the least promising or interesting of fly water. We were all fishing fly. To a man, the Americans were spinning. The lesson was quite simple: if we wanted to catch big kings, the Nush was the place to be. Yet if we wanted to fish it at all, we should have spun. None of us wanted to. Beyond this we quickly grasped that the Nush is the mecca of Alaska 'meat-fishers', who want to catch big salmon by more or less any means. Here, in the midst of a wilderness, we found less tranquillity than a flight path. A tireless cacophony of powerful outboards tore up the river, accompanied by the take-off and landing of squadrons of floatplanes; the whine of a chain-saw deep in the forest; and, finally, all afternoon, the rattle of gunfire from some distant skeet shooters. We trudged into the lodge that night in deep depression. If this was Alaskan fishing, we had made fools of ourselves by coming. Ron Macmillan, the lodge manager, shrugged, 'You said you wanted kings. The Nush is where the kings are. If you want sockeye and peace and quiet, you can have them.'

The next day an idyll began. We flew out to a camp maintained by the lodge at a spot they call Rainbow River, though that is not its real name. Where no private ownership exists, each lodge jealously guards the secret of the locations of its best fishing. We were met by two guides at the seashore who ran the boats up-river to dump our gear at the tents. They led us to a stretch of river standing amid a flat emptiness not unlike Caithness, framed by mountains on the distant horizon.

This looked perfect fly water, an easy cast wide. We ranged ourselves thirty yards apart and began to fish. A few seconds later one rod was bent. Two minutes on, all five of us were simultaneously fighting fish. As the day began, so it ended. By eleven pm, utterly exhausted in the uncanny late night daylight, we had landed ninety chum, sockeye and king salmon. Once one has become accustomed to fishing almost shoulder to shoulder – which is the local fashion although there is nothing to stop anybody wandering downstream to choose a more private spot – it seems delightfully companionable and often very funny. As we learned to cope with fish tearing off line up- and down-river past each other, we became practised in a sort of aquatic highland dance, ducking beneath each other's rods in pursuit. There is a myth that Pacific salmon do not fight. These fish, of between eight and thirteen pounds, almost without exception, fought like fury.

In a few hours we enjoyed more practice playing salmon than any of us had gained in a lifetime. With their hard mouths, these fish needed striking. All that is said about the need for extra reel-backing for Alaska is true – almost every salmon tore the line out within seconds. With a ten-and-a-half-foot rod, even if one adopted the tough tactics that seem acceptable when cast after cast touches fish, it took between ten and fifteen minutes to beach each salmon – those we did not lose, that is. All of us were hooking three for every one we landed. The best of the day was around twenty pounds. All except those we wanted for eating were returned to the water. In Alaska this is the invariable practice, and surely a very good one – to kill fish in such numbers has no meaning. We found, perhaps a little to our surprise, that it cost no pain to put them back, indeed it prevented the guilt that assails any Scottish fisherman today when, by a fluke, he finds himself with a great killing. It was a day of so much fun and laughter and exhilaration that nothing else mattered.

To an English eye, Alaskan fly patterns are garish and unlovely. We christened their more lurid concoctions of silver and purple Mrs Shilling and Barbara Cartland. The most consistent killer was a lumpy ball of coloured fluff like a sheep's eye, that Americans call the egg fly. It was pleasing when experiment showed that Scottish patterns were almost as deadly. Those fish would probably take a bare hook with a feather on it.

One of the most unexpected pleasures of that day, and of those that followed, was the company of the young pilots and guides who took us from river to river and lake to lake. Articulate, eager to please, efficient, most were college students with a passion for fishing and wildernesses – the Alaskan season lasts little more than four months between the spring thaw and fall freeze. Rick, our pilot, was a quiet-spoken little New Englander with a heavy woodsman's moustache and the shoulder-holster pistol that all the guides carry against the off-chance of needing to frighten away a bear. Rick found us some of our best fishing spots, proved an expert at frying peppered salmon fillets for lunch and talked delightfully about his experiences running a trapping line through the long Arctic winter, when he and his wife caretake the lodge.

That second night we sat outside the tents by Rainbow River while the guides cooked dinner, watching the matchless variety of ducks. From day to day, we heard sandhill cranes and willow ptarmigan, watched the loons and drumming snipe and eagles and once even saw an osprey fishing. The mosquitoes, of which we had heard so many dire warnings before we came, proved less of a menace than Scottish midges, providing one coated Jungle Formula or Cutters' Lotion on every exposed surface every few hours. The next morning, we flew off for a day's 'lake-hopping'. This entailed flying to a likely spot, circling at two hundred feet until fish were clearly visible in the water below – in itself a fascinating spectacle. Then we dropped down and started casting, fished until the shoals of sockeye close inshore had drifted away, then took off again for a new spot.

Later in the week we fished a river for wild rainbow trout – again magnificent fighters – and picked up a few grayling and Arctic char. Almost invariably, we used barbless hooks, which seemed to make the fish no more difficult to land. We watched vast shoals of sockeye running through, too much in haste to care for a fly. The Anchorage paper that week reported fishery officials estimating that more than forty million sockeye would run through Bristol Bay. Watching the fish before us, we could believe it.

Fishing in Alaska is a less subtle art than its Scottish counterpart, because the salmon are so much less wary, though just as prone to 'on' and 'off' days. The charm lies in the experience, the low flying, the wilderness. the wildlife. The lodge was impeccably run and catered for by Maggie Macmillan. She showed the genius of Americans for ungrudgingly doing their utmost to please. They take the fishing seriously enough to sell nothing stronger than beer in the house, but we had brought our own whisky to soften the evening poker sessions.

Our last day, appropriately enough, was the best of all. We landed on a desolate patch of coastline, taxied up to the beach and were led by Rick one hundred yards inland to a river estuary. We began to cast. Within minutes we were hooking chum salmon that seemed to fight more fiercely than any of the week. Some led us stumbling down-stream in pursuit, to beach them 200 to 300 yards below the point of strike. There were some epic struggles on trout rods, for two of our carbon fibre salmon rods had snapped on fish that week, and one brand-new reel winder fell off in mid fish. After lunch, tired and sated, we took off again, to land on a lake near a beautiful trout stream where we fished dry fly for grayling for an hour or two. At last, we stood together above a deep hole where the water was crystal clear, peering down upon an extraordinary assembly of king, sockeye and chum salmon, lying a few feet below us. Then we flew back.

Alaskan fishing does not spoil anyone for Scotland because it is so different. It is one of the sporting experiences of a lifetime. We all learned a great deal about playing fish. The Americans, probably rightly, think the British talk too much about the niceties of rod length and not enough about the importance of varying weights of line for different conditions.

Rick said that, if we thought chum and sockeye fought hard, we should come back in late August or September for the silver salmon, the coho, which he considered the toughest of all. Fresh-run chum or sockeye can be very handsome fish, but most of ours were blunt, ugly, red brutes by contrast with the awesome beauty of the Atlantic salmon. The wild rainbows, however, were the most perfectly coloured fish we had ever seen.

It is an unjealous experience, because there is so much sport, so many fish for everybody. It was wonderful to watch the water fountain up from the line as a fish streaked away, as much fun to behold on a neighbour's rod as on one's own. It is important to take one's own party of four or five fishers, to be sure of making up a plane-load. The whole holiday could be spoilt if chance matched one, as a lone visitor, with uncongenial strangers as fishing partners. It is worth giving our combined total for the week, in evidence of the scale and variety of the fishing: 133 chum; 49 sockeye; 3 king salmon; 19 grayling; 14 rainbow; 7 Arctic char; 3 dolly varden char. It was not cheap. But there is a lot to be said for dying poor after fishing in Alaska.

CONFESSIONS TO A GAMEBOOK

ONE SEPTEMBER I was casting a fly on a Scottish river that my father fished forty years back. I found myself wondering how he fared on the same beat, whether he lost a fish in the same pool. I felt frustrated that I shall never know the answer, because he is dead. For the hundredth time I muttered an affectionate curse skywards that he never kept a gamebook properly. I know only the fragments of the past that he recorded here and there in his books – of a war-time shoot where he was one of a team that killed a hundred brace of partridges on the site of Heathrow Airport, of poaching expeditions in Sussex and snipe in India. I shall never discover, however, how fabulously exaggerated were his tales of pre-war salmon or of partridge days in Suffolk or of his own occasional prowess at high pheasants. Most of us like to know as much as we can about those of the family who went before us, and nothing is more frustrating than the absence of written record.

Some people despise gamebooks – which my father did – as mere logs kept by sportsmen tiresomely obsessed with numbers. It is perfectly true that almost all the leather-bound products sold by gunsmiths and tacklemakers are wretchedly designed, allotting most of their space to the bag and allowing only a single grudging line a day for 'Comments'. My father was given one of these for his twenty-first birthday and wrote somewhere that in the first years he recorded his 'paltry little triumphs', then allowed the whole thing to lapse. He concluded that in game shooting '. . . recording individual performance, much of it wishful thinking, is at best self-gratification'. Thus far I can only agree with him. Shooting grouse over dogs, for instance, with the best will in the world one is often uncertain which gun killed a bird. These days, I am teased by the friends with whom I shot twenty years ago, who tell me they frequently conspired to let me claim their birds, to prevent my morale sagging too low. So much for numbers, though I still write in my 'guesstimates'.

What a gamebook can and should be, however, is a sporting diary, a narrative of weather and conditions, incidents and anecdotes. I paste in game cards, group photographs, maps. As the passage of years leaves the memory of reality further and further behind, there is much to be said for an indelible record of the truth of one's own past. Whatever exaggerations each of us allows himself in the course of gunroom conversations, the only unforgivable sin is to lie to a gamebook. If one has shot like a drain, one must write as much; if one lost a fish through stupidity, one must admit it to the blank page. Above all, even if you were foolish enough to tell the picker-up at the third drive that you had eleven birds down, on pain of undying self-reproach you must confess to your gamebook that it was only nine. That is, not counting the two cocks you said you hit, but knew in your heart went on.

Like most men, I show my gamebook to no one. But in

thirty years' time, when my son is bored with hearing me boast about how we took twenty fish in a day out of the Naver in September 1985, if he wishes, he can turn to the book and shut me up by pointing out that it was really only ten. He may also notice that I was not all that young when I wrote at the end of a season, 'If I want to get more invitations, I must learn to shoot straighter and fit into company more gracefully.'

I hope he will fail to notice the mention of a day on which I fired seventy-five cartridges to hit fourteen pheasants. I shall scarcely be proud of the grumpy references to drawing rotten pegs or to the uncontrollability of certain long-dead dogs. Come to that, glancing back through my early teenage pages to write these words, I blush to be reminded that I killed my first pheasant in error one 13 February when out shooting pigeons with my father in a snowstorm. I have a note that he scribbled when I was nine: 'I hope to make gun handling a part of Max before most boys fire their first round.' He was not, I am afraid, entirely successful.

My gamebook reminds me that until a boy is thirteen or fourteen, walking all day through high heather can often prove too exhausting for enjoyment. I try not to get irritated with my own sixteen-year-old son when he finds it boring to cast a fly all morning without result, because I felt the same at his age.

A gamebook enables one to trace a pattern through one's sporting life, to recall at what age one began to understand the magic of trout fishing, which in one's teens seemed so difficult and unrewarding by comparison with wielding a shotgun. Even in the shooting field, it is only as we get older and more relaxed, less apprehensive about occasions, that we can begin to settle down and do more justice to big days. My gamebook reminds me that the common denominator of all the days on which I have shot adequately is that they have been the ones when I stood on the peg at peace with the world, not caring whether I hit anything. I also keep a note of how many days' sport I have managed in each season. Looking back to the pages that cover our time living in Ireland, I sometimes wonder whether I did anything else there but shoot and fish.

At the end of every January I fill a page with an attempt to summarize the season: what I think I have learnt, how well or badly I have performed. Vulgarly, I am afraid, I also write down roughly what the year's sport has cost me. I fancy the figures will make droll reading in the next century, when I can no longer afford any of it. My father kept a note of his costs, too. In 1939, for instance, he was paying £50 for a 500 acre shoot in Sussex, and pretty much the same thereafter until he mustered the astronomic sum of £75 for 1,000 acres on the Berkshire Downs in the early 1950s.

Sometimes it is fun to reflect cynically on what some casual auction viewer will make of my private scribblings a couple of generations from now, when the family has lost all interest in long-forgotten sporting occasions and that great leather game-book, for which my father paid five guineas in Dover Street in 1937, ends up in a job lot in a local furniture sale, with a couple of tattered cartridge bags and a yellowing copy of a Game Conservancy pamphlet on vermin control. Will it seem odd to some stranger that my dead pen reveals such passions?

My father would have laughed and reminded me that the past is another country. He would laugh even more to see me now with a new enthusiasm – seeking to record and preserve on video high spots on the moor and the river, which uner-ringly cause anyone in front of the camera to miss the grouse or lose the fish. But that is another story.

Not so Pukka Sahibs

'THERE ARE ADVANTAGES in being Indian, you know,' said an Indian acquaintance across the bar in Delhi one evening some seventeen winters ago, with the air of a man accustomed to being disbelieved. 'We don't have any of your nonsense about sporting rights and private shooting. If you want to have a bang, you just go out and have one.'

Rajiv, my drinking companion, was one of those Indians who preserve the accent and outlook of the raj, despite being only a few years older than his nation's independence. A lifelong subscriber to *The Field*, he went to bed dreaming of big days at Hall Barn such as he had never known, and no doubt of maharajah's mammoth snipe shoots as well. Despite having been born out of his time and sport, Rajiv's enthusiasm enabled him to make the best of rough shooting in a democracy. The consequence of his remarks to me was that at four am the following morning we were bowling along in the car among the unlit bullock carts through Haryana state, fifty miles west of Delhi, on our way to start a day's sport with a little duck flighting.

Rajiv had borrowed for me an old Webley and Scott that suffered from a violent rattle in the action, while he himself had brought his heavy but serviceable Indian Ordnance model. Weapons and cartridges are considerable problems for anybody shooting in India nowadays, because imported shotguns are prohibitively expensive and good cartridges are hard to come by. Everybody manages by nurturing the English-built guns in circulation, and begging and buying whatever cartridges they can lay hands on.

A few miles short of the lake we were heading for, Rajiv stopped the car in a sleeping village. Were we taking any dogs? I asked. My leader shrugged, 'Dogs? Dogs? Who needs dogs when men are five rupees a day?' We poked about among the darkened huts, until a dim figure appeared, the village watchman, with whom Rajiv exchanged a few murmured words. The watchman disappeared, and we could hear a muted banging of doors and sleepy negotiation. After a few minutes, one by one, three men appeared, doing up trousers and pulling on shirts. They crowded onto the back seat of our battered old car and we set off again up a dust track into the wilderness. Rajiv instructed one man where to take me. Our little party separated to take up station in the reeds at opposite corners of the lake.

With the first glimmerings of dawn came the opening shots from Rajiv on the further shore. Within seconds the water erupted as cloud upon cloud of duck lifted into the sky and began to wheel above the lake. Teal, gadwall, pintail – birds often unidentifiable and sometimes innumerable – were pouring over us. As we began to bring them down, the pickers-up were wading chest-high through the water to retrieve them. During the lulls, they crouched behind us searching the sky. Again and again, seconds before I could see movement myself I felt a hand on my shoulder and a murmur of 'Duck, sahib, duck', as birds swung towards us.

As the cities of India spread remorselessly and the demand for land becomes insatiable, many of the best lakes and marshes all over the country have been drained. Shooting has been declining for many years. Today, I doubt whether that lake where we shot in 1971 still holds birds. The Government has issued thousands – hundreds of thousands – of villages with their own shotguns 'to keep birds off the crops'. Every peasant has become expert at stalking geese and duck on the water and wiping out half a dozen at a shot in a manner Colonel Hawker would have applauded, but modern conservationist opinion is sensibly sceptical about. However, by nine o'clock on that morning with Rajiv, when the last duck had departed and we were counting our very varied and presentable bag, I felt as delighted with Indian sport as any imperial shooter would have been a hundred years earlier.

The only hazard that played on my mind was the matter of the local cartridges. Each time I pressed the trigger of the old Webley, there was a fascinating moment of speculation, waiting to see what would happen next. The right barrel might produce a thunderous explosion, which dispatched a dozen pellets streaking into orbit; the left might yield a mere stammer, as a mass of shot trickled into the reeds. Predictability was not a characteristic in which the morning excelled. Major Burrard or any exact judge of shotgun ballistics would have complained to his MP about those cartridges. But from time to time, both they and I proved capable of killing things.

By now Rajiv was eager to lead the way to the next phase of the day's sport. This was where the tone of the occasion changed, and took on something of the atmosphere of a fourteenth-century chevauchée by a particularly unscrupulous Free Company through one of the more vulnerable regions of central France. We would start, my guide explained, by driving through a few promising areas in the car, guns at the ready for anything we might see. After a few miles, we spotted a flock of geese taking an alfresco breakfast in a field fifty yards from the road. Obeying peremptory instructions, I leapt from the car and began a wide flanking movement to get around behind them, while Rajiv and the beating team mounted a frontal attack. I was only halfway to my appointed post when a roar of gunfire began in the rear.

The geese came skimming over my head. This was the one and only occasion of my life when I have raised my gun to a goose. It came thumping to earth in the dust beside me. I went off in search of Rajiv, to inquire what had precipitated his barrage well in advance of H-Hour. It had not been at all precipitate, he explained, 'As soon as I'd got a firing position, I gave them both barrels low along the ground to try to make a decent score before they took off. With cartridges the price they are, we prefer them sitting if they'll oblige.'

Now that the ground rules for the morning had been made clear, I began to enter into the spirit of the thing. The next hour was a triumph both for the bag and for the party's morale. Every few hundred yards, as we drove, we met partridges and sand-grouse scratching in the dust by the roadside, undisturbed by our arrival and falling like ninepins before our assaults. With the sand-grouse, taking one out of a covey on first sighting was only an aperitif. Poor, silly, home-loving creatures that they are, Rajiv explained that their first idea on being flushed, even after being shot at, is to return from whence they came. As they rose, we shot and then took cover. Two minutes later, back they came for a second instalment and even a third. Some birds would obligingly circle above our heads until sheer gun deafness pulled them down. The partridges, smaller than our own, flew fast enough, but needed only a pellet or two to drop them.

As the sun rose higher in the sky, I began to feel the heat even in shirt-sleeves. We had started the day shivering through enough clothes for a January morning on the Wash. Yet by noon, we were sweltering under a brilliant sun that often blinded us as we shot. Our human retrievers now turned to beaters as we walked among the trees scattered among the sandy fields. At each one, the team picked up a handful of stones and set about bombarding the branches. Again and again they dislodged small coveys of partridges. Reluctant fliers were shot where they sat. Wounded birds were pursued frenziedly across country by anybody who happened to be standing about at the time. We began to run low on ammunition. I wondered whether I should be black-balled for life by WAGBI or the BFSS if they got to hear about this day's work. But Abroad is another country, and all that.

Between attacks, one of our camp followers drew the birds as they were picked up. It was too hot to leave the trail in game, even for a few hours. There were also frequent pauses to ram sticks up gun barrels to clear jammed cases. I had long ago lost track of what shot we were using. At dawn I had been issued with a remarkable assortment of cartridges ranging from No. 1 to No. 7, so that we were armed against every variety of flying contingency. Rajiv seemed able to select the appropriate load between spying the bird and pressing the trigger. I merely pushed in the first projectile to hand.

As the afternoon drew to a close, I missed a couple of scraggy but agile hares, while we added a few more partridges to the bag after a new onslaught of stone-throwing. We drove home with a loaded boot. Peacocks occasionally appeared, strutting by the roadside. They are heavily protected but occasionally and discreetly steered towards the pot. I admired the restraint with which Rajiv drove on, until I remembered that our cartridge supply was running low. He made up for this sporting gesture later, by loosing two barrels at an enormous blue bull, which I fancy would nave needed something like a .400 express rifle to stop it. When we got back to Delhi and Rajiv inquired what I thought of the day, I said something to the effect that it had been truly memorable. If pressed, the comment of the French general after the Charge of the Light Brigade would have fitted the bill admirably.

PORRIDGE AND KIPPERS

AND NOW LET us sing of the hills and the heather, of porridge and kippers and pointers and setters and peat-tinted bath water and grouse curling on the wind. The season of Scotland is upon us again, when every true sportsman who is not translated to the Highlands in body flies there in spirit.

> 'Stranger with the pile of luggage
> proudly labelled for Portree,'

wrote the author of that pre-war doggerel, irresistibly entitled 'At Euston – by One Who is Not Going',

> 'How I wish this night of August
> I were you and you were me . . .'

Whoever could have imagined a railway station inspiring such lyricism? Here is Patrick Chalmers on the identical theme:

> 'Now, when the sportsman is flitting from market and Mammon,
> Now, when the courts, swept and garnished stand silent and lone,
> Now, with her challenging grouse and her sea-silver salmon,
> August, of mountains and memories, come to her own;
> Would you gaze into the crystal, and see the long valleys,
> Braes of the North, and the rivers that wander between,
> Crags with whose coating the tint of the ptarmigan tallies?
> Come up to Euston tonight about 7.15.'

Since the early nineteenth century, Scotland has inspired a romantic passion among sportsmen. The combination of blue hills, blue waters, the wildlife and the Scots people is un-surpassed. I was fourteen when I saw the Highlands for the first time, twenty-four when I almost ruined myself to rent that little moor with some friends. Nowadays, I sometimes think I shall find myself casting a fly rod in my sleep. I am conscious of being merely one of the latest of many genera-tions of Englishmen bewitched by the Highlands.

In the eighteenth century, northern Scotland was almost inaccessible, save by sea, and was perceived in the south as a hotbed of savages and Jacobites. In 1773, however, one Thomas Pennant produced a three-volume account of the country's marvellously rich natural history. A wealthy English-man who read Pennant's book, Colonel Thomas Thornton, took himself north with a vast equipage of dogs, hawks, retainers and weaponry, including a seven-barrelled shotgun. In 1804, Thornton published *A Sporting Tour Through The Northern Parts of England and Great Part of the Highlands of Scotland*. His book may be considered the pioneer among the immense nineteenth- and twentieth-century literature inspired by Britain's northern wilderness.

By the end of the Napoleonic wars, Scotland was recognized as a great British tourist centre. The works of Scott, the visit of George IV to Edinburgh in 1822, the growth of the railways increased its popularity. Queen Victoria saw Scotland for the first time in 1842 and unleashed Balmorality. By that date, fishing for salmon and trout and shooting deer and grouse, were perceived as the finest sport in the British Isles.

They were hard men, the Victorian sportsmen. No Land Rovers bore them to the hill at half past nine. 'It will not be advisable to be upon the ground before six in the morning,' suggested *The Oakleigh Shooting Code* in 1836. 'The grouse-shooter should retire before eleven or he may not feel as he could wish in the morning. This advice is the more necessary if he be not a member of a Temperance Society.'

The pseudonymous compiler of *The Oakleigh Shooting Code* took a disdainful view of those feeble mortals who required ghillies to carry their sporting baggage on the hill: 'A servant is often only an annoyance to the grouse-shooter. A marker, however, may be serviceable provided he can obtain a thoroughbred one – some shepherd lad, whose proficiency may be guessed at by the knowing cunning that glitters in his eye when he is told that his services are required. A youth of this description will lie down when a bird rises, put up his hands to his face like the blinders of a wagon horse and mark a bird down to an inch, a mile off.'

Colonel Peter Hawker, writing in 1830, described the splendours of Scottish sport. But this hard man added dyspeptically, 'Such, however, is the misery of the Highland public houses, and particularly to our perfumed young men of fashion, that I have generally observed nine out of ten of them, however good may have been their sport, come home cursing and swearing most bitterly about their wooden births, peat fires and oatmeal cakes.'

Perhaps it was partly in answer to the complaints of the 'perfumed young men' that Victorians created that remarkable new focus of leisured life, the Scottish sporting lodge. All over the Highlands, in the midst of miles of barren mountain, sprang up edifices of stone or corrugated iron, lined with spartan pine and scantily supplied with water closets, designed to house sportsmen through the summer season.

One of Trollope's wittiest passages, in *The Duke's Children*, sketches the contrast between the most austere specimens of lodge, whose occupants dedicated themselves single-mindedly to slaughter, and the more social variety, where sport took second place to dalliance. The author's Lord Gerald Palliser was not a bit impressed by Captain Dobbes' sporting headquarters, Crummie-Toddie:

'Ugly, do you call it?'

'Infernally ugly,' said Lord Gerald.

'What did you expect to find? A big hotel, and a lot of Cockneys? If you come after grouse, you must come to what the grouse thinks pretty.'

Down the glen from Crummie-Toddie, Trollope situated Killancodlem, '. . . a fine castellated mansion, with beautiful though narrow grounds, standing in the valley of the Archay River, with a mountain behind and the river in front. Between the gates and the river there was a public road on which a stage-coach ran, with loud-blown horns and the noise of many tourists. A mile beyond the Castle was the Killancodlem hotel which made up a hundred and twenty beds, and at which half as many more guests would sleep on occasions under the tables.'

The Killancodlemites did not bother much about sport, though '. . . on certain grand days a deer or two might be shot – and would be very much talked about afterwards . . . At Killancodlem there was lawn tennis and a billiard room and dancing every night.'

Shame on them. It seems a deplorable outcome to an otherwise delightful tale, that the young hero, Lord Silver-bridge, ends up marrying an American Killancodlemite. I have always been more of the Crummie-Toddie persuasion, bent on the hills and the river all day and exhausted to bed at ten pm. But I am teased to death by family and friends who manage to play party games until three am and still turn up fit for the hill at nine the next morning.

One of the greatest pleasures of lodges that have been in the same hands for years is the sense of historical continuity that pervades them. Pre-war novels and Edwardian social reference books discarded from libraries at home in England generations ago fill Scottish sitting-room shelves in random array. Aged and now priceless items of shooting and fishing tackle clutter gunrooms. The old brass-trimmed wooden post-box sits on the hall table. The heads of half-century-old stags that have achieved a kind of immortality peer reproach-fully down upon the sideboard. Estate gamebooks are an unending source of entertainment. I remember one in Sutherland, in which a host expressed exasperation at the interruption of the party in 1939: 'No guests were able to come after September 3rd, owing to the outbreak of war.'

There was a loch on that estate, miles from any road, to which we walked one hot, heather-dusty morning and watched the trout rising. How tempted we were by those innocent fish, which could never have been fished for in history! A year or so later, I was given a book published in 1888, entitled *A Season In Sutherland*. Its author, Mr J. Edwardes-Moss, rented the same estate for season after season, devoting himself for months on end solely to sport. He too, it transpired, puffed and panted up to that same loch and reached the same conclusion as ourselves. 'We anticipated a sort of competition among these unsophisticated fish,' he wrote, 'as to which should be the happy one to possess himself of our flies.' Being an energetic Victorian, J. Edwardes-Moss sent south to the Army & Navy Stores for their nine-foot Duplex-Berthon collapsible boat. With immense labour, he transported his purchase on a deer pony to the loch. He came miserably home at the end of a weary day, with just three minnows. *Plus ça change.*

One of my favourite Victorian books, *The Highland Sportsman and Tourist* of 1886, gives details of every tenanted sporting estate in Scotland, its bag and rent. Mr Edwardes-Moss is duly listed as tenant of '. . . this capital sporting place of 30,000 acres', for which he paid a princely £100 a year. 'The nearest railway station is Lairg, about forty-five miles distant. A coach runs thrice weekly between Lairg and Tongue . . . Supplies may be obtained by post-car from Thurso, which passes the lodge three times a week. There is a postal and telegraph office at Tongue, where a medical man also resides.'

None of us with a sense of history can fail to be conscious of the blacker aspects of the past, wandering among the fallen stones of crofts and whole villages laid waste in the Highland Clearances. There is a melancholy about the hills, a terrible sadness about the emptiness, that marches with the beauty and of which only the most insensitive visitor could be oblivious. Today, however, empty spaces are so rare in this over-crowded island that they have attained a preciousness of their own, which deserves to be cherished and above all spared from promiscuous afforestation. Our descendants will surely think we were mad, if we continue to allow the great northern wildernesses to be polluted by conifers of negligible economic value, an absolute blight upon beauty.

One of the most enjoyable expeditions I ever undertook was a December walk across the hills from Blair Atholl to Inverary, when I was writing a biography of Montrose, Charles I's incomparable Lieutenant-General in Scotland. I wanted to catch the flavour of the Royalist army's famous winter march against the Campbells; though most of Montrose's men scarcely had the benefit of boots and thermal underclothes. In summer, it is necessary to share the Highlands with a host of other visitors; in December, my labrador and I had the hills to ourselves. It was sometimes hard-going, crossing the burns frozen into slopes of ice along the sheer hillsides, floundering through the snow on high ground. But each night, we warmed ourselves by the gas stove in a tiny bivouac tent, and cooked a mess of porridge and beans that was certainly more nourishing than anything the Royalist army found on their march. I felt closer to the country on that lonely trip than ever I did in summer company. I could savour the sort of enchantment Charles St John and other Victorian sporting pioneers experienced, when they too explored the hills with only dogs, rod and gun for company.

There is much pleasure in reading of what earlier sportsmen did, on the moors and waters we know today. Millais, Grimble, St John, Tom Speedy and John Colquhoun were prominent among scores of Victorians who wrote memorable books about Scottish sport. I love that immortal passage of William Scrope's, in *Days and Nights of Salmon Fishing on the Tweed*, published in 1843, about wading in the days before waterproof fishing boots were thought of. 'As you are likely not to take a just estimate of the cold in the excitement of the sport, should you be of a delicate temperament and be wading in the month of February, when it may chance to freeze very hard, pull down your stockings and examine your legs. Should they be black or even purple, it might perhaps be as well to get on dry land; but if they are only rubicund, you may continue to enjoy the water, if it so pleases you.' Phew.

Tom Speedy, another iron man, took an equally bleak attitude towards feminine distractions on the moor. 'Ladies, as a rule, are not "sportsmen", and except perhaps occasionally joining the shooting party on the hill, are in many cases doomed to the monotony of the lodge.' Captain Dobbes of Crummie-Toddie would have approved, but perhaps the most delightful of all Edwardian sporting photographs is that of the tweeded Hilda Murray of Elibank, gun and vast bird in hand, captioned in 1910, 'My first capercailzie'. Today, few women shoot grouse, but many are keen and good fishers and stalkers. My own reservoir of generosity was strained to the limits a couple of years ago, when a novice wife in our party caught five salmon in a week in which I caught none. It is all luck, of course, as I always say, except when *I* am catching fish.

The greatest difference between Scottish lodge life today and in Victorian times is that, for most of us, a week or a fortnight is now as much as we can hope for, where our ancestors expected to spend months on end shooting and fishing. No self-respecting member of the Cabinet, even down to Harold Macmillan's day, would miss his stint on the moors. Remember that dreary egalitarian controversy about the perils posed to Conservative hegemony by 'the grouse-moor image'? Today, Master Nicholas Soames, a gentleman of verily Edwardian sporting appetites, is probably the only member of the House of Commons who continues the great Tory tradition.

The delights of the old night sleeper to Inverness – a magic carpet from the evening carbon monoxide fumes of north London to that wonderful dawn chuff past the deer beside the line and the tiny stations between Perth and Inverness – are no more. It is cheaper and more painless to drive north. On the way home, your son can press hand-lettered signs against the car window to be read by a neighbour in the next lane on the M6 with rods visible – 'How many fish did you get?' Fish ermen being a companionable lot, he will probably get an answer. More intense occupancy of lodges has also contributed to the decline of many splendid Highland fishing hotels, that were once dominated by the scales in the hall and glass cases full of impossibly enormous monsters in the dining room. Today, European and Japanese coach tours have taken over and it is difficult even to get a passable hotel Sunday lunch between Perth and Inverness.

Reading Eric Parker's *Shooting Weekend Book* in bed one night, I noticed a nice example of sporting inflation. Mr Parker, writing in 1943 (when no doubt he sensibly believed that penning works like his own was a contribution to the very culture Western civilization was fighting to preserve), recommended two pounds as an appropriate tip for a keeper, after a fortnight's stay in a Highland lodge, with another pound to the second keeper. Ten shillings, he felt, was about right after a day's driving for thirty-five brace, a pound for a hundred brace and ten shillings for a twenty brace walking-up day. These days, the scale of generosity to keepers that some hosts recommend to their guests imply that the keeper lives on starvation wages for most of the year.

On the credit side, the opportunity to enjoy Highland sport is now distributed among far more people than ever gained a taste of it a generation ago. Contrary to popular perception, if one shares a lodge with a party of family and friends, it makes for no more expensive a holiday than the same period in most Continental hotels. On the debit ledger, sensations are crowded into a perilously short space of time. The Scottish weather is an implacable tyrant. It is agony to sit all week on an expensive riverbank, praying for rain to make the water fishable only to have to leave in a thunderstorm on Sunday, knowing that next week's tenants will be in piscatorial paradise.

For shooting, of course, the reverse is true. It is no good pursuing grouse with pointers in the rain. Fifteen years ago, I aroused the rage of our entire party by driving them out of the lodge we had rented, on day after day of torrential drizzle. 'We don't want to shoot!' they would cry. Yet I forced them into the downpour, because I could not bear to think of going south again without doing what we had come to do. Shades of awful Captain Dobbes. I have always fancied that one reason whisky plays so large a part in the legend of the Highlands is that there are so frequently reasons for employing it to drown sorrows.

I suppose there are people who come home from Scotland in August and September having failed to enjoy themselves: men and women who found themselves in miserable parties or were crossed in love or quarrelled with the cook. I used to shed a tear when we got as far south as Dingwall. I have got over that now. I have trained myself simply to think about going back.

GROUSE FEVER

EVERY GROUSE BUTT possesses a personality of its own. However good the shooting, I feel a touch deprived if I find myself taking up position on a moor behind a mere shield of wooden slats. Give me, instead, one of those works of the keeper's art, a drystone wall semi-circle, topped with a couple of decks of peat and heather. A concrete floor seems a shade overdone. But settling down to begin a day high in the hills, deep inside one's own little sporting rampart, gets the whole occasion off on the best possible footing.

I also like a butt with a short horizon. The longer I have to look at those oncoming birds, soaring and dropping with the contours across a mile of hillside, the more sure I am to miss them when they reach me. It seems easier if they burst over the ridge, thirty yards in front, and the challenge is simply that of pulling up the gun and firing instantly, knowing that a second's hesitation will be too long.

The memories of grouse shooting that I cherish are of sunlit days, shooting in shirt-sleeves. Yet honesty compels me to face the fact that on more than half the days I have shot in recent years, the weather has been something between moderate and appalling. For those of us who wear spectacles, a day of driving rain spells disaster on the moor. It is difficult enough to hit grouse at the best of times, but with water streaming off one's glasses, it becomes plain impossible. I like to think that I am an all-weather sportsman. But there have been at least a couple of days in recent seasons when I have stood huddled in the butt, praying that our host would face reality and call the whole thing off. The gale was driving clouds of grouse out of the flanks, while only a few clusters of bedraggled birds crossed the line. The gun was so wet and slippery that it needed a sharp effort to move the safety catch forward. I was missing almost everything that came my way. The dog was lying shivering in the mud at my feet, oblivious to anything going on above her head. Then again, perhaps it is the memory of shooting on days like that which make the bright ones seem so precious when they come. And the stinkers give us all plenty to whimper about over tea.

Good or bad, driven grouse days are seldom less than notable. Perhaps because I do not get more than six or seven of them a year, I can claim to have a pretty clear picture in my mind of each of the moors I have shot over the past eight or nine years. Snapshots – of this covey or that flanker, this drive or that gun – remain fixed in the mind. At all the shoots I visit, at least half the bag is made by three or four local guns who do nothing but shoot grouse from August to December. More than any other form of shooting, driven grouse demand practice. I have improved from very bad to moderate in recent years. But I still shoot too late, still make heavy weather of crossing birds, still find singletons or pairs much easier than packs. How often one yearns to shoot with two guns on grouse moors, simply to have a chance to make a dent in the packs! I know a boorish Highland peer who always brings a pair, even when everybody else is shooting with one (I asked his loader one day how many his lordship brings when he is invited to shoot double guns. Three? Four?) Most of us make do with wives or children stuffing in cartridges, to speed up the reloading rate. But there is no way of getting in four barrels at any one lot of grouse without two guns.

One of the 'snapshots' I mentioned above shows my neighbour in the butts two years running, a Scottish baronet who conceals his customary good humour beneath a choleric appearance. He stands hunched, his gun lying before him on the front of the butt, hands in pocket, spaniels at feet, until an incoming bird shifts him into instant action. Something almost always falls down. When he is spectating, though, and the birds are coming over me, I feel I can write the caption to the expression on his face in the picture, 'Why the hell do they waste valuable sky, heather, and cartridges letting silly bloody southerners shoot at birds they can't hit!'

Yet lately, I find myself questioning one cherished truism: that grouse are the most difficult of all gamebirds to shoot. I think we should modify that assertion, and declare that grouse *in a wind* are the hardest. Birds flying with or across the wind present terrific problems. Again and again, some of us aim at an overhead grouse in a pack and are embarrassed to see the one behind fall dead. If the wind is absent, however, or if the birds cross the line against it, then surely they become much more manageable targets; indeed, no harder than the average driven pheasant. Personally, I found that one season I was using around five cartridges to kill a single grouse in high wind and rain. But on a couple of still days, my average improved to around one for two or three. Most other guns found the same, and I think this experience is commonplace.

One handicap I could do without on the moor is that of my own absurd height. Grouse butts are not designed for men of six foot six. I face an annual chorus of cracks about my need for a portable butt extender. In reality, I sit on a shooting stick or fold myself double while I am waiting (usually reading a book, for those half-hour waits can pall). Concealment is important on the moor. The trouble sets in, however, when the birds streak forward and I extend myself to shoot. Even the most single-minded grouse is prone to jink at the last moment, with ill-effects on my aim, when it sees two or three feet of Hastings suddenly appear in its flight path.

I don't know whether it is my imagination, but, in general, grouse-beating seems better managed in England these days than it is in Scotland. In the Highlands, it is almost impossible to recruit a team of local beaters, and thus most estates depend upon roving groups of university students, a keen and good-hearted lot, who nonetheless lack expertise, especially as flankers. A lot of birds seem to get back past them. Then again, your elderly Cumbrian flanker is not averse to a quiet sit down in mid drive. A friend with an exceptionally fluent stableyard vocabulary and voice power to match was enraged one day last season by a flanker sitting contemplating his pension while grouse streamed away over his head. 'WHY DON'T YOU WAVE YOUR FLAG, YOU SILLY OLD ******** ******** ****?' bellowed a well-known voice from the butts. The elderly sage leapt to his feet as if he'd been shot. Even a lifetime of Cumbrian pubs hadn't immunized him to that sort of language and volume – and from a gentleman, too. He was still waving his flag with a fine frenzy when the pickers-up started work.

For all the joys of grouse-driving, at most moors one does not have the fun of the walking, which is so much part of Scottish sport. A veritable armoured column of four-wheel drive vehicles wends its way up the hill towards the butts, because nowadays each of us likes to take his own transport, loaded down with personal impedimenta and dogs. This is practical and comfortable, but less sociable. The corrupting bit comes in, however, after leaving the Range Rovers, Shoguns and Mercedes jeeps. More and more moors provide house-to-butt transport, in the form of the all-terrain Argo. We are all great admirers of the Argo for bringing deer down from the hill and taking everybody over sixty to the butts. But I think Argo rides should be banned for anybody under sixty, who is not sick or crippled. If sport is to involve absolutely no physical exertion, why bother to get out of the wagon at all? Why not go the whole hog and shoot from the back of the vehicle or drive grouse over the road? I do not believe Highland hills and internal combustion engines were ever designed for each other. I may be a Luddite or a reactionary about this. But I shall continue to heap scorn on any man short of late middle age who cannot even be bothered to walk up a hill to shoot.

This is carping. The truth is, of course, that, like most shooters, I will sell my soul any time for a day at driven grouse. The thrill never fades, watching those birds turning above the hillside, then falling out of the sky to land sometimes a quarter mile below in the burn, whence the dog will know that she has done a day's work before she returns. Shooting on a famous moor we once took for a day, my loader said kindly, 'It's nice to have some people here who are really keen. His lordship, now, when he's here, settles down in the back of the butt with his tranny and *The Daily Telegraph* and tells me to let him know when there's something worth shooting. It's just a chore to him, you see.' I hope it will never be that to me. At the end of each drive, when a flurry of larks through the line indicates that the beaters are just over the horizon, there is always that stab of regret for the finish. Luckily there is usually another butt, another covey over the hill.

THE SPORTING WIFE

IN NORWAY A few years ago, we met an exceptionally pretty
girl, daughter of a large Scottish estate owner, fishing with her
fiancé. She had just come down from Oxford and looked as if
she would be more at home in a ballgown and Chester Square.
At first I assumed that she was on the Vosso under duress, so
to speak, to clap daintily when her loved one hooked a salmon.
I could not have been more wrong. She proved to be an ardent
fisher and I was later told in London that her reputation as a
setter of snares, executor of game and general mistress of the
wild places was legendary. Her fiancé's fortune and good
looks had done rather less to win her hand, it was said, than
the assurance that, once married, the two of them could devote
their lives to casting fly rods around the world together.

Women, when they choose, are often better fishers than men – perhaps they possess a more highly developed sense of rhythm. I suspect, however, that many take up a rod only in self-defence, to make the best of it when their husbands insist upon an annual migration to Scotland. If it were otherwise, one would see more girls trout-fishing on English rivers and lakes at weekends, instead of which they usually prefer (or are chained to) the garden or the children. Even the most devoted countrywoman, even in this age when we are preoccupied with sexual parity, tends to possess the instinct for hunting or, more frankly, killing, in lesser measure than a man. The fact that so many women love fox-hunting does not diminish this argument since the joys of fox-hunting have relatively little to do with killing foxes. My own wife will happily cast a fly if we are together on a river and, a year or two ago, much enjoyed hooking two salmon in ten minutes on a day when I could do nothing.

I do not think she would regard it as a great deprivation if she was told that she could never fish again. But it is infinitely agreeable for any woman to demonstrate that, when she chooses, she can wipe the eye of lesser (male) mortals. Among Barbara Cartland's many qualities, determination and courage rank high. There was a story of her on the Helmsdale a few years ago now, mercilessly teasing the men in her party every evening in the lodge about their inability to catch fish in bright sunshine and low water. One of them, supremely provoked, was rash enough to mutter something about, 'Well, I'd like to see you do any better.' The next morning, the pink Rolls-Royce bore the prodigious novelist majestically to the riverside. A few casts later, she hooked her fish. Ten minutes on, the triumphant procession returned in state to the lodge, having made its point. That's show business for you.

Most women find shooting an unrewarding spectator sport. My wife declares that there is a certain sameness about watching me miss grouse. I have tried to make it more interesting by instructing her as a loader. But when I break the gun she tends either to be preoccupied by watching the last covey fading into the distance or irritated by finding the spent cases flying into her face. She says she is a doer, not a watcher and would much rather be hunting, a sport that commands her respect in a fashion that driven game-shooting emphatically does not. So, when I see a girl hanging onto a man's gun arm from first drive to last on a shooting day, I am enough of a cynic to suspect either young love or a somewhat precarious relationship. I have seen an American tycoon standing on a peg with a former international beauty queen nibbling his ear throughout the drive and somehow he still shot well. The best shooting schools, though, do not recommend the technique.

One icy cold January dawn in County Kerry, I was crouching beside a lake, waiting for duck with a clutch of other guns. Next to me was the long-standing girlfriend of one of them. I said I admired her fortitude and that no power on earth would get my wife to turn out for such a rendezvous. 'Yes, well, yes,' she said rather glumly, 'but that's the difference between being a wife and, er, something else, isn't it?'

The belles of every shoot, of course, are the pickers-up. Most of the best dog handlers seem to be women. They are eagle-eyed in their observation of the performance of the guns; sometimes uncharitable in their dismissal of pathetic and ill-founded claims from the line about that bird which was 'hard-hit and coming down in the spinney'; the sternness in their treatment of their dogs, fails to mask the obvious fact that they dote on them. They are an essential ingredient of the day. Their efficiency can sometimes be overdone, from the viewpoint of guns with dogs of our own at heel. But those teams of labradors handled by doughty ladies in unisex Barbours and floppy hats (why is it usually men who are foolish enough to suppose that they can control spaniels?) are one of the most enjoyable spectacles at most shoots.

Relatively few women themselves shoot, and those who do use mostly 16 bores or short-cartridged 12s. I have only once seen evidence to support the view that they are incompetent or dangerous – a dog was on the receiving end. On the whole, women who shoot are a good deal more efficient than the rest of us, like that indomitable Yorkshire grouse-shooter, Barbara Hawkins, or those splendid Victorian authors and sportswomen, Lady Breadalbane and Hilda Murray of Elibank. But most are content to leave driven game-shooting to men. They are more enthusiastic about stalking, and a lot of the best rifle shots seem to be girls. They enjoy the relationship with the stalker, and perhaps also the artistry of pursuing and shooting a single beast more than the noisy mass executions in the coverts.

One of the tests of relationships in most sporting households is to discover who does the plucking. In our younger days in Scotland, my wife says that I put her off grouse for life by making her take part in rather maggoty plucking and drawing parties outside the kitchen door after tea. For years, I sat in the garage at home plucking away, sometimes fifty or sixty pheasants in a season. Nowadays, I am afraid, they go to the butcher. As a pastime, plucking has lost its novelty and I settle down over the dustbin only in an emergency. My wife says she has too much to do getting her tack ready for more worthwhile pursuits: 'You shoot them. You deal with them!' She does, however, perform the most important sporting rites of all in an exemplary fashion. There is no hand from which I would rather receive a delicately roasted partridge. That is by far the most skilled and important challenge for the sporting wife.

In Praise of the
Yeoman Dog

ONE DECEMBER MORNING at a shoot where I was a guest, a visiting American gun arrived trailing a stranger and a leash of labradors. The dogs looked and behaved like guardsmen, forming fours and sloping arms at the hint of a whistle and generally conducting themselves in a fashion unlike everybody else's dogs, including mine.

They were present on approval, we were told, to be shown off by their trainer. The successful officer candidate would be crated up and shipped off to Georgia, there to spend the rest of its days picking up quail. We never learned those dogs' names, but they were readily distinguishable by price: there was the £1,000 dog, the £1,100 dog and the £1,200 dog. At tea-time, inevitably, the £1,200 dog was declared the winner (or not, as the case might be) and there the matter rested until the same time the following year, when the American guest appeared once more. How was his king of labradors, we demanded? Ah yes, the dog. He shuffled his feet as much as American billionaires ever do and said, 'First time I shot a bird over him, I said, "Go geddit!" Off he went, and we haven't seen him from that day to this.' We would have chortled, but we were all too busy feeling sorry for that hapless labrador, presumably still trying to find someone to tell him the way from Augusta to Heathrow.

I waste a lot of money on expensive shooting gear and fishing tackle and gardening gadgets. But I have come to the conclusion that, for people like me, there is much to be said in praise of the yeoman dog. I mean, by that, the gundog of honest but humble parentage, who grows up knowing that life is a struggle, all flesh is grass and that one has got to produce a day's work for a day's meal – a Thatcherite dog, in other words. I know lots of friends who own vastly expensive gundogs of impeccable pedigree and appearance – huge golden retrievers that will make them fine rugs some day, spaniels with bloodlines that would provoke the Prince of Wales to touch his forelock – these are the dogs that win field trials and get their pictures on the front of *Country Life*. But for those of us who can give our dogs less attention then they deserve most of the week and most of the summer, who cart them from town to country and back, board them while on holiday, use them to beat a cover rough shooting as well as to pick up, then I am not convinced that a hot, highly-bred animal is the right answer.

My first gundog was mostly labrador, with a pointer grandfather, a beautiful head, and rather too bony a body to be graceful, 'Very svelte dog you've got there,' fellow guns would declare speculatively, as they examined Stokeley and tried to remember whether the Kennel Club had authorised a new breed lately. Peter Moxon kindly trained him and ended up warning me not to expect too much. But, like most dog-owners, I shall never forget the first time I dropped a hen pheasant, out hedge-walking on a late December afternoon, and saw that streak of black energy haring past me up the hill.

After a few seconds' erratic chase, Stokeley pinned the bird and came trotting back towards me with it. I walked on air to the car, knowing that I'd got my dearest wish – the makings of a retriever.

Stokeley was never a properly controlled dog. Looking back at all sorts of experiences in the shooting field that I thought funny at the time, I can see how tiresome he and I were to our sporting hosts and guests. 'Whose is that asterisked asterisked asterisked black dog running *straight* into the next drive,' I bawled, at our own shoot one morning. 'Yours, Max,' murmured a still, small voice behind me. Oh dear, oh dear.

In those days, though, when I spent most of my days rough shooting, Stokeley's nose and dedication were priceless. I loved him for his irrepressible high spirits. He seemed to enjoy living in the car and a succession of hotel rooms as I took him with me round the country about my business. During the week in London, he ran dangerously behind my bicycle to Richmond Park for exercise. An exceptionally fortunate wanderer, a dozen times he went roving, and was returned from unpromising locations such as Vauxhall Bridge.

On the hill in Scotland, when we were short of a pointer, on his day he would hold a point over grouse with surprising patience – ancestry coming out, I think. There was a day when I shot a ptarmigan high on a crag and it fluttered away to land a quarter of a mile below us, out of sight. I was sure we would never find that bird. But five minutes later, Stokeley was back, bird in mouth, tail wagging like a windmill. In Ireland, amid those miles of gorse and thorn, he was in his element, digging out pheasants from the sort of cover only spaniels are supposed to prosper in. His light build gave him a tremendous turn of speed, which could be a menace if he ran amok on a driven day, but was perfect for coursing a running pheasant. I have never liked the very heavy cast of aristocratic labradors, which possess the characteristics, and sometimes the temperament, of Sherman tanks.

Like so many dogs, Stokeley eventually paid the price of an over-indulgent sex life. One morning in Ireland, he didn't return from a nocturnal ramble. I picked him up days later, stiff and cold, on the railway line. I carried him up Mount Brandon to bury him, where we had pursued grouse to no purpose but infinite pleasure. He possessed most of my own characteristics, impatience and impetuousness prominent among them.

His successor, Francie Fitzpatrick, an Irish liver and white spaniel, was a very different proposition. My wife adored her (as she does to this day), because she is pretty and sweet-natured. But I can claim no more success than most of my friends in controlling a spaniel shooting or in making her pick up.

Francie has a splendid nose. If I run very fast behind her – or not quite so fast, now that she is an old lady – I can sometimes get a shot rough shooting. But while she will worry a dead pheasant or chew a grouse or nuzzle a woodcock, no power on earth will make her bring a bird back. Just once, and only once, has she done so. Out alone with her on the hills of Sutherland, I shot a long grouse which landed fifty yards out in a loch. So much for that one, I thought. Then, to my astonishment, Francie plunged in. She swam out, picked the grouse, and brought it back to my feet. 'You see?' she said, like the dowager leaping from her wheelchair in Alan Bennett's *Forty Years On*, 'I can do it perfectly well really, it's just that I'm so rich I don't have to.' I regard it as an indication that shooting men are growing more honest, that one sees fewer part-time countrymen these days who profess to be able to manage spaniels, delightful dogs though they are for the house or the beating line.

In my crosser moments, I would have given Francie away, once she had conclusively demonstrated that she would not work for me. But my wife, who often declares that I am not a proper animal person, tore several strips off me when that suggestion was made. 'You don't just pick animals up and put them down like that,' she said, 'when you have them, you keep them for life.' I pointed out with impeccable logic that this was not at all her line when she found herself with the wrong horse. But she loved Francie, and Francie loved her. I retired hurt from that encounter.

In canine terms, I suppose Francie's background might be described as Anglo-Irish gentry. But for my own next dog, I went determinedly back to working stock, to the daughter of a very good picker-up I knew. I had seen her mother in the field for years and much admired her performance. Tweedie, the daughter, was a shy and rather nervous dog when she came to us, too angular to be handsome. Her trainer in Norfolk was not much impressed by her and, to begin with, nor was I. However, as the seasons went by, in an extraordinary fashion she acquired not only the physical, but also the temperamental characteristics of old Stokeley. Very lean and leggy, in her prime she could give a greyhound a fair race. But she has also developed into an admirably sensible, down-to-earth gundog. At the age of eight, she has, at last, reached the age at which I no longer need to peg her at my feet – or not often, anyway. She goes, she finds the bird, she brings it back. What more can you ask? Day after day, one sees the owners of very expensive black and golden labradors urging, pleading, cajoling them to fetch a pheasant. Will they, heck. I don't think it is lack of education – they have all been to very expensive schools – it is surely just the wrong sort of breeding to cope with their owners' peripatetic lives.

One day in January, with a friend and our sons, I walked the outside of one of the thickest covers in the East Midlands – a perfect harbour for a fox, a terrible place to get a bird out of. Tweedie flushed eleven woodcock and four pheasants from that maze of holly, scrub and bramble. I told her I was proud of her, and I was, too.

Tweedie will never bequeath us puppies, I am afraid. She and Francie were spayed after one sexual disaster too many. There was the episode when we returned from holiday and I rang the kennels to say that I would be over in the morning to collect our two dogs. 'You don't mean two,' said an aggrieved voice at the other end, 'You mean thirteen.' That little surprise dispelled our illusions that puppies were brought by the stork, and made us feel uncommonly foolish. One morning a year or so later, my wife went to let out the two dogs, and was astounded to see three emerge. The third, a sheepdog, had gnawed through the side of a solid, purpose-built wooden kennel building to get into the seraglio. His owner, a doughty local farmer, displayed a glow of pride when we sent for him to fetch the dog, and the bill. 'Gaw!', he exclaimed, amid the impressive wreckage of the kennel, 'I can just see the bogger doing it!'

When we choose our next dog, which I hope will not have to be for many moons yet, absolute sexual frigidity will be considered a virtue as important as a sound, workaday view of pheasants.

A Stalk
Without a Stalker

THROUGH THE FIRST two seasons of our dogging experiences in Sutherland, one of the pleasures of each day on the hill was the sight of the deer on the high ground above us.

Ben Stumanadh, the mountain that dominates the moor, is shaped like two horseshoes placed back to back, with deep corries on both the northern and southern approaches. The resident deer population fifteen years ago must have been approaching 150 hind and calves. By late August, stags were moving onto the ground. By late September, there were usually some good beasts on the hill.

I knew nothing of stalking, save what I had read in books. But I was eager to learn. I mentioned earlier that when my Bisley days were over, I exchanged my old full-bore target rifle for a .308 telescopic-sighted Parker-Hale. There was no stalker on our ground, but the right to shoot two stags went with the sporting lease. We did nothing about the deer in the first year or two. But a neighbouring laird asked to shoot a stag after we had gone south and killed one of the best beasts shot in the Highlands that season. From his lodge window, he had been spying the herd diligently across the loch, and knew what was out there. We, of course, did not. Insistently, I nagged our crotchety old keeper to take me to the hill. He would have none of it. He said it was a waste of time. He was paid to take out grouse-shooters, not novice deer-slayers.

Night after night around the dinner-table at Tongue House, we talked our way around the deer issue. I said that, keeper or no keeper, I was determined to try my hand. Others did not rate my chances. One thing led to another, until money was mentioned. Bets were offered, and finally taken. By bed-time, I had undertaken to shoot a stag on Ben Stumanadh and £25 of other peoples' money said that I would fail.

Privately, I must admit, I cherished hopes of pulling off the triple – stag, grouse, salmon. It was with this ambition in mind that I rose early, at five am. Soon after dawn, I was making my way along the lochside between Loyal and Crag-gie, my footsteps chasing away the morning mist, rifle slung across my shoulder. The hills can seem very lonely in those early hours, even when one knows and loves them as well as I did that stretch of Sutherland. The problem I had so cockily set myself to solve the previous night seemed very formidable now, with not a deer to be seen around the foot of the mountain.

I marshalled my slender stock of stalking lore, gleaned mostly from the pages of Victorian memoirs. I needed to come upon the deer from downwind. Now, it was blowing from the north. The shortest ascent of the hill, up the north corrie, seemed therefore unsuitable. I began the long walk around the base of Ben Stumanadh, to approach the summit along one of the southern ridges. Once upon a time, the place must have been stalked seriously, for there remains a derelict stalkers' bothy at the foot of the corrie, surrounded by one of those places of vivid green grass, which occur in many parts of the Strathnaver region, and mark the sites of forgotten villages and shielings. I once saw an eighteenth-century map of the area that showed iron workings at the foot of Ben Stumanadh. I am not a superstitious man, but those broken stones and stretches of green sward amid the wilderness always make me feel surrounded by the ghosts of forsaken clansmen in their plaids.

Now I began to prepare for the steep climb and to think about what I should do if, or when, I found the deer. 'Always advance on deer from above, as they are much less apt to look up than downhill,' wrote John Colquhoun. The previous afternoon, I sat casting from a boat on Loch Craggie, listening intently to the counsel of the charming retired keeper who acted as our ghillie, Donald Macdonald. He had spent forty years on the neighbouring estate. While he was not a stalker, he knew his deer very well. Donald harangued me about the need to take more care of the hinds than of the stags, to watch for the way scent could cheat direction amid the swirling air currents in the corries and, like Colquhoun, he warned me to stay above the beasts.

At that moment, as I breasted a small shoulder of hillside with my reflections, I was suddenly confronted by a herd of deer 200 yards in front of me, every head staring hard in my direction. I dropped flat in the heather, but I was upwind of them. They turned at once and began to trot, then to canter away up the hill. There were some thirty or more hinds and calves and, yes, a single stag at the rear of the party. I waited until they had disappeared over the ridge, then got to my feet once more and walked on.

I reached the lochside from which they had bolted and gazed upon the mass of tracks in the black peat. Many times we had looked down from the high ground on deer watering at this loch – I should have been watching for them. I began to clamber towards the crest in their wake. Perhaps 200 feet up, I had a remarkable encounter. I crossed a horizon to find myself face to face with a golden eagle, perched on a rock barely twenty yards away. He stood for perhaps five seconds before spreading his wings and lofting gracefully off around the mountain. Many times we had seen the eagles above us as we shot. Sometimes their passage drove the grouse to sit specially tight for our pointers, but I had never, and have never since, been so close to the great bird.

I reached the spine of the ridge, with a marvellous view for miles to the sea in the north, across to Ben Loyal and Ben Hope in the west. I crawled cautiously forward, to peer down into the corrie. I could see nothing. The deer must have crossed over onto the lochside. But, then, as I moved forward a little further, suddenly there they were, perhaps 300 yards below. I dropped flat on the rocks, almost crying with excitement. I eased off my field glasses and pack and laid them among the scree. Easing back the bolt of the rifle, I rammed a round into the chamber and put up the safety catch. This time, the deer were upwind of me. Remembering a few fragments of military fieldcraft, or perhaps of John Macnab, I began to crawl forward flat on my stomach, down the bare 45 degree convex decline between myself and the beasts.

When next I raised my head a few inches, half a dozen hinds were staring straight at me, 150 yards away. Where was the stag? I crawled on, measuring every yard, not daring to look again at the deer. Then, to my horror, a trickle of rocks slipped beneath me. Within seconds a miniature landslide cascaded towards the deer. The herd sprang to life, leaping down the corrie away from me.

There, behind them, was the stag – an eight-pointer of moderate size and no obvious distinction. Few stalkers would have let me do it, but I fired down into his back as he ran, aiming just behind the neck. On he went, without evident check. Then, fifty yards on, as I knelt in supplication, the stag suddenly slowed and stopped. I stared, fascinated, for a moment as he turned and looked back towards me. Forcing myself to take time, I thought of Donald's lecture in the boat on the loch and fired just behind his shoulder. The stag stood stock still, alone now, while the rest of the herd was half a mile away. While the shot was still echoing, I sprang to my feet and raced down the hill towards him, ejecting the spent case as I ran, thrilling to see the beast motionless, a hundred yards from me, then fifty. He walked two steps, lurched and keeled over to bounce in the heather. He looked at me once from where he lay, as I came up to him, then that was that.

I sagged with weariness, physical and emotional, as I climbed laboriously back to the ridge to retrieve my pack and glasses. Then I sat down beside the carcase and drank coffee from my Thermos. I talked to the beast as the sun started to appear over the hill, because I felt an intimacy with him at that moment that no grouse or trout could match. Stroking his hide, all the clichés of stalking I had ever heard or read passed through my mind. When I saw him fall, I had felt a sudden sadness and a sort of shame – not regret, because the thrill of success was too strong – but a sense of assassination. When the big rifle jolted against my shoulder, it felt as if this was no contest. My first bullet had gone into his back, the second had made a neat hole in the flank beside his chest. I looked the beast in the eye, told him that he could only present the problems of a rabbit on a larger scale, then got to work with a sheath knife. It took me about half an hour to gralloch him, largely because, for the first fifteen minutes, I could not muster the courage to dig in my hands. Then I started down the corrie.

Knowing nothing of the business, I had brought no rope. Having tried unsuccessfully to hoist the brute onto my shoulders (this was where our relations began to deteriorate), I settled for dragging him by his hind legs. Yes, I know now that I should have pulled him front first. I did not know then. It was nine am when I shot him; it was eleven when I reached the foot of the corrie, after bumping the carcase across burns and over ridges, through the rocks and the heather. Utterly exhausted, I left my companion where he lay and trudged the last mile back to the car, to enlist the aid of Hughie, the most long-suffering young gardener in the Highlands, to get him to the road.

I had imagined myself motoring in triumph up the drive with the beast across the bonnet. In reality, by the time we got him into the game larder, everybody else had departed for the hill.

'Och, he's an old beast and you did well to shoot him,' said Donald Macdonald, to my intense relief, as an inexpert judge of deer. I followed the guns and shot lamentably all afternoon, dimissing any slender hope of adding grouse and salmon to the bag. Indeed, I have not achieved the triple to this day. I fell asleep over tea and scarcely woke for dinner.

In the years since that morning in Sutherland, I have shot a few stags alongside some fine Highland stalkers. But no beast has come close to giving me the thrill, and the challenge, of that lone, ignorant, amateur pursuit of the deer on Ben Stumanadh. We hang our hats on his head in the hall at home, and stalking friends ask why I troubled to have such a poor specimen mounted. Both the beast and I know the answer to that one.

The Tweed 'Auxiliary'

TOO MANY FISHING writers cause their didactic tales to climax in triumphs over lack of water, heatwaves, salmon disease, floods, hurricanes. It was on the morning of the last of three back-end days on Tweed that I made up my mind to write an honest fisherman's tale, which ends with my defeat.

I had never fished in late November. Driving to the river on an icy winter morning, I found the experience disorientating. Pheasants skurried away from the car into the snow. I fumbled for ear defenders and began trying to remember my number in the line. Geordie, the ghillie, recalled me to the business in hand with, 'You'll have to work for your fish this week – the water's terrible low.' The paraffin stove in the hut was already lit. Wearing two pairs of gloves, a brace of Huskies and a ski jacket, I looked like a Michelin man – but, I was warm enough to wade.

The day started inauspiciously. As I cast across the Elshie pool, I realised that my line was absurdly light for a fifteen-foot rod. A closer look revealed that the reel held a sea trout line. All that day, I was sweating to throw a decent distance. A second problem also emerged. As I toiled at the rod, trying in vain to shoot line, I saw that the upper rings were jammed with ice. Snapped off once, the miniature icicles reappeared every few minutes through the day. The river, I think, was marginally warmer than the atmosphere – never good news for salmon. Geordie summoned me out of the water, saying, 'We'll try the boat in the stream.' He embarked upon that curiously Sisyphean labour, rowing hard up-river for a couple of hours to hold me steady in the slow water at the tail of the long Elshie pool. 'You see that ripple?' he said, after a while, 'the best lie is just in front of the rock. If he's there, he'll have you.'

A few seconds later, I snagged bottom. Then the bottom began to pull steadily away from me – I was playing a salmon of around twelve pounds. 'You shouldn't have any problems with him here,' said Geordie, glancing around the big stretch of open water. But I remembered the Findhorn in September.

That day, I was shooting grouse high on the hills above the river, watching the water fall as two days of rain drained away. At tea-time, with an hour before my train south, I ran down to the river, assembling my rod as I went. Within five minutes, I was into a good fish. Three minutes later it was gone. So was the fly. In my wretched haste and impatience, I knew that it was my own knot which had failed. Is there a greater folly?

This Tweed fish, though, pulled steadily and was thrashing on the surface. God, the excitement of preparing to land a salmon again. Geordie reached for the net. The rod sprang and straightened. We were alone again on the river. My spirits sagged. I sat fingering the bare hooks. 'Go on,' said Geordie, 'get that fly back on the water.'

We pulled the boat into the bank for lunch empty-handed.

We saw my host, Charles, walking towards us along the far
bank. 'Is that a salmon he has over his shoulder or is it his
jacket?' asked the ghillie. 'It's a fish!' Charles had winkled
one out of The Doors. He talked about the difficulty of
waggling a fly around the pool's eddies at low water and how
interesting the problem made the fishing. I felt a pang of
shame. To hell with interesting difficulties, I was looking for
uncomplicated solutions.

The beauty of the steep banks of Makerstoun on a clear,
frozen, sunny November afternoon overcame my impatience.
The lines of leafless beeches against the ice-clear sky; the
mallard and goldeneye climbing and banking above the water,
offering every kind of tempting shot; the marvellous sunset
with the colours shifting through reds, blues and greys of
every hue, were irresistible. There is nowhere like the Borders, with the pheasants flitting to and fro across Tweed,
looking at their bronze best against the snow.

'How many do they rear here, Geordie?'
'About 1,600.'
'And what do they shoot?'
'Nearly the same.'
'Good heavens, we think fifty-five per cent is marvellous in
Northamptonshire, but then we don't have your perfect
woods.'

The last hour, into the darkness, it was so cold that we felt
we were risking hypothermia for nothing. Surely no fish
would take in such conditions. My morale flagged at tea-time,
walking into that most delightful of fishing hotels, the Ednam
House in Kelso. Big, deep-bellied men were comparing the
size and merits of the big, deep-bellied salmon lying on the
floor. I blushed to think myself the only non-scorer in the
dining room. Alastair Brooks, the proprietor, comforted me
by remarking that only about half of his two dozen fishing
guests had brought salmon home and said, 'You've nothing to
be ashamed of.' But I knew how poorly I had been casting. I
had not deserved to catch a fish.

Next day, armed with a new and more appropriate No. 11
medium-sinking line, I was fishing better. The weather was

marginally warmer and we were not afflicted by icing problems. The sky was as beautiful as ever. In thermal underwear
even the wading was not too painful. Charles generously left
me to fish the most promising stretch of the upper pools and
took himself off to the very topmost corner of the beat. From
a distance, between ten am and half past, I watched him
charm out of the river a salmon of around nine pounds, and a
sea trout over eight pounds. He was casting beautifully, and
he deserved them.

That evening, walking once more into the hotel empty-
handed, I felt a sorry sense of failure. I gazed upon all those
crowded photograph frames, full of triumphant Tweed fishers
and their enormous spoils with captions like 'Fifteen by
lunch', 'Twenty-nine pounds and twenty-six pounds', 'First
fish' (this being larger than its captor) – all the traditional
appurtenances of the Scottish fishing hotel. It was increasingly
plain to me (over the third dram) that I was being punished
for taking time off for fishing when I should not have done,
for casting poorly and so on and so on. The punishment was
hurting.

At half past nine next morning, as Geordie pushed us out
into the Elshie stream, he said, 'You should get a fish here
today.' There remained three hours before my train south.
The weather was warmer today, four or five degrees above
freezing, with a perceptible thaw. It took us over an hour to
fish that first pool. We covered the fast water twice, after
Geordie spied a fish showing. We changed flies three times.
Then we went down to The Red Stane for twenty minutes.
'. . . Never, in fact, from one end of the year to the other, does
this pool want for occupants,' wrote Stoddart in 1853, describ-
ing the annual slaughter done to salmon in its midst with
leister and lantern, but today, nothing moved. How much
more difficult it is to believe in fish, when one glimpses not
more than two or three broad backs on the surface all day!

At The Straik, where the water cascaded in half a dozen
places between rocks exposed by the river's fall, Geordie
pointed to the strongest stream. 'Start wading at the top here,
and casting across. There's an eighty-five per cent chance
you'll get a fish. They lie in a deep cleft between the ledges.' I

began to throw the heavy fly inelegantly across the current, wading clumsily and very carefully among the big, slippery rocks. This was no day to fall in. Recovering the deep-sunk line from the pool after each cast seemed like towing a corpse off the bottom. After five minutes, the line straightened. I was into a good fish. I wound the slack on the reel, and took up a steady pressure. The salmon began bucking hard, jerking to and fro on the end. I was much happier with the stronger drag on this old Hardy Perfect reel, than the easier action of the Grenaby that allowed Monday's fish to run so free. I edged sideways to the shallows of the pool, guided by Geordie, who had hastily prepared the boat. He said, 'If he runs down into The Doors, we'll have to row after him.' Stoddart's *Guide* offers its own dire warning about the perils of playing a fish in this pool: 'Many is the woeful face mirrored by shining Tweed above this cast, when down, at the rate of a racehorse at full speed, rushes the aroused fish, snapping, like the touch of fire, the tackle of the angler and carrying with him the daintiest fly that the fingers of Forrest ever put wing to – all, bit and harness, with high hopes and stirring fancies, into the abysses beneath.'

Verbosity was in fashion 130 years ago. Now, I settled to savour every moment of that wonderful sensation, holding a big rod against a salmon of at least fourteen pounds. After five minutes, the fish was tiring. His purple flank showed on the surface. Geordie advanced with the net. The fish twisted on his side – and was gone. I leaned against the side of the boat, clutching my despair. 'I try not to be a complaining sportsman, Geordie, but that was bloody unkind. I thought I was about due for a fish after the past couple of days.' 'You should have eased up on him as you brought him in. That's when they're most dangerous – at the very end,' said Geordie. 'Anyway, you get back in that water. There's plenty more where that one came from.'

Thus I waded miserably away to the head of the pool and cast as I began to compose this piece, about the frustrations and disappointments of salmon-fishing. There was Charles with three on the bank and me with none. What a week.

The line began to swim away. As I tightened, I realised

that I was holding a bigger fish than I had caught in my life. I strained against that salmon for ten minutes, as it hugged the current deep in the rock cleft. Then Geordie netted it, all nineteen pounds of glorious hen fish. My hands were shaking with excitement, tension, relief. 'She's full of eggs,' said Geordie. 'Do you want to keep her?' 'I'm afraid I do – I've worked too hard to let her go.' There was an hour to the train. 'Get back in there,' said Geordie, 'there's more yet.' 'I'm perfectly happy with what I've got,' I said, truthfully. Geordie said that I shouldn't be. Though by profession a forester, he possessed in full measure the qualities of the best ghillies – confidence, knowledge, enthusiasm. Few possess them all.

Five minutes later, he netted a fresh fifteen pound salmon for me. Five minutes after that, there was another beautiful silver-blue eight-pounder. I went home in an ecstasy of pleasure and fulfilment. 'That's salmon-fishing for you,' said Geordie, 'your luck can turn at the very last moment. Never, never give up.'

The reader will have discerned by now my enthusiasm for measuring my own sport against that of our ancestors. I turn again to Stoddart's *Anglers' Guide*: 'Much of the detriment to the sport, and undue exultation of the mere novice in angling in the parts of the Tweed I allude to,' thundered this Victorian worthy, 'arises, no doubt, from the nature of the casts or pools and the necessity of fishing them from a boat under the guidance of the local fisherman . . . To this auxiliary, it is impossible to refuse a large share of the credit for skill and craft claimed by the rodsmen who entrust themselves implicitly to his directions. He is, in fact, the mainspring of their amusement, by the assistance of whom the veriest bungler . . . may, on the first essay, hook, play and haul to shore half a score of salmon.' Stoddart would have nodded triumphantly at the demonstration of his thesis, beholding me on Tweed's bank that morning. Even if it was my rod that landed those fish, it was Geordie's spirit.

GUINEAS AND TIGERS

ALMOST EVERYONE WHO practises field sports some time feels a yearning to try them in Africa. The colonial experience is still very close. If the number of English homes with elephant's foot wastepaper baskets is in decline, the supply of Edwardian family photograph albums, sepia images of triumphant great grandparents astride large corpses, seems undiminished. My great-uncle Lewis, whom I much admired as a child, devoted half his life to slaughtering wildlife in southern Africa. My father crossed the Kalahari in the early 1950s and did his share of shooting for the pot with Lewis's old rifles. I have pictures of them both, showing off large, dead beasts. In Rhodesia in the early seventies, I met an old Afrikaaner farmer who remembered Lewis well: 'Ah, I never forget Major Hastings going out hunting wearing a cartridge belt and his tennis shoes and damn' all else.'

In our generation, an acute sense of the decline of Africa's game makes almost all of us doubtful about the merits of killing large animals. A game warden whom I met in Salisbury during the Rhodesian guerrilla war once asked me if I fancied shooting an elephant – this, at a time when numbers were getting out of hand in some of the game parks near the operational areas. It cost me only a moment's thought to decline. I recently met a very rich American family, who were showing visitors photographs of their daughter's graduation-present trip to Tanzania, where she had shot samples of almost everything bigger than an antelope. Seeing the carcase of a hippo somewhere in the roll of honour, I asked why it had been executed. 'Oh, we needed it as bait for the lion', her father said. There is a sound and honourable case – honourable for the host country, anyway – for letting rich foreigners pay very large sums of money to shoot African wildlife under controlled conditions to finance game conservation. But I know few English sportsmen who want to do it themselves. To our generation, unlike our parents and grandparents, it seems privilege enough to be able to watch game in the wild.

It is still delightful, however, to pursue small game through the African bush, one's head full of Selous and the old Badminton Library books. I had a few memorable days chasing guinea fowl in Rhodesia before it became Zimbabwe, before even the guerrilla war turned nasty; in the days, indeed, when the social atmosphere among the farmers south of Salisbury was that of middle England transplanted across the Equator. The log fires were always blazing in the hearths of those comfortable, thatched farmhouses. There were the starched clothes and generous hospitality that go with having plenty of available hands to do the ironing and make the spare-room beds. At the end of long, dusty tracks, on which every crevice of the car became coated with a film of red earth, one saw the long cattle fences; the pretty girls exercising well turned-out horses; the signboard at the junction of the road that signalled a corner of England in Africa; and there was the certainty of a steak and a whisky – this last, even at the height of sanctions. Listen to the music of the place names: Marandellas, Macheke, Inyanga, Selukwe. We were happy here, said so many voices from England and 'when we's' from Kenya and escapers from socialist reality in colder climes. So why do so many people – including the journalists like you – want to rain on our parade?

For all their reservations about my reasons for coming to their country (and my political pessimism about their future) those Rhodesian farmers were kind to me, and I thank them for it. I shot their spring hares by night off the back of a pick-up with exceptional inaccuracy – strange little animals these, half hare and half miniature kangaroo. I stalked a reed-buck or two to no purpose, save to skin my elbows, crawling in a sleeveless safari jacket through that long, unyielding dry grass. Mostly, though, I joined guinea drives.

The gathering of the guns for a guinea fowl shoot southwest of Salisbury parted with English tradition only in substituting sandals and shorts for brogues and plus-fours. The familiar pack of labradors, setters and spaniels nosed around everybody's heels. 'It's all nonsense about the climate not suiting them,' I was told. The accents were those of Stockbridge or Wetherby, of the first drive in Perthshire or a back-end day on the Sussex downs. Only the Hollands and Purdeys and Powells seemed to notice the change of latitude, with their rust streaks where the climate had attacked them.

There are guinea shoots, they tell me, where the birds are driven with military precision over the guns. I never went to one of those. Ours were more in the nature of guinea chases, since those perverse birds are happiest running a four-minute mile through the high grass, chasing in and out of the great red rock kopjes that landmark the bush in such startling fashion. Sharp-eyed and lazy about exercising their wings, guineas can be induced to do the sporting thing only by cunning tactics.

We all piled into a couple of pick-up trucks and began to cruise cautiously along a track through the bush, every eye watchful for the glimpse of a flock. After fifteen minutes, somebody spotted around fifty birds, already scurrying hard across a field towards a distant tree line. Our host gave the orders: 'Right, four guns out here, lining the road, everybody else stay in the truck and we'll try and get round the pack and push them towards you.' The daughter of the house appeared round the corner on a smart pony, out for her afternoon ride. She was dispatched at a canter to try to head the birds off. Energetic hunters went running in all directions. Guinea fowl linger for no man and masterly improvisation usually means doubling after them, while trying to ram a couple of cartridges into the gun, and stop a frantic dog overreaching himself.

By now, there were guineas scuttling along the front of the standing line of guns. One shooter broke forward, chased his bird into the air and promptly shot it. Honour satisfied, he then returned to his place on the track. A single covey, if such one may call it, skimmed low through the line amid plentiful gunfire. More birds were running by. One rose at my feet and flew hard for the trees behind. I missed with both barrels. Two guns were disappearing over the horizon at a smart lope, in pursuit of a breakaway group of birds. I suddenly noticed a single guinea perched on a rock high above me, peering down on our activities with magnificent disdain. A wife, hitherto invisible in the high grass, could be heard loudly, but without ill will, accusing someone of peppering her. Everybody, it was plain, was entirely happy.

For eight guns to shoot a dozen guineas in an afternoon is good going. At a highly organised shoot, they sometimes get forty or fifty. A Kenyan acquaintance who read a piece of mine about guinea shooting experiences in Rhodesia shook his head and declared that it wasn't like that at all. I said it might not be where he did *his* shooting, but this was how it was, on a warm August afternoon south of Marandellas.

The pleasure of those little expeditions was immensely enhanced by the sightings of game: duiker, steenbok, reedbuck, even an occasional kudu or sable. We stumbled upon the odd covey of francolin, which always caught me unawares. The sun was hot enough for shirt-sleeves, but never so warm as to burn. The conversation was a charming hybrid – mutterings that Harrods didn't seem to be quite what it used to, in among an explanation of the difficulties of keeping a crocodile in a swimming pool from a man using one as a temporary reptile house while he got his safari park going. Somebody else capped that story, by complaining that a crocodile had eaten his wife's Pekinese.

Those farmers rated the duck flighting the best sport the country could offer. On one estate I visited, they had shot 2,000 the previous season. They eulogised the trout-fishing in the Eastern Highlands, where the fish averaged two and a half pounds. But already, the guerrilla menace was creeping closer. More and more steel mesh security fences were being erected around those warm, friendly farmhouses. The idyll, it was plain, was approaching an end.

I never got to those legendary streams up at Troutbeck. But I did get a day at the tiger fish up on Lake Kariba, which the old African hands rated second only to Nile perch for sport with rod and line. A good specimen of tiger can run fifteen to twenty pounds – much smaller than the perch, but, pound for pound, marvellous fighters.

It was often difficult to concentrate upon spinning a bait from a boat when, along the lake shore moved a constantly changing parade of buffalo, impala, hippo or water-buck from the Matusadonna Reserve.

It was August, the worst time for tempting a tiger. The surface of the lake was also ruffled by a light breeze, which the fish dislike. I must have been making the hundredth cast of the day when the rod was suddenly wrenched forward in my hand and I found myself recovering my balance in the boat, then getting over the shock of losing my first tiger, and the bait. However, we had found a feeding shoal. For the next two hours, almost every cast produced a take and every strike reminded me that a greedy fish was by no means a fish in the boat.

Tigers have very bony mouths, in which it is difficult for hooks to get a purchase. The boatman kept his whetstone by his side all day, sharpening his hooks every half-hour or so. 'More fish are lost here from blunt hooks than from bad fishing,' he said. A sharp hook, a very fast strike and relentless pressure are the only combination to hold a tiger. My first fish was small, as they go, around three pounds, but fishing with light tackle, he still gave me an exciting three or four minutes – shooting under the boat, leaping out of the water full of anger, tearing out line as he ran. Finally, I heaved him in without benefit of a landing net. From then on it was a fighting afternoon, in which I lost three fish for each one I landed.

Before Lake Kariba was created, the tiger of the Zambesi river were famous. On the river, the fish tend to be lean and tough; smaller than those in the lake, but better game. On the lake, a record fish of thirty-four pounds was taken a few months before I fished there. In winter, the best of the sport is to be found in the shallow water, but there are endless hazards created by sunken and floating trees to snag a line – all the foliage of the forest that lingers from the fifties before the lake was created. It seems that every tiger fish in the shallows of Kariba has learnt the knack of twisting a line around a sunken tree. At the time I was there, there were still occasional rumbles and upheavals as the lake bed settled, together with chains of bubbles breaking on the surface at intervals, from hot springs a hundred feet below.

In the old days, most fish were taken on a spoon. But the introductions by the Zambians of a small, sardine-like fish – kopenta – changed the pattern on Kariba. The tigers began to feed hard on these and we used kopenta all day on the lake, as we spun or trolled. I landed nothing bigger than a four-pounder, but local fishermen told me the bigger fish behaved little differently. They fought ferociously for a few minutes, then collapsed. They lacked the stamina for a sustained contest. The struggle was generally decided in the first few minutes, when the fish leapt. If it could smash the cast, it would do so then. There is a vicious quality about the fight of a tiger, which comes as novelty to anyone who has only played trout and salmon.

Some sportsmen love spinning from a boat. I have dabbled in big game fishing a couple of times, once off Kenya and once off Mexico. My chief memories of both expeditions were of feeling horribly hot and seasick. I hankered for a Scottish riverbank in a bracing breeze and a Barbour jacket. Yet, in the midst of Africa, the setting for sport of any kind is irresistible. The rich red sun sinking slowly across the water, the absolute stillness of the evening, the indefinable scent of the continent in the air. We had broken a few casts and lost many baits, but I had seven tigers in the boat for my pains. I was somewhat crestfallen to return to our island camp and discover somebody flourishing a splendid-looking nine-pounder. It was a few hours and a few drinks before he disclosed that he had run it over with the boat.

DUCK SOUP

MORE THAN A few shooters who kill pheasants, grouse or partridges without a moment's scruple, feel a twinge of unease about ducks. They seem such good-natured, clubbable creatures. They are also uncommonly hard to kill. Most of us, at one time or another, have stood on a peg or crouched behind a hide opposite a wounded duck, reproached by those kind eyes for ten minutes, until the bird's head sags and drops. My own guilt is compounded by the fact that I generally shoot indifferently at ducks. I find difficulty judging the speed of the oncoming bird. Not only do I miss a lot, I also wing more than my share, which I see flinch and then fly on.

Ducks are much in sportsmens' thoughts, because more and more shoots are rearing them. In the past, outside days in

October and early November were reinforced by partridges, hares and various. Today, most shoots are entirely dependent upon the birds they release. Since nobody tackles pheasants seriously until late November, it is increasingly popular to raise a few hundred ducks to add a drive or two at the beginning or end of autumn shooting days. Many of us, I think are ill at ease with this practice and feel a pang of dismay when the word comes in mid afternoon, 'Let's go and have a bang at the quackers.'

The guns muster in hides or cover around a lake. The keeper and a couple of pickers-up with dogs move in and hustle the ducks off the water with a round of exhortation, clattering of feed bins and general appeals to duty. Sometimes, to everybody's embarrassment, the birds won't fly at all. Once, in my younger days, I became so exasperated by standing around a lake in Surrey with a dozen others, watching the duck swimming round in circles, that I hijacked a handy boat and paddled out across the water in a rage to shift those birds. Immediately afterwards, this seemed quite funny to all of us. Looking back on the moment, I am less proud.

On the birds' first airborne circuit, the guns can usually pick up a dozen without immense difficulty, though my neighbour at a big shoot inquired innocently at tea-time, 'Having trouble seeing those ducks, were you, Hastings?' Then the gloomier phase sets in. The birds begin to wheel higher and higher, indeed at extreme shotgun range. A barrage of more or less ineffectual banging sets in. From time to time there is a cheer from the hides, as somebody flukes a really high bird. Some duck simply continue to circle at intervals, unscathed. A lot of birds are pricked. Some manage to slip past the guns, and drop back onto the lake. This provokes another round of dustbin banging and shouts from the keeper's team to shoo them back into the air.

After half an hour or so, the whistle goes, and picking-up starts. This is a protracted business, if it is done properly. Wounded ducks are back on the water, swimming among the unwounded survivors. Sorting out the cripples and persuading tired dogs to chase them around the lake, is quite a performance. A few divers can keep going for half an hour, unless a gun can get close enough to put another shot into them – itself a tricky business to get right, with birds on the water.

My own feelings about reared duck, I must confess, may also be jaundiced by the memory of a last drive some years ago in Hertfordshire where, before we marched upon the mallard, stern warnings were issued to avoid shooting the tame call duck. Now, this being a dark and grey evening, in among all the birds and the banging and an excess of enthusiasm, I was dismayed to see a white object, indisputably a call duck, plop dead into the water with my name on it. Ah well, I thought, no one need know. It was half an hour later, while tea was being served in the blue drawing room that, in a scene worthy of Wodehouse or Saki, the keeper entered bearing the murdered call duck and deposited the corpse silently upon the carpet at my feet. Somehow, my name has since been forgotten when guest lists are compiled for that shoot.

I am not yet single-minded or honourable enough to refuse to take part in shooting reared ducks. But I can't say I much enjoy it, or know many shooters who do. If one is going to shoot duck – and serious wildfowlers are some of the finest sportsmen I know – then surely flighting them wild, on the foreshore or a flight pond, is the way to do it. 'His nature is subdued to what it works in,' wrote Millais of the foreshore shooter, 'the loneliness of his life, its hardships and its chill and depressing surroundings sink into his soul . . . he becomes more and more of a class apart . . . To him the howling of the wind in the chimney or the first flakes of snow drifting across the leaden landscape, are more attractive than the comfort of his fireside . . .'

Colonel Hawker began his great eulogy of duck-shooting, 'This amusement is generally condemned, as being only an employment for fishermen, because it sometimes interferes with ease and comfort; and bucks (who shoot as they hunt, merely for the sake of aping Adonis at breakfast or recounting their sport over the bottle) shiver at the idea of being posted, for hours, by the side of a river or anchored, half a night, among the chilling winds in a creek.'

I have only a little experience of the foreshore. I remember a misty and ineffectual morning on the Wexford Slobs and a few early morning outings on Irish river estuaries. There is a little pond on our shoot and we feed it to some effect through the summer and clear the worst of the rushes and dead trees after each winter's storms. Half a dozen evenings in September and October every year, two or three of us picket it.

I love those autumn vigils in the failing light. Each year, I record in my gamebook the times of the first and last duck dropping in. These do not vary more than ten or fifteen minutes from year to year and thus we have a pretty good idea when it is worth taking up position. I always claim the same spot, shielded behind a bulwark of chainsawn logs, hidden beneath a big, evergreen bush. In my earliest days at this business, I armed myself with a duck-call, and quacked away whenever I saw birds circling overhead. Nowadays, I don't bother. With a pond like ours, if they are going to come, they come.

The first mallard or two often take us by surprise. The guns have been lulled into a reverie, gazing on the water and listening to the pheasants clattering noisily up to roost in the trees all around the spinney. More often than not, the duck drop in with a quick flutter of wings and are settled on the pond before we have got our guns up. After they have ruffled their feathers and shaken their wings, they glance up to see a human face peering at them from the bank, and, irritably, take off. They leave too low to get a shot, but they wake us up.

After that, for twenty minutes a succession of singles, pairs, and flights of half a dozen or more drop in and we rattle them to more or less effect. Often, with three guns positioned in a sixty degree arc on one side of the pond, it is impossible to know which of us has hit a bird. The moment one falls, we send in a dog. Frustrating experience has shown that, in darkness, if we wait until the end of the flight to chase a runner into the rushes, it will be lost. In the case of my dog, too, some obscure canine trades union principle causes her to go on strike when the light goes. No power on earth will persuade her to jump into that chilly pond once night has fallen.

We have never troubled with decoys. Although I am not a

goose-shooter, I much enjoy the grim comedy of Sir Ralph Payne-Gallwey's tale of setting out a tethered live goose as a decoy, upon whom fell a gaggle of bean geese. 'They ... crowded round the decoy, cackling vociferously and, without more ado, beat and pecked their relation to death. They then walked off a few yards, regarded the corpse fixedly for some moments and calmly sought food and repose. Whilst this tragedy was being enacted, my punt was stealing nearer and nearer, until eventually the slaughter of the decoy bird was avenged and twenty-eight of the visitors were laid low.'

Hawker delivers a withering denunciation of wildfowlers who seek to shoot duck without getting their feet wet, so to speak. 'If ever there was a chance on the shore, or in a fen, to see a flock of fowl well pitched, send a gentleman sportsman after them and he generally comes back without a bird, while a common fellow would get a shot and kill three or four. Why is this? The gentleman thinks his crack(ed) shooting is to do everything and will not go low enough, for fear of dirtying his knees, while the rustic, not minding dirt, or anything else, pulls off his hat, crawls to the fowl and is generally sure of getting, as the other is of *not* getting, a good shot.'

Flighting is a much less bloody business than Hawker's or Payne-Gallwey's devastating salvoes at sitting birds. But it remains a very exciting form of shooting – waiting, poised to seize a fleeting chance in the dusk, ears cocked to hear the birds quacking high in the sky, then, as they peel off and swing in towards the water, one strains to judge the exact moment at which to fire, when the birds are committed and every gun will get a shot. On our inland pond, we have never noticed a significant correlation between wind, moon and duck, such as is usually decisive on the foreshore. I have stood shivering in a howling gale on a dark night and seen nothing come in. But then, on a warm, still evening with a rising moon, we have shot seven or eight mallard.

Like most office-working sportsmen, we find our flighting activities are determined by weekends and we cannot choose our meteorological moments like a shooting farmer or coast dweller. We never collect more than nine or ten duck on a good night – more often four or five – and maybe a couple of late-flighting teal, slipping in just when we have decided it is too dark to go on.

My reference guide about timing is the one recommended by that bible of duck-shooters, *The Complete Wildfowler*. At intervals I glance at the palm of my hand. If I can still see well enough to define the lines on it, the light is fit for shooting. When it has gone, we plod up the hill to the cars and go home for a large drink.

To me, shooting duck in this fashion is fine sport, while harrying tame mallard is not. Maybe I am being unreasonable in drawing a distinction. Perhaps it is partly because, in the dark, I don't have to look those wounded birds in the eye, but, either way, I am a flighter, and not a driver of ducks. Nor, I am afraid, do I have the iron constitution and commitment to be a punter.

Punt-gunning, the favourite sport of Hawker and Payne-Gallwey, is a dying art now, but I take my hat off to those men who still practise it. Just once, a veteran punting friend named Geoffrey Ivon-Jones took me out in Poole Harbour. Geoffrey is a great all-round sportsman, for many years a fine falconer, who also built his own punt. On one notable occasion, he went out on the Wash with Prince Philip and James Robertson Justice. Our own expedition began inauspiciously, with my leader in fine fettle at three am as we set out from home with the punt on the trailer and myself – who can take thirty years off him – yawning and groaning. On the seashore, Geoffrey shepherded me into position amidships, established himself aft and took up the paddle. Then we set off in search of duck.

It was three hours, as I recall, before we approached a raft of wigeon. I was so cold and miserable that all sensation had long since departed. Geoffrey, prone in the stern, was using the short setting poles with unstinting vigour. On shore, I had been carefully instructed in the aiming and firing of the vast gun, mounted on breeching ropes. Its great brass cartridge, hand loaded by Geoffrey, must have weighed a couple of pounds. There is a delusion among the ignorant that a punt-gun is a brutal method of slaughtering big numbers of 'sitters'. In reality, the gunners seldom average more than five or six duck an outing through the season. There are plenty of blank days, not to mention frightening ones for punters on the Wash, when the wind gets up while they are on the water. In the old days, when professional wildfowlers made a living punt-gunning, two or three were drowned every season, regular as clockwork. Millais again, 'Out of the four professional puntsmen on the Moray between the years 1880 and 1890, two were drowned and one was completely crippled with rheumatism . . . During the same period, on the Forth, there were four professional gunners above Blackness, possibly more, and two of these also met death by drowning.'

That morning in Poole Harbour, I lifted the breech of the gun, peered along the top of the barrel and pulled the lanyard. There was a thunderous explosion, after which I remembered nothing much more for some minutes. I had forgotten all Geoffrey's careful instructions about keeping my nose a hand-span away from the breech when I fired. Few spectacles could have caused more delight to the League Against Cruel Sports, as I reflected when I regained consciousness, than that of a gunshot after which the birds flew away unscathed and the gunner lay writhing in the bottom of the punt with a bloody lip.

Geoffrey, an exceptionally good-natured fellow, paddled us home without a murmur of reproach. I fell asleep in the car as he drove us home, leaving him, no doubt, to pass the journey reflecting that young blood wasn't what it was in his young days.

LONG POND

'GOOD MORNING MR HASTINGS, I'm Bud,' said the old punter. He grunted and mumbled a little as he started the recalcitrant outboard motor, told me to move my gun barrel off the prow and stow it so that it would not be vulnerable to the passing reeds. Then we began to motor briskly along the channel between the big reed beds, a mile and a half towards the spot where we were to lay the decoys and wait for the duck.

This was a very different sort of punting expedition from that day in Poole Harbour. We had set off from a little island, four miles out from the shore of one of the Great Lakes, surely one of the oddest little enclaves of sporting privilege in Canada. It is a club, an exclusive partnership shared by a handful of sportsmen. The cluster of wooden bungalows set on stilts in the midst of the marsh was established in the nineteenth century. The walls of the clubhouse in which visiting shooters eat are lined with fading photographs of posturing Victorian and Edwardian duck-shooters and long dead grandees of two continents who have stayed there.

The presiding genius of the club is Billy, an old man who has been looking after members from his dimly-lit hut, cluttered with sporting and boating impedimenta, for two generations. Set alongside narrow walkways, raised on piles above the water, stand a dozen or so private bungalows, each one owned by members, many of whom only visit them to shoot two or three times a year. For the season is short, a mere two months from mid September to mid November, when the lake freezes and the desolate little hamlet on the marsh is locked up for the winter.

Between times, members drop in by boat or floatplane for a day or a week of shooting on the club's privately owned marsh, some 3,000 acres of it. At breakfast, they observe one of the club's many little rituals: drawing for position from a velvet bag containing numbered tokens. 'It's all very civilised here,' said my host, 'we don't go out at dawn or any of that stuff. A bell is rung at nine a.m. precisely and no boat may set out before it goes.'

There were only four of us on the island during my day's visit. After an elegantly presented breakfast in front of a log fire, a little before nine each of us clambered gingerly down into his punt, in truth more of a canoe, with a swivelling seat amidships for the shooter. Most of the punters have known the lake for years. My helmsman, Bud, was a sixty-nine-year-old retired ironmonger. He loved the lake, he loved the duck, he loved the club members. 'There's old Mr Hellman,' he said proudly, 'won't go out with anyone but me. He's been one of the greatest shots in Canada in his day, but now he's eighty-three and he misses and he doesn't like anybody to hear about it. So he goes with me, because he knows I won't tell. It hurts to miss, when you've been a great shot all your life.'

The channel had narrowed to a few feet now and the reeds were brushing our faces as we cruised between the beds. The punt bumped and scraped the mudbanks. The lake was lower than anyone could remember it for years. If it continued to fall, the marsh would become impassable for shooters in a week or two. At intervals, we changed course at neat sign-boards placed at the crossroads of the channels. Each of our four guns had been allotted a position. We were heading for Long Pond. I asked Bud if we should not have a better chance of seeing duck if we had started earlier in the morning. 'Sure,' he said, 'but that's the point. We're only allowed to take twelve ducks on our licences, so nobody is in the business of trying to make big bags. 'We'll do OK.'

The punt grounded decisively on a mud flat. Bud heaved himself over the side and began to drag us towards the next patch of clear water. I felt embarrassed that, lacking waders, I was obliged to recline on my throne and let the gentle old man do the hard work. But eventually, with a lot of grunting and heaving and pushing with the paddles, we made it.

'That patch of reeds should do us,' said Bud. 'You see all those duck getting up? They're definitely coming in there.' One by one, we began to throw out the beautiful wooden decoys, the work of a celebrated local craftsman. When fifteen or so were sitting nicely, bobbing into the breeze, Bud tugged the punt the last few yards into the bank of eight-foot high reeds. Taking out a scythe, he trimmed the cover to his satisfaction, tucking clumps of reeds into the slits specially made for them along the sides of the punt.

'You shoot sitting or standing?' he demanded. 'Standing,' I said. He himself climbed over into the mud and stood leaning onto the punt to hold it steady. I loaded the splendid old Purdey that my generous host had lent me. It fitted perfectly, so I had no excuses. Within a few seconds, a mallard moved fast over our heads and I dropped it into the water a few yards from the punt. I felt that quick surge of relief about being off the mark. Shooting in an unfamiliar place in un-familiar company, one is always afraid of making a fool of oneself.

'On your left, on your left,' hissed Bud. I lifted the gun, missed with the right barrel and found myself unable to fire the left. Cursing, I began to wrestle with the gun. Try as I would, I could make neither the lever nor the trigger work. It seemed irrevocably jammed, and we were forty-five minutes from the club. Bud sympathised, then pulled out a radio with a chuckle. 'Never go without this, at my age, in case we get into trouble,' he said. He spoke into the handset. 'Billy, can you bring the buggy and another gun for Mr Hastings?' I was hugely relieved that reinforcements were close at hand. We sat down to wait.

In the next three-quarters of an hour, we saw a wonderful procession of wildfowl. Mallard and teal, wigeon and geese swooped in, settled on the water among the decoys or curled through the warm blue sky above our heads. The weather was more appropriate for June than early October. Shirt-sleeve order would have suited the occasion, but for the need for camouflage. Bud fumed in frustration on my behalf. I laughed. 'You're a patient man, Mr Hastings,' he said. I told him that no one had ever said that to me before. It was simply that here, in this remarkable place, unlike anywhere I had shot before, the experience alone was enough. I didn't mind much whether we made a bag.

At last, Billy arrived with the second gun. We drank a cup of coffee from the Thermos, and sat down to wait again. Now, the ducks seemed few and far between. 'I was afraid this would happen,' said Bud. 'There comes a time when they just settle down someplace on the lake, and quit flying. You can't hear anybody else shooting now, can you?'

A lone teal came in and I dropped it. With the long pauses between birds, our vigilance began to relax and I failed to get the gun up to several passing ducks. We could hear the geese, but they did not fly over us again. Suddenly, a single beautifully coloured wigeon settled on the water among the decoys twenty yards in front of us. 'Get up, you old fool,' I called to it. It did so, and I promptly missed with both barrels. 'Yeah, some people feel like that,' said Bud with a shake of his head. I looked puzzled. 'You know – they won't shoot a bird on the water.' I muttered that I might have done, if I had known I would make such a mess of it in the air.

We began to drop odd mallard around us. But now, we were running into difficulties. The birds were falling into the thick reed beds and we had no dog. Twice, Bud plodded off into the mud and the cover, to return empty-handed. 'It's no good,' he said, 'it's like a jungle in there.' Why were there no dogs? 'No place to walk them on the island,' Bud said.

I missed a retriever, not only because a dog always seems such an integral part of a day's shooting, but also because it was irksome to leave birds on the marsh. We were now well into the afternoon, scarcely a duck was moving and I had a plane to catch. 'I'd like you to have seen the marsh on a really good day,' said Bud, 'it can be wonderful here, sometimes.' I said, truthfully, that it seemed pretty good to me just as it was. We packed up to go home, seven ducks down.

Clattering back to the island, Bud pointed out that the water had fallen another inch or two during the few hours we were shooting. Mud flats hung out of the water in places he said had not been dry in years. My host was waiting on the walkway by his cottage as we came alongside. He had shot a dozen ducks and made his way home by noon. He showed me how to push the trigger of the jammed gun forward to clear it. I, too, could have had my dozen. But it didn't seem to matter. The memory of that curious and desolate place, not the score, was enough to carry home.

A SHOOT IN THE SHIRES

THERE ARE DAYS when to be a shooter in the hunting Shires seems to possess most of the social advantages of running a billiard parlour at Ascot. There are moments, standing at one's peg on a still, misty December morning, when the clatter of massed hooves in the distance fills one with the same sensations as an Indian brave about to finish off the wagon train hearing the trumpets of the Seventh Cavalry tell him that, once more, he is to be cheated of victory in the last reel.

Seriously, though, the Shires always have been and – I hope – always will be primarily fox-hunting country. It seems only just that they should, in an age when, elsewhere, so much of the English agricultural scene overwhelmingly favours shooting. Recall the disgust of the legatee in J. K. Stanford's *The Twelfth*, who inherited '. . . a hundred-acre farm in the middle of our Friday country, which was wired up like a ruddy canary's cage'.

If Norfolk and Hampshire are landmarked with their great swathes of kale and maize, it seems fair enough that every second field in Northamptonshire and Leicestershire should have its hunt jump, its hedges cut down to make a tidy leap, if also poor shelter for a hen pheasant in a high wind. It is only in our less reasonable moments that those of us trying to shoot up here sometimes lose sight of these lofty and admirable sentiments.

With the exception of a few great historic shoots such as Belvoir Castle, the Shire estates in the nineteenth century were planted overwhelmingly for fox-hunting. The paradox today is that, with constantly growing numbers of shooters eager to rent ground, and farmers anxious to increase income, more and more acreage inhospitable to pheasants is being leased by people like us, shooters making the best of it, since we happen to live up here.

Our shoot is one of the vast number all over the country now, that rely upon the efforts of an incredibly hard-working part-time keeper, and a fair amount of do-it-yourselfing. Morris, our keeper, worked on the estate for many years and retired shortly after we started the shoot in 1982. Ever since, he has worked endless hours for sheer love of the thing, with a lot of help and support from his daughter, Marjorie. The two of them are exceptionally skilled and lucky rearers of pheasants. While Morris does not have the time for a lot of vermin control, every year he brings our poults out of the release pen in splendid condition, with very few casualties. For a small shoot like ours, rearing less than a thousand birds, this is immensely important.

We four guns who make up the membership of our syndicate – each inviting a guest every shooting day – built the first release pen with our own hands and still do most of the covert-clearing and game-crop sowing that is necessary. I think we all enjoy the shooting much more as a result, because we know the ground so well and have been so intimately involved. I fall in our duck pond – the dirtiest and smelliest in England – at least once a year, while wading to pull out rushes and dead trees. My wife thinks I enjoy the swim. She is wrong.

Most Shires syndicates are trying to make the best of difficult conditions. A few are shooting big blocks of forestry, which present driving problems of their own. Many are rearing pheasants on ground with limited areas of woodland, where the only way of creating enough drives to provide a decent day is to plant as much game cover as the budget runs to. How we yearn for some of those high hills and deep valleys from the West of England!

Our own shoot extends to almost 2,000 acres, but of this only some 50 acres are woodland. The remainder is open country with closely shorn hedges that make us chronically jealous of those splendidly overgrown Berkshire and Hampshire field boundaries ten yards wide. On idle autumn afternoons, I have walked miles around our outlying hedges with a dog, out of curiosity to see what they hold. The answer is next to nothing. All our pheasants concentrate tightly around the woods. This makes them easier to hold, but also much restricts the possibilities of the drives.

When we started the shoot eight years ago, we took advice from the Game Conservancy about how to plan drives and plant game cover. Much of it was very sensible, and has worked well, but there is no substitute on any shoot for trial and experience. For two years we had a strip of kale on a hill 500 yards from the main woodlands. Scarcely a pheasant did we shoot out of it. It was too cold for game. Each generation of shooters has to learn the same lessons anew – pheasants will fly where they want to, and nowhere else. Nowadays, we shelter our game strips on hilltops with round bales, and this is an improvement. But they seldom offer much sport after early December. Near our main woods we have three modest strips of artichokes, which we planted ourselves, each walking behind a blade of the plough with a bucket. We have tried hard to persuade the estate's agent of the virtues of the Game Conservancy's conservation headlands, which much improve the stock of wildlife at negligible cost to corn yield by leaving an unsprayed perimeter around every field. Thus far he is un-impressed.

The best shoot I know in the Shires, in Leicestershire, excels chiefly because it has the right sort of woodland and enough of it. Driven off the hilltops its birds fly marvellously. Its chief problem is that none of the neighbouring farms is keepered, but all are let. Thus there is a steady haemorrhage of pheasants to rough shooters feeding over the boundaries, which even constant driving-in cannot wholly prevent. It is little use appealing to neighbours' goodwill over issues such as this – everybody these days is simply too determined to get his hands on whatever sport he can.

The main problem for almost all Shires shoots is to make pheasants fly well. There are one or two notorious local estates where vast numbers of birds are reared and equally vast numbers are killed head high, to the apparent satisfaction of the shoot captains. Most of us compromise by running small shoots, recognizing that whatever we do, we can never turn our tract of Northamptonshire into Castle Hill. Each year, we shoot around fifty-five per cent of the birds we rear. On our four main days, we expect to get the right side of a hundred twice, the wrong side twice. Recently, on our best day ever, we shot 140. A year or two ago, we tried a few partridges, without success. They simply vanished. I think one has to have a full-time keeper and rear substantial num-bers to do well with partridges, and get them over the guns.

Our costs are relatively high – more than £13 a bird in 1988 – because even a part-time keeper must have the use of a Land Rover to feed them, and, somehow, each year there are new capital expenses. We have considered and rejected possi-ble economies of scale by rearing more pheasants. We do not believe that the ground would hold them, at least not without planting a lot more expensive game cover. As it is, to make the most of our woodland, we have to make a drive of a belt of trees that runs for half a mile beside an increasingly busy minor road. I hate doing it. I am always terrified that a dog will be run over, even though the guns are kept well off the highway. We have to shoot that belt, though, to make a day and get at the pheasants and it is a characteristic irony that the birds fly better out of it than any drive on the shoot. I simply dread the day when the editor of *The Daily Telegraph* is held responsible for landing a dead pheasant on the top of a passing car.

There is one significant bonus about Shire shooting over Norfolk or Hampshire: because there are relatively few of us, beaters are easy to come by. There are plenty more people glad of a day out than local shoots need and there are none of the headaches about mustering a beating team against stiff competition that seem to beset the great shooting counties. The company of our long-established beating team is one of the greatest pleasures of the shoot. They are brutally frank about the shortcomings of our marksmanship. We are pretty honest about the inadequacies of their dogs. In other words, we understand each other pretty well. On the debit side, however, in the Shires good pickers-up are like gold-dust. There are plenty of dog owners who want to pick up, but the good ones are booked up season after season for the big shoots where they will have a chance to see 300 birds killed rather than our modest 90 or 100.

Each day we pray for wind. In a wind our birds will fly as well as any in the country. Without one, all too often they are coasting in second gear over the guns. Working in a restricted area, many pheasants fly back behind the beaters towards home. We recognise this reality by having at least three guns walking at every drive – they often get the best sport. At any shoot I would rather be a walking gun than be sent to stagnate on a peg where there is precious little chance of a shot. Too many drives at too many shoots refuse to recognise that they can really entertain only five or six pegs in front of the covert and the outsiders are redundant.

In the Shires, inevitably, more time is spent discussing foxes than anything else. Most of us long ago acknowledged that putting hounds through the coverts does a shoot no harm at all – indeed, it can do good by shaking up over-tame pheasants – but we sometimes become a trifle choleric about the sheer number of foxes we see (five in one day is our record). We don't shoot them, but the temptation is strong.

The League Against Cruel Sports will never need to set up sanctuaries in the Midlands. The whole region is one vast fox park. This is still the land where the fox is king and my hunting wife expects me to leave out bread sauce and gravy with our chickens for those pampered predators. Pheasants and their shooters have to do the best we can with what is left behind the brush.

BAG AND BAGGAGE

ONE MORNING A greasily worded circular dropped
through my letter-box, from a gentleman asking whether a
distinguished fisherman like myself had ever stopped to think
that some of the useless old tackle in the attic might be worth
real money. Old Hardy and Farlow catalogues, for instance,
could even have some modest cash value. I gnashed my teeth,
to think of a few widows and orphans who might be foolish
enough to take this dealer at his word and accept his money.
I may not know much, but I know what old Hardy and
Farlow catalogues are worth, and line driers and Super Silex
reels and fly books and every other kind of sporting para-
phernalia. My father was good enough to pass on to me a
considerable collection of loot of this sort. But widows and

orphans are often unaware that fishing and shooting produce classics and antiques as surely as any other historic pastime. They may thus fall prey to the sort of sharks who are cringeing enough to address their circulars to 'distinguished fishermen'. Grrrr.

Field sports give birth to an unrivalled selection of impedimenta that passes from generation to generation. Fox-hunters have to be content with their hunting horns and old whips. Father left me a splendid, leather-cased, silver sandwich case, but my wife told me dismissively that nobody would be seen dead carrying anything of that sort on their saddles these days. The supply of tasteful accoutrements for shooters is much wider. I like those charming, old silver game counters, of which I inherited a couple. My father declared in a book which he dedicated to Prince Philip, that nobody bothers to use them nowadays. This provoked a friendly, but firm, letter from the Prince himself, who remarked that anybody who has the interests of the pickers-up at heart still carries a counter. But then again, Prince Philip has to account for somewhat more dead pheasants than most of us.

I find flasks a mixed blessing. The silver ones dent, the caps leak and even the expensive glass ones seem to break at the neck with monotonous regularity.

Many shoot captains possess elegant silver or ivory position finders. I know a few meticulous shots who use those plastic butt markers to note the position of every dead grouse as it falls. But many of us are too over-excited under the pressure of a drive to remember where the dog was last seen, never mind to draw reliable maps of the birds' last resting place.

I rejoice in possession of three of my father's admirable Payne-Gallwey cartridge bags, which cost a fortune nowadays. Cartridge bags improve greatly with the patina of age and regular treatment with saddle-soap. Thirty- or forty-year-old ones look better than even the most distinguished modern product straight from the window of Holland or Purdey.

I also own one of those big brass-mounted cartridge magazines. From a utilitarian point of view, however, this is a doubtful asset. It is much simpler to pull cartridges from their cardboard cases as one needs them. Likewise, it is mostly young shots rather than old ones who bother with cartridge belts. Most of us can load a gun much more quickly straight from a Barbour pocket. All that leatherwork, though, becomes more valuable with every passing year and one of the pleasures of a shooting day is to go forth equipped with aged, beautifully-made accoutrements, just as I like to record the day in a big, old, leather gamebook, which will be irreplaceable when I reach its last page. The practical modern gadgets, such as ear defenders and gunsleeves, lack the magic of good harness. They are just tools.

I am a mere infant about sporting gadgets, compared with my father. I inherited his Manton percussion locks and powder flasks, his nets and cartridge-loading gear, periscopes and monoculars and whole cases of sea-fishing and coarse-fishing tackle that I have never used. There were twenty-four rods of various shapes and sizes in his collection, some of them useless greenhearts, but also including such classics as the Grant's Vibration, the Wee Murdoch, the A. E. H. Wood Palakona. There were eighteen or nineteen reels, cast tins, carved wooden tackle-holders, spinning gear, and flies in such profusion that I could ground-bait the Spey with them for years without making much impact on the stock. There were patent knives and pliers in sufficient strength to equip a butcher's shop and hats and coats and boots to stock a department store sale – all the latter, alas, too small for me.

Although a mere amateur compared with Father, I should like to think that I have made a promising start in the gadget department. I bought a couple of anti-midge hoods like bee-keepers' nets for Alaska a few years ago, though I have never used them. The advance of carbon fibre has provided me with an excuse to add seven or eight rods to the rack and a few trout reels to match – no need to increase the wonderful armoury of old salmon reels. I have bought a lot more flies, not least because it would be both foolish and sacrilegious to squander those old gut-tied flies on the river. I scarcely use any of the old fly boxes, either. Most are black japanned designs or early aluminium ones with fiddly little springs and lids that bend and stick. The best fly box today, surely, is the simplest of all, the one in which hooks are stuck into an unadorned layer of plastic foam.

Most of us find modern fishing waistcoats invaluable, though I have clipped the manufacturers' badge off the breast of mine, because, for the life of me, I cannot see why any fisherman should wish to spend his days on the river advertising a tackle-maker. I fish draped in the usual assortment of clippers and thermometers and tweezers. My priest I often take shooting as well as fishing, because I am a poor hand at finishing off wounded pheasants tidily, and a priest does the job rather better than the average beater's stick. A few seasons ago, my sister-in-law gave me a splendid insulated salmon bag, for carting fish back from the river. For a while, I became convinced that bag had jinxed my luck. Not a fish did I hook, while others were reeling them in all around me. But the jinx is broken now and that excellent bag has brought a lot of fish tidily home.

Father's collection of guns reflected a passion for them as works of art, which I have not inherited. To my infinite sadness, I had to sell his shotguns, because they were all too heavily cast for him, as a left-handed shot, to be sweated across for me. And anyway, those short-barrelled Churchills look ridiculous in the hands of a man of six foot six. Why is it that, if one is selling a left-handed gun, it seems to command a lower price because of this eccentricity? If one is buying, the story is very different. I own only two shotguns of my own – together with couple of boys' guns and the odd rifle. Oh, and I kept Father's muzzle-loaders, though, unlike him, I lack the courage to fire them.

Yet, for all the complaints I receive from the family about the weight of sporting gear I acquire, I remained awed by the sheer excess of Father's collection. How could any man conceive a need to go on buying gun-cleaning kit until he possessed more than sixty jags and brushes, some of them for calibres of weapon he never owned? What would make him collect spinning baits when he rarely spun, until he ended up with dozens of identical, mint-new plugs, devons and tobies that look as if they have never seen water? The answer, I am afraid, is what I call ten-minute disease. This is caused by finding oneself in the West End of London with ten minutes to spare before or after lunch, within walking distance of

Hardy or Farlow, Holland or Purdey. It seems so feeble, when one's face is known, to walk in, look around and walk out again without buying anything. 'The pleasures of fishing are chiefly to be had in rivers, lakes and tackle shops,' wrote Arthur Ransome sixty years ago, 'and of these the last are least affected by the weather.' Over a forty- or fifty-year span of active sportsmanship, the cumulative haul (and financial damage) from ten-minute disease becomes astonishing. Then, when you have gone to meet the great tackle-maker in the sky, the men who send circulars to 'distinguished fishermen' – or their widows – move in and set about the carcase.

HIT AND MISS
IN ARGYLL

AT DAWN IN August, the corridors of the great Scottish night trains used to be alive with sporting expectation: plus-fours and guncases everywhere, dogs shouting their heads off in the goods van, formidable tweeded ladies sniffing the air like so many practised retrievers. At eight a.m. on a December morning in the early 1970s, the coaches were almost empty and the handful of unsporting passengers peered at a lonely rifle case as if it might bite them. The little Argyllshire station was deserted but for the head stalker who had come to pick me up. There were no tourists, no house party at the lodge – just the snow on the hills and the deer I had come for.

Knowing the Highlands in their friendliest mood in summer is no preparation for meeting them in winter. England is always recognisable, familiar, whatever the season. The Scottish hills seem to become so much bigger, so much more formidable in the lonely months when most of us abandon them.

Angus, the stalker, who drove me to the foot of the hill in the Land Rover, had been warned that he was dealing with a novice hind shooter. Like most Highlanders he was all the friendlier because of it. Never in a dozen seasons would we get a more perfect December day to look for hinds, he said. The hills were set in a brilliant blue sky with a light wind and a little mist. The lochs glittered miles below us. As we began to plod upwards through the snow, the view stood clear to the summits. A cock grouse burst angrily off the ground and planed away towards the loch. My arms swung instinctively round after him. As other birds broke forward, one felt mean to be bothering them now, off-duty. The stalker talked about the growing problems on the forest with hikers' access. In the summer, he said, they now came in their scores and hundreds. The problem was not that they disturbed stalks – they were usually good about observing requests to stay off the hill on stalking days – it was that their constant presence was driving the deer off the ground altogether. The controversy about public access to the great northern wildernesses threatens to become a major political and environmental issue in the years to come.

In the hills, one becomes absorbed by the effort of the climb, the images all around. It is easy to forget the purpose of the expedition. I was taken unawares when Angus suddenly dropped in mid step and motioned me down behind a hummock. Inching forward, he took a long look through his glasses and whispered to me to get the rifle out. I crawled up behind him.

'There's a dozen hinds just over the top. I want you to take the one lying straight in front nearest to us,' he said. I slid up onto the brow. There, sure enough, were the deer – feeding along the hillside sixty yards away. I shifted the rifle to find a comfortable position, put my thumb on the safety catch and squinted through the sight. The beasts were up and away, trotting rapidly towards the skyline. I watched them go through the crosshairs and then relaxed.

'They won't move far,' said my companion, easing himself upright and getting ready to move on. No sign of concern there, yet I knew that it was my sharp movements and slow approach to the aim that had cost us a fair chance of shooting a hind. I remembered that charming Victorian book by 'An Old Stalker' entitled *Days on the Hill*. It tells his story of a lifetime of triumphs over the odds – these being, almost invariably, the 'gentlemen' holding the rifles. There is Augustus Grimble's tale of the sportsman who failed to keep prone as he approached deer, which promptly bolted. 'Why, what on earth could have put them away?' demanded the frustrated rifle. 'Why, you was just *walking* when I was *crawling*,' replied the stalker sardonically. There is, too, that legendary stalker's demand of the laird, before taking a guest to the hill, 'Do you want him to see deer, or shoot a stag?' Yet, the annual Highland miracle is the patience of most stalkers and ghillies, who spend their lives teaching Englishmen a little of their craft. They need it most on days with a tyro like me, when any success is their achievement.

We moved off along the saddle, slipping sometimes in peat hags brimming with snow, stepping wide across the burns in spate. People who are translated straight from trains from London into the heather are out of breath by eleven a.m. I was puffing along behind Angus, wondering if I dared suggest a pause, when we found the deer again. This time, I had my arm in the rifle sling and was well poised before I moved forward onto the little ridge behind which we had approached. I took care to lie flatter than before as I marked the hind I was to shoot. She was feeding head down towards us. I steadied the beast in the sight and waited for her to turn. As she did so, I fired and she dropped stone dead.

The relief of not having failed was greater than any positive pride. I had not let Angus down. I could breathe again. Watching him gralloch that hind so tidily, I thought of the bloody butcher's mess I had made on that day when I was alone on the hill, and cut open a beast with my own hands. I am a great believer that anybody who practises field sports should be willing to do the dirty work afterwards, if need be. But this morning, I was glad to have somebody else do it properly. I asked Angus how he could judge that this hind had wanted shooting. He muttered something about the shape of her head and the general look of her. But, of course, the real answer is the one every part-time countryman hates to hear – you judge by spending every day of your life on the hill, though I think even professional stalkers can sometimes fail to notice that hinds have calves, amid a great herd of them.

We left the hind to be collected by the Argocat, summoned by walkie-talkie. Ponies are a marvellous survival, on those forests that still use them. But the Argo and the radio make life much less complicated for stalkers. Now, I felt, time for a few more: three hours of light, deer everywhere, only a breathless walk between one carcase and the next. How was it that J. K. Stanford had Colonel Hysteron-Proteron define stalking? 'Pottering about on one's stomach after sitters . . .' In the West of Scotland, the stalker provides the fieldcraft, but I cannot say I have ever felt that the rifle had done less than a day's work by the time one shot one's beast.

We trudged on through the snow. The mist began to drift across the hill in patches. I remember a day stalking with that ardent pursuer of deer, Duff Hart-Davis. We climbed for hours through thick mist and blinding rain, myself praying for our leader to admit defeat. But, as we ate our soggy piece, Duff and the stalker spied deer through a window in the weather, far up the hill. We clambered on for hours, as it seemed, until Duff and his wife Phyllida left the stalker and I to make our way across the last quarter mile. We were crawling down a scree, completely blind, when the stalker whispered that we must be close to them. At that moment, the mist opened like a curtain, to reveal deer all around us. I dared not move, and took a desperate shot lying on my back with the rifle barrel between my feet. The stag fell down and I preened myself. But Duff, of course, felt compelled to conduct a post-mortem. After a few minutes, while I was assuring the rest of the party that I took shots like that every day, he looked up from the carcase and demanded, 'Max, did this beast die of fright? We can't find the wound.' Eventually, they found the bullet in that stag's spinal cord, eighteen

inches above the aiming point. My reputation as a rifle shot
has never recovered, among the Hart-Davises.

That dying afternoon in Argyll, after a long detour around
and above the herd's new position, we found ourselves high
up, in the bed of a deep burn. The hinds were wide awake
and restless. We crawled painstakingly downhill, with long
pauses while we stopped and watched. The snow, melting
beneath our bodies, soaked deep into our tweeds. The morning's walking now seemed easy. The crawling had me gasping
for mercy. We came on one group of beasts and I took the
rifle out. But as Angus studied the hinds, he saw nothing that
deserved a shot. Then, as we neared another group, once
again a movement stirred them. They were away. Almost an
hour's painful effort had gone for nothing.

Yet, it was now that the fascination, the concentration of
the day, became more intense. The fickleness and wariness of
the beasts made them seem so much more desirable a prize as,
again and again, apparently on a whim rather than any firm
fear, they moved away from us. A rich, red sunset grew on
the hills opposite us as the light went down. Infinitely patient,
my companion said that we would try one more circuit above
the hinds, further still along the hill. There were more checks
and pauses as stragglers from the herd lingered along our
path, an impassable rearguard. Then, at last, we were among
a thick fall of boulders that offered us cover all the way down
to the deer. We edged in until my guide motioned me up to
the rock behind which he lay. As I brought up the rifle, I saw
a hind broadside on, less than a hundred yards away. I took
rock-steady aim, knowing the beast was as good as dead. I
pressed the trigger. She bounded away, clean missed.

Angus said it was because I had rested my rifle barrel on a
rock. I said I would test my 'scope-sight the following morning as I was sure it must be out of true. But, of course, I knew
in my heart that he was right. Together, we walked back
through the dusk towards the Land Rover. The sense of
failure now eclipsed the pleasure of the morning's success. To
waste a cartridge missing an easy pheasant is a small personal
defeat, quickly wiped out by the next kill. Yet here, now, I
had been led all day by a sure hand who asked me only to

perform the last rites. It is the sense of letting down the stalker that burdens the heart of a rifle who misses his shot. Angus, of course, talked all the way back about how many other people he had seen miss deer. Stalkers learn perfect manners before they learn to shoot.

I can never understand why shooting a stag commands such a high premium in Scottish sport, while estate owners find it difficult to get paying rifles to shoot their hinds. Hind-stalking is no whit less difficult – often harder, indeed – and the emptiness of the Highlands in winter can make the experience more memorable than any stalk through the summer heather. The pursuit of big heads seems as meaningless as most of us would find it, these days, to shoot an elephant. Sport should surely be measured by the difficulty of the quest, not the size of the quarry. That morning, Angus' matter-of-factness over our little success had dampened my exhilaration. Yet, as we drove home, the same quiet calm revived my fallen spirits. As with every sport in the world worth the name, failure spurred my determination to try again, and to do better, another day. The Highlands are infinitely patient.

REFLECTIONS ON A DECEMBER
PHEASANT PEG

FOUR. FOUR? NEVER having shot here before, one has no
way of knowing whether this is a real four – middle of the line
and the pheasants – or whether one will have to spend a
quarter of an hour watching birds curling right and left sixty
yards in front of the peg, that miraculous Red Sea parting
that occurs with such frequency on pheasant shoots.

Do they believe in giving the guns a good first drive here,
to sweeten the time-wasters to come? Or will it be ten
pheasants and a jay, with another dozen disappearing around
the corner of the wood? In the wind we've got today, most of
them are bound to favour the left of the line, but this is one of

those shoots where the positioning of the pegs was sanctified in 1906 and has never been modified since for hurricanes or forestry.

That's the third bird to scuttle out onto the grass, inspect us and disappear back into the wood again. I have always liked that Patrick Chalmers' verse about the Christmas cock pheasant:

> 'A sage of fourth season, he knows the red reason
> for sticks in the coverts and "stops" in the strip,
> And back through the beaters he'll modestly slip.'

Is that a picker-up in the reeds behind us? As usual, there is nobody one is less pleased to see, having one's own dog. Yet fate always ensures that on the day one is dogless, the shoot is picker-upless as well. Are those duck coming in behind? Those pigeons look as if they might turn this way. Who is somebody shouting 'Over!' at?

Those were wasted cartridges, the gun hopelessly off-balance, the pheasant halfway to the next county. If there is one vice worse than coffee-housing, it is falling into a philosophical stupor, lulled by twenty minutes of distant tapping. Now the problem is to settle down again, to forget that moment of being all arms and legs and pretend the next bird is the first of the day.

A flush on the left. Two high, fast pheasants dead in the air above my neighbour, one of the straightest hitters in the county, whom I heard a disgusted local peer describe recently as 'the greediest shot in the Shires'. This reputation is earned – like that of many deadly killers of driven pheasants – by a willingness to raise a gun to anything that moves around him, whether head-high or mountain-high. It is both delightful and frightening to watch him shoot – he possesses an elegance, matched by absolute dedication to the business of killing pheasants, which is unnerving to those of us less efficient at it.

A barrage of banging and, in two minutes, twenty pheasants are lying dead, three around me. I am having one of those patches when I can hit anything on my right and next to nothing on my left. This is self-perpetuating, of course, because the belief is in my mind when I raise the gun. Another cock. I've hit it, but it's planing down and will run. To send the dog or not to send the dog? If one waits until the end of the drive to follow runners, half of them are never seen again.

Go on, Tweedie. There's no danger of upsetting another drive. I love watching her course a running pheasant, grab it inelegantly and canter back. I have ruined her as a disciplined gundog by using her to hunt hedges, letting her run in and every other vice in the book. I bear that badge of the incompetent dog owner's shame, a spike and chain. But to shoot without a dog, any dog, is misery and she will get the birds. If she sees a pheasant tower a quarter of a mile back, she will bring it when I send her. It is only memory, or brains if you like, that she lacks. If she has not seen the bird fall, she does not really believe in it. The pheasant is still blinking when she brings it back and I take it from her to finish it off. The best reason for wearing gloves shooting, even on a mild day like this when the leaves are dancing on the stubble, is to avoid being gored by the spurs of an old cock leaving one a last reminder of himself.

I swing the gun to face the unmistakeable sound of a pheasant breaking out of the undergrowth, to discover that the identical noise is being created by Tweedie shaking the ditchwater off herself. Sound is often as important as sight in getting the gun mounted quickly onto a bird, especially rough shooting or when the pegs are immediately in front of a covert. That is why most of us hate wearing ear defenders. But being half deaf myself already, I put up with them. The other day, I heard somebody condemning a great grocery tycoon who shoots four days a week, and won't turn out for less than five hundred pheasants. 'It won't do you any good saying anything to him,' said another of the party cheerfully, 'he can't hear a word anybody says any more.'

The sun is glowing too bright for comfort behind the right of the line, pushing birds away or encouraging them to slip through low. There have been all too many bright, sunny days this season – good to be out on, but bad for the pheasants. I also agree with my brother-in-law's strongly held view, that there are too many overweight pheasants about. Over-fed birds are no more athletic than over-fed people. One of the most obvious differences between tame birds and wild ones is that the latter are leaner and fitter.

A deluge of pheasants going through on the far left, most being missed. I remember too many days like that of my own, firing a bagful of cartridges to bring down a pathetic fistful of pheasants and being naive enough to believe that the rest of the line hadn't noticed. How odd it is to behold the various fashions in which pheasants fall out of the sky: cart-wheeling, drifting, hovering frenziedly, bouncing through the tree branches or throwing back their heads and stopping dead in the air, as my left-hand neighbour surgically arranges almost every time.

The flow of pheasants has ceased and the beaters' sticks now sound quite close. I check the cartridges in my pocket. Twice already this season I have insulted my host by running out in mid-drive and having to dash pleading to my neighbour for more. I heard a tale lately of a gun in the hot seat at a big drive who ran to his neighbour, a notoriously unsporting 'big shot', to beg a handful of cartridges when he ran out. 'You've had quite enough shooting,' said his neighbour crossly with a shake of his head. The grandee finished the drive himself on the suppliant's peg.

The most frustrating aspect of seeing a shoot only as a gun on a peg is that one knows nothing of what is going on, of what country lies beyond the face of the wood. Conversely, half the pleasure of one's own shoot is to know every tree and spinney and beater so that, even standing outside, one can guess exactly who is doing what and where, identify each curse at each dog, each yell of 'Forward!' (for we are coarse enough to enjoy a little shouting at each other).

A cock pheasant comes straight over me, very high. I spend ten seconds looking at it before I raise the gun and miss with both barrels. It was all that gazing that did for me. One December I was the only gun under seventy at a marvellous shoot in Bedfordshire, where the others were pulling down astounding pheasants with untroubled consistency. 'Ah,' said Michael Rose at the West London Shooting School when I ruefully described the experience to him, 'that's because, at their age, they can't hurry even if they want to!' Now, there's a hen swinging across my front. I take it on the left and it cannons on to plump at my neighbour's feet, which almost certainly means that I shouldn't have fired at it. I know how unpopular 'poaching' makes one, having been both culprit and victim. But I think most of us are, some time. Crossing birds always pose a dilemma and one is usually excused by an apology afterwards, which at least shows that one was aware of a doubt.

The first of the beaters is coming out of the wood, shooing a final clutch of pheasants into the air. Most turn straight back, to another burst of fire from the back gun behind them, so often the most enviable position of the day. The estate manager of a big shoot I know in Hampshire is permanent back gun. I am certain he kills more pheasants in the season than the best shot in the line. There are more than a few shoots where the host would be doing guests a favour to allow one of them to walk behind, rather than send a boy or a brother-in-law to do so.

A final hen coasts past me. I kill it behind with a blush at myself. It was higher after crossing the line than it was in front, but still too low to be worth shooting. I had fired out of momentary boredom. As usual with those birds, one feels guilty for having shot at them – and doubly foolish if one misses, as so often happens.

The mad canine scramble across the field begins, as the pickers-up move in. The cluster of beaters files away towards the next drive, to hear the stops' report on the guns' performance. Already one has forgotten the pheasants one hit. The mind is fixed on the photographic memory of those missed, above all that high cock. Would a hasty jerk before firing the left barrel have done it or was I off-line altogether? As with so many birds, I suspect this one was pricked. It gave that fractional flinch in the air just after the gun went off. Those who say cheerfully, 'Oh well, they'll all be there for another day,' are usually wrong. At least ten per cent of the apparently unwounded survivors who got through the line are dying a couple of woods away, bait for the foxes.

Our host seems to be calling something. Yes, inevitably,

with that note of despair so familiar to all shoot captains, it is, 'Guns, this way, please.' How odd it seems that chairmen of large companies, managers of great estates and razor-sharp professionals who count in millions every week, on shooting days cannot number accurately from one to nine and are stricken with deafness to instructions every Saturday from November to January (although I have always liked the story of the rural grandee rubbishing an acquaintance, upon whom the worst insult he could heap was to declare him, '. . . the sort of man who shoots on a Saturday').

Hunched in the Shogun, one resolves to do better next drive. There are five more – all the time in the world to improve, to startle the rest of the line with the superlative brilliance of one's performance. Oddly enough, I seem to remember that same happy surge of faith in better things to come still going through my mind five hours later, when someone said we were going home for tea.

CHANCING A SNIPE

THE IRISH ARE not usually thought of as snobs. Yet by happy accident for some of us, local shooters in that peerless sporting society display a patrician disdain for snipe. Irishmen will risk death or mutilation – or at least get up uncommonly early in the morning – for the chance of a pheasant. They will course hares wherever they can find them. They will defy the law, the elements and probability to hook a salmon. But they cannot be bothered to stumble through miles of featureless bog, to waste cartridges and energy and suits of dry clothes, to catch a snipe when he is at home.

Thus it is, that, for a relatively few discriminating farmers and visiting Englishmen, there is still marvellous sport to be had in the Irish bogs. I did my share of snipe-shooting – or maybe snipe-missing would be more appropriate – in the two years we lived in Kilkenny. I gained a taste for it and go back for a couple of days in January whenever I can.

I was thinking recently, though, that we office types quickly become too soft for snipe. Mickey, a frequent sporting host of mine in Kilkenny, along with his farming friends, are only a couple of years younger than me. But they keep in practice, and I do not. One day, Mickey had me flighting a duck on the big estuary before eight in the morning and we finished with a dusk flight twenty miles away at six in the evening. During the ten hours in between, we had walked half a dozen bogs for snipe and taken five minutes at lunch-time to eat a sandwich, standing, off the roof of the car. By nightfall, I was done for. Who says the Irish are lazy? Not when game or a horse are at stake, they're not.

'The pursuit of snipes is declined by many, who plead their inability to kill them,' declares Colonel Hawker. 'Snipe shooting is like fly-fishing: you should not fix a day for it, but when you have warm, windy weather, saddle your horses and gallop to the stream with all possible despatch.'

We workers, however, find ourselves compelled to 'fix a day' for snipe as much as for anything else. I am only grateful for the number of times the snipe and I have been in accord about scheduling a rendezvous. I have got to know a fair few of the Waterford and Kilkenny bogs that Mickey, George, John and the rest invade from time to time. These expeditions start with a strategy discussion the previous evening, to recall which patches they have lately been warned off for life, which farmers still need a bottle of Paddy to keep on-side and which bogs have been found out by those villainous murthering swine from Tipperary, otherwise their oldest and dearest friends. The secrets of good snipe places are jealously guarded. Even if most Irishmen are not snipe-shooters, there are enough of them to pose a peril, when legal possession belongs to – or is recognised by – very few.

After the abortive duck flight, which ended with a couple of teal floating out to sea, because I don't bring my dog across the water on aeroplanes, we took to the first snipe bog. With the party's customary generosity, I was nominated flank gun, to walk ahead and on the coastal side along the estuary, with the best chance of a shot. This was a good bog, but it reached for a mile and I was walking all the way through the thickest, blackest, dirtiest mud flats in Ireland. I learned one important lesson in my early snipe outings, when I tiptoed around all day trying to avoid getting wet and usually fell in up to my waist around three pm: the truth is, it's going to happen sooner or later, so you might as well get it over. Five minutes along the estuary this morning, I was stuck over the calf in the mud and had to crawl out on my knees in my stockings, clutching the boots. Then, that was that over. I simply walked for the rest of the day feeling as if my feet were encased in a layer of chilled engine oil.

There was a double bang behind me and a couple of snipe were twisting, soaring, swooping past. I hit one, which fell forty yards out in the icy, fast-flowing estuary. A dog, an old black retriever, to its undying credit was persuaded to swim out. A chorus of encouragement, cheers, jeers, misdirections and stones (at the snipe, not the dog) urged it on. Five minutes' work brought back dog and snipe and everybody felt justly pleased with themselves.

After this, however, matters began to deteriorate. That bog was full of snipe. But most of them broke wide across the river, miles in front of the line or behind me. We banged our way through the reeds for the best part of a mile, all trying long, wild shots. A couple of dead birds simply couldn't be found, for all the dogs' patient questing. Most of the rest got away. Over the years, I doubt whether I have ever averaged better than a snipe for every six or seven cartridges. It is so fiendishly difficult to make a predictable swing at a bird whose speed and course are varying wildly. Even when the beating line put a bird straight over me, as forward gun, often it seemed to hang still in the sky above my head and I filled the air in front of it with shot. Then there are the contour-chasers, dodging around gorse bushes on the fringes of the bog, needing the quickest snap shot or a cartridge is wasted. 'If they spring from nearly under your feet,' says Hawker, 'remain perfectly unconcerned, till they have done twisting and then bring up your gun and fire, but, if you present it in haste, they so tease and flurry, that you become nervous and, from a sort of panic, cannot bring the gun up to a proper aim. If, on the other hand, they rise at a moderate distance, down with them before they begin their evolutions.' I have never noticed the slightest consistency about which way snipe will fly with, across, or against the wind, but I agree with Hawker that a long snipe is often easier to shoot than a snipe at very short range. If you hit one – ah, the satisfaction.

Walking back to the cars, Mickey and George drove a steep, thickly gorsed and wooded bank, in search of a wood-cock. The other three of us walked along the bottom, watching for a flushed bird going back. The beating was as tough and rugged as all Irish cover driving, accompanied by the sound of constant stumbles and curses and searches for the dogs in the undergrowth. Glory be, a woodcock broke out, flew as high and fast as ever a woodcock should, back along the edge of the marsh and was dropped by a fine shot behind us.

Mickey once took me to Kerry for a couple of still, blue, frozen January days that gave us some of the best sport in the most serene setting I have ever known. We found a lot of woodcock at the foot of laurels and holly bushes and hedges. We shot only a handful. The best I remember came at dusk – a lonely bird, flying out of a pine wood that we were guarding. It was so dark that, when I fired, I was shooting at a shadow, but, somehow, it came down and the dog found it after a hard search. I share wholeheartedly Colonel Hawker's view that '. . . the pursuit of woodcocks, with good spaniels, may be termed the fox-hunting of shooting! A real good sportsman feels more gratified by killing a woodcock, or even a few snipes, than bags full of game that have been reared on his own or his neighbour's estate and one who does not, may be considered a *pot-hunter*.' For all my earlier strictures about the difficulties of controlling spaniels for woodcock shooting, they are unrivalled.

Back in Waterford on this January morning, we drove for twenty minutes to the next bog, beside a little sandy seaside bay, where the geese were pottering on the foreshore, watch-ing the breaking waves. We parked by a cluster of old stone farm buildings, surrounded by the usual crop of derelict refrigerators, bedsteads and farm machinery. I once expressed astonishment that one sees so much brand new farm machinery in Ireland. It was an Irishman who commented succinctly that this is because the old machinery is maintained so badly. George diverted across an acre or two of heavy, cattle-trodden mud to make our peace with the farmer's wife at her front door. Then we walked down to the beach, crossed the little stream and settled dispositions for the next drive. One man and a dog would bring the bog towards the other three of us, crouched behind bushes, 'And don't move beyond that rusty old strand of wire and the posts there in the middle,' said George, 'that's the boundary, and the fellow on the other side is a terror.'

The view to the sea and the scent of the salt on the wind were perfect and we enjoyed them while we waited for birds. We watched our beater walk into the bog on the far side, a quarter of a mile away, and start to navigate a zigzag path through the reeds and gorse towards us. Within a few seconds, snipe began to come forward, almost all of them swinging to my right. Everybody got to work. Five minutes later, we had seen twenty come past the guns and shot four of them. There was the usual protracted pick-up: the dog working hard to find those elusive, tiny corpses. Then we were away to the car again.

I have shot snipe a couple of times in the West, in Clare and Galway. The huge horizons out there can become depressing, as one trudges across miles of bog, hour after hour, feeling the low skies pressing down upon the earth, impatient to close the door upon the brief winter daylight. The sort of small bogs we were shooting today in Waterford and Kilkenny, never more than half a mile across, give me much more pleasure.

In a day's shooting, one seldom gets through more than five or six of them, often as much as ten or fifteen miles apart. The physical exertion is very great for heavy breathers like me – even compared with a day on the hill in Scotland. Plod, plod, plod, trudge, trudge, trudge. Every alternate footstep has to be dragged heavily out of the mud, usually at the very instant that somebody shouts, 'Over!' and there is one of those damnable birds coming straight at you, while you're struggling to get the safety catch off and remember whether the gun is even loaded. I take my hat off to first-class snipe shots – the Crippses and Lamberts and Teignmouths I knew in our Kilkenny days. If you can hit snipe consistently, pheasants and grouse begin to look pretty manageable. Try it some time – if you can, before the fiftieth birthday party.

LITERARY DIVERSIONS

SOME FATUOUS MODERN educationalists argue that history does not matter. Yet, for most of us, part of the pleasure of being British is derived from a knowledge of what the British have been, and done, over the past millennium or two. In the same key, if on a more trifling note, one may suggest that the rewards of any sport are multiplied by a sense of its past. If it is pleasant to own family gamebooks reaching back over generations, it is even more satisfying to know the history of the rivers one fishes, the covers one draws, the hills one shoots: in other words, to know the literature of sport.

For many sportsmen, all this goes without saying. But I am still surprised by the number of fox-hunters who have never fallen under the spell of Surtees and Trollope, nor even read such modern books as Raymond Carr's delightful *English Fox-hunting*; likewise, there are fly-fishers unfamiliar with Skues or Grey; shooters who have never heard of Major Burrard's *The Modern Shotgun*, nor read Hugh Pollard's irresistibly witty *Sportsman's Cookery Book* ('. . . very small roach caught by very small boys may be boiled in a pie dish with vinegar, peppercorns, onion, etc., and served cold as a breakfast side dish, but only the small boy should be obliged to eat them.'); there are countrymen who have yet to explore W. H. Hudson and Richard Jefferies. How much more interesting it becomes to cast a nymph into a summer chalk stream if one knows the tale of the great debate between the purist dry-fly disciples of Halford and the sturdy pragmatism of Skues, the little London solicitor and pioneer of nymph-fishing. There is scarcely a corner of the Highlands that John Colquhoun did not penetrate before he wrote the two volumes of *The Moor and the Loch* in the mid nineteenth century; and Stoddart discusses every significant river (and its most celebrated fishers) in his *Anglers' Guide* of the same period.

I was lucky enough to inherit a substantial collection of sporting books from my father and I have added to it over the years by recourse to the catalogues of specialist dealers. To pick up such a book as Augustus Grimble's *Deer Stalking*, published in 1886, with its woodcut-illustrated advertisements for Turner shotguns at fifteen guineas and for Charles Lancaster's 'Rifled Guns for Hollow-Fronted or Solid Conical-Shaped Bullets', is to plunge immediately into the Victorian world.

One of the earliest sporting books I own, by an odd fluke, is a review copy inscribed to 'The Editor of *The Morning Herald*'. It is a whimsical compendium of sporting lore entitled *The Oakleigh Shooting Code*, published in 1836. This gives succinct hints upon everything from dog feeding to gunsmithing. There are plenty of clues to the intensely competitive nature of shooting at the period, when each man strove to be on the moor or at the covert before his neighbour. Among the rules Oakleigh's pseudonymous author proposes for a grouse-shooting syndicate, he suggests that, 'No gun shall be fired before six o'clock in the morning on the 12th

and 13th of August, nor before eight o'clock in the morning,
nor after five in the afternoon on any other day.'

Hawker, of course (who took very good care to be in the
woods before anybody else), is indispensable. In *Instructions
to Young Sportsmen*, the choleric, arrogant Hampshire colonel
anticipated by a century and a half the moans of our parents
and grandparents about the decline in sporting standards.
'Nowadays, every common fellow in a market town can det-
onate an old musket, and make it shoot as quick as can be
wished; insomuch that all scientific calculations in shooting,
at moderate distances, are now so simplified that we, every
day, meet with jackanapes-apprentice-boys who can shoot
flying and knock down their eight birds out of ten. Formerly
shooting required art and nerve – now, for tolerable shooting (at all events for the use of one barrel) nerve alone is
sufficient.'

Hawker was arguing, of course, that the speed of detonation
of the new-fangled percussion locks rendered redundant the
delicacy of judgement required to assess aim, with the slower
detonation of the flint-lock gun. His book vividly paints the
life of a sporting squire of the early nineteenth century, with
nothing to distract him from the business of the chase. 'Many
people who wish to secure all the partridges they can during
the month of September, make a point of shooting every day
and are quite disconcerted if they lose even half a day's sport
. . . but if your object is to get a great deal of game on the
same beat . . . do not go out above three days in a week.'

There was no aspect of shooting on which Hawker did not
offer a fierce opinion, though he left the matter of dress to the
discretion of the sportsman, '. . . in everything further than
always to appear like a gentleman.' He averred – correctly I
think – that '. . . although we are not all blessed with such
nerves as to aspire to being first-rate shots, yet I have no
doubt but almost every man may be taught to shoot tolerably
well.'

My own delight in Scottish sport has been many times
increased by familiarity with Charles St John's *Wild Sports
and Natural History of the Scottish Highlands*, J. G. Millais'
The Wildfowler in Scotland, Hilda Murray's *Echoes of Sport*,

Lady Breadalbane's *The High Tops of Blackmount* and others of their period. Nor should one despise modern works such as Duff Hart-Davis' history of stalking, *Monarchs of the Glen*, and Ronald Eden's *Going to the Moors*, which stirs a stockpot of information on Scottish sport, its past and its literature, with some entertaining illustrations. When we lived in Ireland, I gained equal pleasure from books like W. H. Maxwell's *Wild Sports of the West* (read the tale of Anthony the otter hunter, if nothing else) and more recent odds and ends such as Gerald Fitzgerald's *Pot Luck*, and the doughty Captain Drought's *A Sportsman Looks at Eire*.

My father sought to persuade me, as he believed himself, that the four indispensable books for a fly-fisherman were John Waller Hills' *A Summer on the Test*, Skues' *The Way of a Trout with a Fly*, Dunne's *Sunshine and the Dry Fly* and Plunket Greene's *Where the Bright Waters Meet*. I think he may have added Negley Farson's *Going Fishing* to the list in his old age. I was also instructed to note the omission of Isaak Walton, whom Father regarded as a pompous old ass. I agree with him, and suspect that, like Dame Juliana Berners, the supposed fount of all sporting literature, Walton is more often cited than read. Myself, I would be ashamed to claim a fishing library that did not include a couple of John Ashley Cooper's books, and some of the modern classics on lake tactics, such as T. C. Ivens' *Still Water Fly-Fishing*. I also much value Maunsell's good old *Fisherman's Vade Mecum*, that simple primer which is becoming somewhat long in the tooth now, but contains all sorts of practical advice for the game-fisherman, at a loss on the riverbank. And speaking of books that are more referred to than opened, I will now myself cheat, by quoting a defence of piscatorial activity that often comes in handy in domestic disputes, from a book I have not read, Best's *Art of Angling*, published in 1798: 'It is undoubtedly the most rational, innocent and entertaining amusement that exists; neither hurting families by the expenses which attend it (as many other sports do), nor running the professor of it into any kind of danger whatever.' Best, I fear, neither studied Strutt and Parker's price lists, nor waded the Spey in high water.

Sydney Buxton, who published his *Fishing and Shooting* in 1902, summarised the key principles of dry fly-fishing in a single paragraph that I do not think can be bettered today:

'Keep yourself and your rod out of view; remember that the first cast, after crawling into position, is all important; wait for a good opportunity, as regards wind, sun and fish, rather than impatiently take a bad one. Keep always in mind that your artificial fly is competing with the real article. Don't hurry your casts; pause often. Keep your eye on the fly; always expect a rise at each cast, or assuredly the fish will rise when your attention is distracted, and be missed. Stick to a particular fish. Go rather for the fish rising at the side or under the bank than for the one rising in midstream. If the fish will not take the fly at one angle, try him at another. Never throw a long line where a short line will suffice. 'Strike' or not, as nature teaches you . . . limit your flies as much as you can; the standard patterns will serve, the others will only confuse. Never hesitate, through laziness, to change your sodden and fatigued-looking fly for a fresh and dry one. Do not be hard on the hooked fish, keep an even strain. Finally, take your cruse of oil, and your opera-glasses.'

Shooting has produced much less memorable literature than fishing. This is a reflection of the reality that one is only a sport, while the other is an art. There is also far more to be learnt about fishing technique from reading about it, than about shooting, where there is no substitute for putting a gun to the shoulder. Among the shelves of shooting books in my library, few have given as much pleasure as that droll, witty work of Hugh Gladstone's, *Record Bags and Sporting Records*. Though more than sixty years out of date now, its charm is ageless. Gladstone was a tireless collector of whimsical sporting information, such as, 'The statement that Amenhotep III "killed 102 fierce lions in the first ten years of his reign" (1400/1390 B C) is sufficient to whet the appetite for research in ancient history.' Where else but in his pages could one discover that on 7th July 1905, Sir Ralph Payne-Gallwey, using a Turkish bow, shot an arrow 367 yards at Le Touquet? I commend Gladstone's chapter entitled 'The press and shooting', which makes my own trade today seem well-informed and responsible.

Speaking of Payne-Gallwey, what shooter could deny himself the pleasure of reading that marvellously entitled work *High Pheasants in Theory and Practice*, in which the great sporting baronet describes how he experimented with dead birds hoisted aloft on kites manned by hapless gardeners' boys. These (the birds rather than the boys) were then shot and retrieved for exhaustive target analysis. My first edition ends with twelve blank pages, headed 'Notes on Guns, Loads and Shooting', which make me feel a failure, as one of Sir Ralph's readers, because I have never dared to fill them in.

For more solid fare, I hope that my enthusiasm for Hugh Pollard's *History of Firearms* reflects more than merely old family friendship. We may take J. K. Stanford's *The Twelfth* for granted, though I confess I find his other books hard-going. Among the minor pleasures of shooting literature, I would include Noel Sedgwick and Patrick Chalmers' pleasant personal collections, Hare's *The Language of Sport*, Everitt and Watson's *Shots From a Lawyer's Gun*, Jonathan Garnier Ruffer's *The Big Shots*, Colin Willock's *The Gun Punt Adventure* and Major Jarvis' *Scattered Shots*. Many of the Major's whimsical reminiscences concern his time as Governor of Sinai after the First World War, but my own favourite among his stories concerns a Norfolk shooting day in his old age when, like most of the English rural upper-middle classes, a lifetime of shooting had rendered him stone deaf.

'After lunch we beat a wood for pheasants and then moved on to a second wood for the last drive of the day. This enclosure was quite close to the house – a most admirable arrangement, as it meant tea and whisky-and-soda immediately after the end of shooting, which is a very thoughtful and satisfactory conclusion to the afternoon. I was at the extreme right of the line and my host, having carefully put me in position, walked away some thirty yards and then, in that hushed voice one reserves for churches and when speaking of death, turned around and said something about birds going to the right – some people can never learn by experience.

'One thing, however, was obvious, and that was that I was to look out for those artful old birds who would hope to escape the line of guns by passing well out to the right. The drive started. The birds began to come over, and the warning I had received was based on extremely sound grounds, for the majority of pheasants tried to pass me on the right. I had made up my mind to do my utmost and I succeeded far beyond my expectation, for, of the odd-thirty, wily ruffians who tried to evade the line I dropped no less than fifteen and this was a particularly good effort for me. As each bird fell I heard, or thought I heard, a curious noise that sounded like a tea-bell, which more or less fitted in with the general scheme of things. At the end of the drive my host came up and asked how many I had down.

'"There are two to the left," I said, "four in front, but I think one's a runner, and," proudly, "I got well onto those birds going to the right that you told me about. I think there are about fifteen down."

'"Oh, my God!" he yelled, "you didn't take those birds to the right, did you? I told you particularly *not* to. Every damn bird has gone through the new vinery."

'And they had, and what is more, they had fallen quite as accurately as I had shot. I do not think one had missed the target, and when a pheasant goes through a glasshouse, he is not content with removing a single pane, but takes a minimum of four, with quite a lot of the wooden framework as well.'

I suppose I enjoy that story more than most, having been in the soup myself for sporting offences of one kind or another more often than I care to remember.

Most good sporting collections include the *Fur, Feather and Fin* series, and the Lonsdale and Badminton libraries. These, like Walton, tend to be more revered than read. Wildfowling has changed a trifle since Walsingham and Payne-Gallwey declared in the Badminton *Moor and Marsh* volume that '. . . swans are useless birds to the gunner and scarcely worth following should they be seen. We have done some execution on swans, both sitting and flying, with a rook rifle and have now and then taken a shot at them from a fowling punt with a swivel-gun.' However, the same authors' volume on field and covert shooting is by far the most entertaining of the series. Try some samples of their reflections upon the characteristics of shooting hosts, the martinets and the worriers. 'It is said of the late Lord —, a man of notoriously violent temper that, on finding a scarcity of partridges in a field wherein he had expected good sport, he would in a fury throw himself on the ground and *gnaw the turnips* ... We recollect a disciplinarian (a bad shot, too, besides being deaf) ... who, when walking-up a wood, peppered a boy, and was thus addressed by a keeper:

"Beg pardon, sir."

"Well, what is it? You will put everything up if you shout like that."

"Beg pardon, sir, you have wounded a boy!"

"Wounded a what?"

"A boy, sir!"

"Careless idiot! Serve him right for getting in the way! Send him home at once, and tell him not to let me catch him out again today".'

The Payne-Gallweys, the Bromley-Davenports, the Hesketh Pritchards serve as constant reminders that, in sport, there is nothing new. I reflected one day on the hill in Scotland how easy it is, in the tension of the moment, to mistake a bee for a grouse and raise a gun to it. On a recent armchair winter evening, I noticed that Sydney Buxton made the same observation almost a century ago: '... sometimes, a large bumble bee does, for an instantaneous second, look uncommonly like a distant advancing grouse.' Sporting jokes, I fear, also change very little from one generation to the next. Gladstone quotes some elderly chestnuts. Each of us in turn is innocent enough to suppose himself a pioneer when he tells the tale of the French gun waiting for the running pheasant to stop. That yarn was first perpetrated around 1815. 'You silly black bugger, you've lost him!' the story about the ghillie whose politeness snaps with the visiting maharajah, cannot be of much later vintage.

It must be said that the literary grace of many sporting classics leaves much to be desired. Looking along the serried ranks of twentieth-century books on fishing and shooting, I am amazed that so many indifferent writers troubled to put themselves between hard covers. The motives of most, I suspect, were the same as my own: to re-live, by the fireside,

days on the hill and the river. I possess a shelf-full of almost
unreadable nineteenth-century sporting encyclopedias. To
most of our generation, Whyte-Melville's novels – even
Market Harborough – are hard-going. Some of the most celebrated memoirs are triumphs of substance over style. It is
fortunate that Colonel Hawker's shooting was not as laboured
as his punctuation. Today, also, some books have become
absurdly over-valued by collectors and dealers, merely because they are illustrated. Philistines buy them, for the sole
purpose of stripping out and framing the hand-coloured
plates. For this reason, I despair of making up some in-
complete sets of books from my father's collection at tolerable
prices. But I cherish the treasures that I possess. As a spiritual
link between the sport that we enjoy today and that which our
ancestors knew, their pleasure never fades.

UNSPORTING OCCASIONS

AT THE END of a pheasant drive, one remembers birds missed much more clearly than those hit. In the same way, memorably awful sporting days stick in the mind, when some marvellous ones are fading. One of my own first fishing recollections is of a rare occasion when my father took me down to the river in search of roach and perch. I lost the bread paste somewhere between the car and the first cast and we all went home in tears.

Looking back over more recent sporting occasions, I can remember precisely in which field a borrowed hunter took off with me clasping the saddle and one stirrup, from which I was speedily ejected, breaking the saddle; the exact moment at which I watched somebody's large foot snap the top joint

of a salmon rod; the day I wrecked the end of my barrels by
firing them with a lump of mud obstructing the tube; and lost
an unmarked dog halfway between Aberdeen and Inverness.
Some of these little mishaps took place ten or fifteen years
ago, but the images remain as vivid as these affairs do for us
all.

I have a theory about holidays, that it is nonsense to
suppose people travel in search of peace and quiet. Instead,
they want to return with a veritable Norse saga of disaster
and tragedy, with which they can beguile the long winter
evenings and think how lucky they are not to have to see any
more foreigners. British passengers on Channel ferries on
their way back from the Continent always resemble defeated
armies retiring from a stricken field.

Most of us have very clear memories of days when we shot
really, seriously badly. I took a couple of hours off from the
Thurso, when staying in Caithness one September, to go after
grouse. Admittedly the keeper's dogs were hopelessly wild
and I was offered only long shots, but nineteen cartridges for
an empty game bag . . . There was a day in Surrey when the
guns and the beaters found themselves doing different drives.
You might think that we laughed. But by that stage everybody
had had enough cock-ups for one day. There was the ill-fated
Norwegian trip, when we were asked to practise that unspeakably dreary brand of fishing, bouncing a prawn on the
bottom. Ever since that blank week, members of the party
who meet again greet each other solemnly with the inquiry,
'Are you bouncing your prawn properly?' Never again, never
again.

Days of sporting misfortune divide themselves into two
kinds. There are those that stem from technical failure: a
broken firing-pin in the middle of the best drive of the season
(more common than we sometimes think – I always keep a
spare gun handy in the car nowadays); achieving a hopeless
tangle trying to cast in a high wind (usually with a ghillie
looking pityingly on); leaving the ammunition behind on an
epic stalk (which a stalker once did to me, though, arguably,
it was my responsibility to make sure).

The second variety of mishap is social. There are few

blacker fates that can befall any of us, than to find ourselves trapped for the day – or worse, the week – on the moor or the river in unsympathetic company. There is a story of a guest arriving late at an unfamiliar shoot and searching for the guns. He demanded of a passing yokel, 'Excuse me, my man, but have you seen a party of gentlemen hereabouts?' The yokel cackled horribly and replied, 'Gentlemen? Gentlemen? We haven't seen a gentleman on this shoot these twenty years.' My friend Mr John Carleton-Paget often accuses me of stealing his stories without due credit. I am happy to acknowledge this is one of his more printable ones.

There is nothing worse than a silent shooting lunch, where eight men chew their gloomy stew, wishing to God they could get back to the solitary dignity of the pegs. It must be said that some very spectacular shoots are run by some pretty unlovable characters. A year or two ago, my wife questioned me when I walked in at the end of the day.

'How was the shooting?'
'Great.'
'How was the company?'
'Terrible.'
'When will you learn that it's better to shoot fifty pheasants with friends than five hundred with strangers you don't like, and who don't like you?'

She's quite right, as usual, and I hope I am getting more discriminating about invitations as the years go by (and friends tell me some hosts who haven't asked me back feel that they, too, are getting more discriminating about their guns).

I know a few sporting guests who are saintly about finding themselves out of the shooting all day. I admire them mightily. I am perfectly happy if I get a good bang at one drive in the day – less happy, if not. I am perfectly reconciled to the luck of the draw. But I feel grumpier at those shoots where the draw is quietly seeded or where the guns are placed. Seeding is always noticed and placing guns is liable to divide first- and second-class guests. A friend who went to shoot at a local lordly estate came back in a rage, saying, 'We shot 300. I got 15 – and I didn't miss much.' The son of the house was home for the weekend. His father simply placed him in the middle of the line, young house guests around him, and then distributed the other guns on the edges. This is not endearing.

Northumberland is the most marvellous sporting county in England, but I have never forgotten shooting there ten years ago with a man who had taken a couple of days and treated the rest of the guns like the peasants at Crecy, saying 'I'm going to stand *here*' – *here* being the middle of the line – 'The rest of you can arrange yourselves over *there* and over *there*.' Jolly cross our host became, too, if the wind caused the cream of the birds to fly over other people. I don't think anyone but himself shot there twice.

A day's stalking in the West of Scotland ranks high in my own list of blighted occasions. We had taken a famous forest, which had lately changed hands several times, much unsettling the staff. The stalkers were not a happy group of men, which did not make for a happy holiday on the hill for the rifles. By our last day, for all the marvellous beauty of the place, we were impatient to be gone. With Johnny, one of the stalkers, and a young teenage pony boy, I drove in the jeep four miles up the lonely track past the loch, to the foot of the hill. Then we climbed hard for a couple of hours, until, at last, we gained a sight of deer. I shot a stag. The boy was delegated to drag it down the hill to the jeep, while we worked on along the ridge. Johnny told Billy, the young lad, to drive the jeep a mile or two down the track and then wait for us. 'Do you think he's up to driving?' I asked doubtfully, for Billy was both very young and more than a little nervous. 'Anyone can drive a Suzuki,' said Johnny.

Three hours later, after much walking and crawling and climbing, we got another beast. A beautiful Royal stood stock still for ten seconds after the shot, and I held it in my sights with an ignoble pang of yearning. Johnny laughed, 'You shoot that stag and they'll have me looking for another job in the morning.' Then the stag cantered away and we set out to drag the dead beast down the hill to the track, a mile below us.

It was a long, long afternoon. The going was hard, and we had to pull up some stiff inclines and flat, rocky stretches. It was going on seven o'clock when we came in sight of the track. There was no sign of the Suzuki. Then, through the glasses, I glimpsed it a mile uphill. 'I'm afraid it looks as if it's ditched, Johnny.' Glumly, we pulled the stag the last quarter mile, then walked to the irretrievably bogged and abandoned vehicle. 'Thank God the boy's had the sense to go for help,' said Johnny. After twenty minutes waiting, I said I was not so sure – 'I'm going to walk down the track a while.' Half a mile on, I found Billy, the lad, sitting miserably on a rock, nursing his shame and holding back the tears. I felt sorry for him, but not half as sorry as I felt for us. Billy had had four hours moping in which to get some help. All I needed, as the light began to fail, was an hour's march to the farm to find another vehicle, recover the stags and the jeep, then get home. I plodded into the lodge in the middle of dinner, any pleasure in the beasts dispelled. I was simply so tired and fed up that I stumped off to bed.

I haven't shot a stag since, come to think of it. The dragging business lacks charm. But then again, perhaps it is all these little mishaps that make the good days, the great days, feel so great.

BACK-END DAY

'AAARIGHT! LET'S GET on wi it!' The irresistible Scots inflexions of Morris, our keeper, break up the knot of beaters on the drive, who file away into the laurels to start the long beat past the big house and the water-tower, through the covert a quarter mile forward to the release pen. I am in my favourite position, walking gun on the drive twenty yards back from the line of tapping sticks, Tweedie walking tense as a cocked flintlock at my heel. At last, in these dying days of the season, we have a decent frost whitening the grass and decking the skeletons of the trees and a steel-blue sky overhead.

A protracted cry of 'For-ward!' from the laurels is immediately corrected to 'Baaackkk!' A fast cock-pheasant carves a diagonal above the drive behind me, heading for the wood-yard. I loose an ineffectual barrel at it. With those snap shots, there is no margin of error. A hundred yards ahead of me, a couple of hens slip low out of the side, unshot at. It doesn't matter. We'll catch them in the afternoon. There is a quick, distant barrage from the forward guns. A bird or two has begun to show at their end.

A wood-pigeon flits through the trees. Both the next walker and myself take a punt at it and the bird flutters out of the sky. I am always dismayed by those shoots where guns in the line are too proud – or too reluctant to risk failure – to take a shot at pigeons, jays, magpies overhead. Pigeons are much harder targets than pheasants and the man who hits them consistently can hit anything.

As we cross the track above the water-tower, the beaters re-group and Morris gives a whistle to start them down the hill. Another cock gets up with a fine cackle of protest, and flies back over the beaters, missed by me. It wasn't very high, but it was pretty wide and, especially at a small shoot, I think it is fair enough to take a shot at a tricky bird, even if it isn't up in the clouds. Apart from anything else, it gives Kevin and Phil and the rest of the beating line something to smirk villainously about when they see me miss it. We, in our turn, start moaning about the standard of beating, now that the day of the beaters' shoot is so close. We claim that their minds are on their own future bag, not on our present one.

I halt on the rubbish dump while the beaters press on through the pen, and take a few birds going back. The pleasure is great, now, in late January, seeing birds flying seriously at last. All of us have been frustrated by those still, damp days in November and December, when pheasants really did not want to get up and, correspondingly, guns did not really want to shoot them. There is a clatter of gunfire from all around the wood now. By the time the whistle goes, there must be more than twenty pheasants dead, which is a fair number for us at this time of year. Morris marches up, clutching a brace of birds and looking aggrieved. 'What happened out in the field, then?' he demands. 'The bogger out there must have fired twenty cartridges and nothing to pick up. And you weren't doing so good yourself.' 'Come on, Morris,' I say, 'we can't all be Lord de Grey. Anyway, what about that bloody spaniel of yours running fifty yards ahead of the line all the way through the wood?' Morris' face breaks into his charming, I've-got-you-but-you've-got-me grin. 'Ah well, there was a few birds there, wasn't there?'

We cluster around the Land Rover for the customary ten-minute comfort stop, at which a bullshot of my manufacture is administered. A few years ago, its ingredients included two bottles of vodka. This has since been reduced to one, as the guns have grown older and more infirm. The dilution has markedly improved the subsequent shooting and probably made us all less liable to charges of being drunk in charge of a shotgun. There is no shooting drink better than a bullshot on a cold morning, except possibly Berry Bros's incomparable King's Ginger. Over the years, we all get in the habit of repeating ourselves. It is about now every shooting day that one of our number, nursing his second mug, announces that this is the best drive of the day other than lunch.

Beating the long belt of trees beside the road, it is a pleasure to see four or five birds soar forward, which would not disgrace any shoot. Bang bang, bang, bang. About half fall down. Was it Lord Walsingham or Lord Ripon who said that, for a man to call himself a good shot, he must be able to bring down three in five of the targets he shoots at, under any conditions? I know a few guns who achieve this sort of consistency, but they are firing ten to fifteen thousand cartridges a year. The rest of us have our good days and our bad. Several times recently, I killed a pheasant for every two cartridges. But one afternoon, a friend suggested that we take our sons to walk round a thick covert on his land. Without going into the grisly details, by tea-time I had fired 13 cartridges and shot just two woodcock. I could see the perfect cartoon caption in an imaginary bubble hovering above my companion's head as we walked home – 'They say Hastings is keen on his shooting, but he doesn't look much of a shot to me!'

Well, this was a disappointing drive. We walked through a spinney, clear-felled a couple of years ago, and since replanted and overgrown with brambles – a bad place for man and dog. Fifteen minutes stumbling and shoving yielded just three pheasants: two got away too low for a shot even from me in my most ruthless mood. One was missed, climbing away high and wide towards the park. For those of us walking, the shortage of birds is less frustrating than for the forward guns, who have to stand a hundred yards apart to cover the ground here. Hanging about on a peg during a blank drive is irritating in a way that walking a field or spinney is not. But we are a pretty relaxed lot – we only expect sixty or seventy pheasants at the end of the day, and we're well on the way to making those.

The next drive, The Sewer, always produces a few birds and today is no exception. Most of them climb steep and back. The rest slip out over the farm buildings, barely barn high, into the next spinney. This is where it is such an advantage to be one of the home team and such a liability to be a stranger. The home team know exactly what the birds will do and where it is safe to shoot them between the grain drier and the pigsty. The visitor is hesitating, unsure whether he is expected to drop pheasants on the roof of the dutch barn (he is), or whether that bird going hard along the field below the track is meant to be shot at, and where (between the hedge and the ditch, yes it is).

The last yards of the drive bring the beating dogs' yells and yelps and shouts at each other to a crescendo. One of them is glimpsed streaking out of the cover, across the track and into the next wood (which, thank heavens, we're not doing today) in hot pursuit of a pheasant forty feet above its nose. Everybody cheers, then the whistle goes. I apologise to the gun I placed on a corner where pheasants always fly and on this occasion did not. I ought to know better than to promise any visitor that he is in the hot spot. I do, however, tell friends whom I invite to shoot, roughly how many pheasants we hope to get in the day because I don't want them to drive miles into the East Midlands cherishing hopes that will not be fulfilled. 'Couldn't get the boggers out,' said Morris succinctly, as we walk to the last drive in the failing light – 'You need more bloody beaters in there.'

The afternoon cold is starting to grip. Two Huskies and a Barbour do not seem too many. I direct the guns to their places. Although we draw for numbers, we do not put out pegs. This is partly so that I can adjust peoples' positions in the light of wind and conditions and partly because pegs can seem pompous at a small shoot. Also, of course, they would represent more work for Morris and his daughter, Marjorie, who do more than enough for us already.

We plunge once more into a belt of laurels, this time between the village and the big house garden. Here, we are almost totally dependent on the dogs to find the pheasants, although my brother-in-law was once enchanted by the spectacle of Morris lying prone on the ground beneath the bushes, in an effort to spy birds. A cry of 'Baaccck!', and again, 'Baaaccckkk!' from the beaters as two cocks in succession turn away over the trees and are pulled down in fine style by a gun on the village green. One more hen over me, and dropped, before the final whistle. Then we are gathering ourselves up at the cars before going in for tea. It is all over for another year.

As usual, it seems only yesterday that Morris and I were looking at the poults in the pens in October and wondering when they would get themselves some proper tails. Even Morris might be persuaded to admit that, in the end, it's been a pretty good season and he is pleased with the number we have shot. Now, let's start counting the days until we can get at the salmon again.

A FUTURE FOR FIELD SPORTS

TEN YEARS AGO, I was one of many followers of field sports fearful for their future. Before long, it seemed likely we should have a government that would legislate against them. Today, the prospect – let us be honest and say the threat – of a Labour administration has receded. Disreputable behaviour and fearsome factional infighting among the anti-field sports groups have diminished their credibility even among those newspapers that consistently give unfavourable publicity to fox-hunting and shooting. The odds in favour of field sports have improved.

The debate, however, will never go away. A great many people, most of them living in cities, find the notion of hunting birds or animals intrinsically repugnant. I used to

nurse a fantasy that, one day, I would make the definitive
television film about field sports, convincing critics once and
for all of their importance in managing the countryside. I no
longer believe this is possible. The spectacle of upmarket
sportsmen with upmarket accents pursuing wildlife will
always seem unattractive to many modern citizens, especially
those with no personal experience of the countryside. Driven
game-shooting, in particular, does not look sympathetic on
film, with wounded birds fluttering about behind the guns,
dogs pursuing broken-winged pheasants, overweight businessmen being ferried to their pegs by Range Rover to have
overweight pheasants driven over their heads at low level.

The fox-hunters, of course, will always be in the front line.
Their sport is conducted in full public view. They arouse a
hostility among the opponents of field sports that is driven
much more strongly by social antipathy towards those who do
the hunting, than by real interest in the welfare of foxes
whose numbers are increasing. Yet the fox-hunters themselves
make less than the best of their own case. They argue that the
justification for their sport rests upon the need for controlling
foxes. In reality, of course, there are far more foxes in countries where they are hunted than in those where they are
not. In non-hunting areas, they are ruthlessly controlled. In
the Shires, they are preserved with cheerful disregard for the
interests of chickens and other non-combatants. It would
serve hunting well, I believe, if its supporters focussed upon
their role in *preserving* the fox population, as well as *controlling*
it. The argument sometimes advanced by fox-hunters fighting
their corner on television or in the press, that they are perform-
ing a necessary public service by killing foxes, has never
carried much conviction. They would sound far more plaus-
ible if they declared proudly that they are continuing a fine
English tradition that contributes to the sense of community
and the balance of nature in the countryside.

The greatest threat to shooting must come from the new
obsession with big bags and the growth of commercial shoots
that seek to offer the opportunity to kill pheasants and partridges on much the same terms as a golf club offers members
a round: birds are presented under rigidly controlled, artificial

conditions. Any idea of wild sport or physical exertion (even by the wretched pheasants) is dispelled. There is a story of an English guest gun, invited to a French shoot. He was caught in a traffic jam on the autoroute and arrived an hour late. He was astonished to find his fellow guns still waiting patiently at the rendezvous. His host brushed aside his excuses. 'There is nothing to apologize for, *m'sieur*,' said the intrepid French shooter dismissively, gesturing towards a large lorry rolling up the drive, 'The birds were caught in the same jam. See, here they are now.'

A year or two ago, I was a guest at a tycoons' shoot on a 2,000 acre island amid one of the North American great lakes. The first surprise of the morning was to meet the dogs, each of which wore an electronic collar and aerial. Were they radio-controlled, ho, ho, I asked? The handlers showed their scorn for my ignorance, 'You never seen shockers before? If the dog runs in, you give it a quick charge.' The line of guns walked through the woods, past vast pens housing thousands of hysterical birds awaiting the call to duty. The pheasants we shot that morning had been released just an hour before. Most of the partridges were literally kicked into the air by the dog handlers, from beneath the rocks where they crouched while the pointers marked them. Even some of the local guests declined to raise a gun to shoot them. The day was a frightening example of what field sports can become in their most corrupted form.

Game-shooting in Britain has not, mercifully, plumbed the depths that it has attained in the United States and on the Continent, with birds released from their cages immediately before being shot. But there are strong grounds for fearing the evolving trend towards commercial shoots. These lack the sense of being a traditional part of country life, involving local people. They offer none of the uncertainty which is so important to sport, that makes the occasional blank drive, the empty-handed return from the river, as much part of a sporting year as the big day, the basketful of trout.

Ten years ago, it was widely agreed among British shooters that the Edwardians' enthusiasm for big bags had been incorrigibly vulgar and its absence was unregretted by their modern successors. Today, however, the age of the 'big shots' threatens to return, financed by businessmen perfectly willing to spend £10,000 or £15,000 a day to entertain their friends in a fashion that they think will impress them. When the British public begins to notice what is going on, as it surely will, then all our sporting interests will be at risk. On the continent, legislation has already been passed in one country and is threatened in several more to prohibit the shooting of birds for a specified period after their rearing and release. The pressure for similar legislation in Britain will grow, enabling those hostile to field sports to make disturbing inroads, if the new commercial shoots continue to develop along present lines.

This is especially sad, when so many sportsmen are passionately devoted to the wider cause of conservation. Shooters and fishers and fox-hunters may justly claim that they were taking The Environment seriously long before organisations such as Greenpeace and Friends of the Earth were thought of. The Game Conservancy has a research record second to none, in studying the habitat of British wildlife and considering means by which species survival can be improved. Almost all shooters take the view that they will kill only birds and beasts that are plentiful. Wild partridges are cherished and very selectively shot, wherever they are still found.

The Conservancy is constantly monitoring the balance of wildlife, and most field sportsmen closely heed its views. It was the Game Conservancy which recently conducted important research on the impact of releasing chukar partridges for shooting. When Dr Dick Potts and his team found not only that chukars do not themselves breed in the wild, but also that their presence has an adverse impact on wild partridge breeding, it was immediately agreed that chukar releases should cease. No sportsman wants to be party to any practice inimical to countryside management and conservation.

There remain a few areas of Britain where hares are a scourge. But on many shoots nowadays they are shot sparingly or not at all because modern agricultural practice has diminished the numbers.

Statistics suggest that woodcock numbers are increasing, yet there is a growing reluctance among British sportsmen to raise a gun to these most charming of birds because of dismay at the slaughter inflicted upon them on the Continent.

It is a great pity that the public was never convincingly told of the role of the field sports organisations in persuading the otter-hunts to abandon their activities as soon as it was plain that otters were a threatened species. It was true that the damage done to otters by hunting was negligible – loss of habitat was the key problem, coupled with river pollution, above all by the drug Dealdrin used in sheep dipping – but no field sportsman wanted to go on pursuing otters when it became clear that their numbers were in serious decline. It was a classic example of the poor public relations of field sports, that the 'antis' were able to project the end of otter-hunting as a triumph for their lobby, when, in reality, it was the leaders of the British Field Sports Society who persuaded the otter-hunters that they should disband or transfer their attentions to the genuine menace of wild mink.

European abuses now pose a serious threat to British sport. There is such dismay about the reckless massacre of birds conducted by Italian, Greek and French gunmen – sportsmen seems an inappropriate description – that there is a growing threat of intervention against *all* hunting by the EEC in Brussels. There is an important job of education to be done here by British ministers – to make Brussels understand the critical difference between the anarchistic approach to sport in some EEC countries compared with the care with which shooting and wildlife management are conducted in Britain.

The hostile publicity towards field sports generated by abuses, whether in Britain or abroad, however, makes it all the more important that sportsmen in Britain should grant as few hostages to fortune as possible. That is to say, every episode in which people are discovered conducting illegal badger digs or killing hunted foxes in the midst of populated areas, does disproportionate damage to the wider cause of sport. The principal fields sports organisations often seem reluctant to take the initiative in condemning those responsible. The MFHA, for instance, almost invariably supports in public the behaviour of members who find themselves battered by hostile publicity. But when masters of hounds or shooters or fishers have committed acts that damage the image of field sports, it seems only right that field sports bodies should make it clear that their behaviour is unacceptable. For instance, while some of us believe that it is right for man to hunt, others do not. Surely the lay public is entitled not to be confronted at close quarters by the spectacle of hounds killing a quarry. I appreciate the great practical difficulties of controlling hounds when they are running. But the publicity that follows a hunting incident in mid village, of the kind that occurs once or twice every season, converts a steady stream of ordinary people from neutrals into 'antis'. If we are not seen to keep our own house in order, the danger of others doing it for us increases. Of course it is true that neither BFSS, nor BASC, nor the MFHA has any statutory authority to impose penalties upon individuals. But it seems important that nobody should be left in doubt of these bodies' opinions about sporting malpractices. At present, they are most often seen in a defensive role, fending off public criticism. Unlike BFSS and BASC, the MFHA is an administrative body whose ultimate sanction – expulsion – would carry considerable power, if the Association wished to use it, or if it introduced a lesser penalty of suspension. As it is, only very infrequent 'censures' have been issued. Some thoughtful fox-hunters feel that the MFHA sees its role much more as a Masters' trades union than as a body creating standards and imposing them on the sport.

Many of us would like to see the field sports organisations giving a strong public lead about what sort of conduct is, and is not, acceptable. Wilson Stephens, former editor of *The Field*, wrote a powerful and sensible article in that magazine in January 1989, condemning commercial shoots and urging that field sports organisations take a lead in creating and sustaining a code. BFSS and BASC could gain credit for an important contribution if they declare publicly and prominently what are, and are not, acceptable limits on pheasant/ acreage densities and release/shooting dates. If, instead, they wait for a torrid newspaper 'exposé', growing public concern and eventual ministerial action, field sportsmen will be left merely to make limp excuses after the event. Even if BASC and B F S S lack statutory powers, it would make a substantial impact on many shooters if they were formally warned that, by participating in the more deplorable commercial shoots, they are breaking every principle of sport, conservation and the countryside. Peer pressure can be effective.

In a less serious vein, the image of fox-hunting is injured by followers holding up traffic without apology, or hacking to the meet two or three abreast with a queue of cars behind. Only a small minority of fox-hunters do this. But their thoughtlessness generates lasting rage and hostility. Both Masters and field sports organisations issue general warnings against this sort of behaviour. But one seldom hears of hunt followers being ticked off on the spot, far less sent home, for transgression. More serious still, perhaps, is the problem of hunts continuing to meet in heavy winter weather, churning up the land in a fashion very unwelcome to farmers. Many fox-hunters express fears that the reluctance of farmers to allow them access poses a much more immediate threat to hunting than demonstrators and saboteurs. Hunts are also increasingly restricted, even in the Shires, by the great expansion of leased shooting. Those who are paying farmers large sums of money for shooting rights naturally expect first call on the land, and more and more Masters find their dates and meets restricted by shooting timetables. There is no obvious remedy to this when farmers need shooting income more than ever before, and hunting brings in nothing. However, with a little goodwill, hunts and shoots in the same country should surely be able to fix dates to suit both.

It would be wrong, of course, to imply that fox-hunters behave any worse than the rest of us. They would point out, quite rightly, that other sports have their own embarrassments. Which of us, hand on heart, can deny shooting a low pheasant or two last season? What about the anglers and lead shot and carelessly discarded nylon? At regular intervals, shotgun accidents are reported with relish in the papers and tabloid editorials question whether guns should be allowed in private houses. Unjust though the fox-hunters' share of the burden may be, they are the most conspicuous field sportsmen and so bear the brunt of public dismay. The rest of us are customarily able to remain out of sight in the woods or on the riverbank. It is irrational that the public should become so exercised about the sufferings of furry foxes or over-populated seals while remaining indifferent to the silent agonies of fish. But that is the way it is, and probably always will be. Rationality does not come into the matter.

It is also much easier to make the case for fox-hunting in counties where hunts retain strong roots in the local community. That long-suffering Master of the West Percy and admirable country writer, Willy Poole, has endured my company with his hounds on a few occasions, when even my bumpy horsemanship has not marred the pleasure of the day. In the hills of Northumberland, every farmer is committed to keeping the foxes off his lambs and the hunt's determination to kill them is not in doubt. One morning with Willy, I saw five foxes killed. Some Shire packs would be glad to manage that in a fortnight. More to the point, the West Percy hunt followers are delightful local Northumbrians, and many of them are riding across their own land. No one can level the charge that these are 'city swells out to cut a dash'. It might be good for fox-hunting if more was heard of hunts, such as the West Percy, that still retain a clear relationship with the tradition and purpose of the sport – even if they are not hunting a great jumping country – and a little less publicity fell upon the fashionable Shire packs, marvellous 'goers' though some of them are.

The broadening of the 'antis' assaults to embrace fishing has alerted supporters of the most overwhelmingly popular field sport to the political dangers. Shooters, fishers and hunters find it difficult to make common cause, but progress is being made.

The wider the social sweep that field sports embrace, the better their chances of survival. The public case for hunting and shooting is too often put by men who – through no fault of their own, but mere accident of accent and background – are least likely to command public sympathy. It is the hunting farmers, the shooting footballers and fishing showbusiness stars – the Charltons and Bothams and Corbetts – who are likely to make the most sympathetic impression in television debate. We need to work closely with the growing host of clay-shooters, many of whom become game-shooters as soon as they can find the land and opportunity. The immense political power wielded by the American sporting lobbies shows the way we must surely go to mobilise sporting opinion effectively in this country.

Masters and shoot captains should insist that all those who hunt or shoot with them belong to one or other field sports organisation. The Ministry of Agriculture should be explaining to the public that, as farm incomes are squeezed, farmers must be allowed to earn money from field sports, if they are to be able to manage their land for the common good. Shooting will never provide a farm income substitute, but it can be a useful supplement on the margin, likely to become more popular with the introduction of 'set aside'. There is a risk here, as elsewhere in the shooting field, that some farmers will overdo it and go all out for big numbers and big income. Everything possible must be done to discourage this development.

In a wider sense, there is an immense job to be done, of making the public understand the direct link between field sports and conservation, in a fashion that, at present, only the Game Conservancy seriously undertakes. Very few town dwellers perceive, for instance, that it is the fact that most land and sporting rights in Britain are in private hands which ensures that our countryside and wildlife are incomparably better managed than in those parts of Europe where a free for all prevails. Frankly, we need a much more hard-nosed approach.

One significant caution may also be entered: it seems unwise for field sports to become entangled with the interests of the gun collectors and 'survival' enthusiasts. During the 1988 debate on the new Firearms Act – an unwelcome piece of legislation – the gun enthusiasts and the field sports bodies in some measure made common cause. I think this weakened the field sports case. Most game-shooters feel as doubtful as the general public about allowing civilians in peace-time to possess automatic weapons. The argument that civilians must maintain the historic right and opportunity to practise with contemporary military small arms has become anachronistic as these become more lethal and specialised. The new, fully-automatic SA80 seems a quite unsuitable weapon for private possession. What if the next generation of army rifle is a laser weapon? Degrees of lethality *do* matter. The old Lee-Enfield was interchangeable as a sporting and military weapon. The SA80 is designed explicitly to kill people, and has no other possible application. It would scarcely be at home in the hands of a stalker. It seems important to place as wide a political distance as possible between the suburban 'survival' enthusiast, who likes to spend his weekends fantasising on the range with an assault rifle, dressed in combat fatigues, and the sporting gun or clay-shooter.

The future of field sports will surely hinge upon how well they are seen to be conducted by the public at large, however inappropriate we may think some of the factors that influence opinion are. It is dismaying that so little support today comes from the Conservative Party. I have always believed that, when so much of the party's cash is contributed by supporters of field sports, it would do no harm periodically to remind ministers of their political debts. This is likely to be more effective than a mere appeal to traditional political loyalties, when it is recalled that the Prime Minister herself abstained on the bill to ban hare-coursing, when this was last voted upon in the House of Commons. Some Tory MPs are explicitly hostile to field sports. Most modern suburban Conservative ministers and MPs see votes to be lost in assertive support for field sports and none to be won. They yearn for political silence on the issue. I heard a vivid account recently of the selection process for a new Tory candidate in a rural constituency. Among several hundred applicants, most professed indifference or even hostility to field sports. Several, fumbling to say the right thing, kept referring to 'blood sports'. One man, sensing himself losing the struggle and clutching at straws said hopefully, 'Well, you might like to know I'm a great chum of old Evelyn Hayes just over the county boundary. Did you hear that he'd shot 150 foxes on his own land last year?' This unsuccessful applicant was a rarity among modern Tory politicians, in acknowledging any acquaintance with the land at all.

It is a measure of the field sports organisations' political apprehension, that they are unwilling to see any legislation on shooting or fishing reach the floor of the Commons. Many people, for instance, would like to see a change in the shooting seasons, to match the historic shift in the weather pattern – 1 November to 15 February would be widely approved dates for the pheasant season, for instance. The field sports bodies, however, are unwilling to encourage any measure that would bring the matter before Parliament lest it open Pandora's box to expose a host of other, hostile votes. This seems a pity. Legislation on field sports needs periodic updating to keep pace with changing circumstances, as much as any other aspect of life. If a government of the present complexion cannot be trusted to introduce sensible amendments to sporting law from time to time, then it is hard to see any future administration proving more sympathetic.

Yet, if there are sometimes grounds for dismay about the treatment of field sports by politicians and the media, there also seem overriding reasons for optimism. We have emerged from a historic period of more than thirty years in which 'the nanny state' dominated Britain. Successive governments of every hue took it upon themselves to tell the public what was good for it – industrially, financially, socially. The consequences were disastrous. Since 1979, the public has undergone a profound change of heart, based on an understanding of the pass to which the nation had been brought by collectivist policies. In the new climate of freedom, of belief in individual choice, the right of hundreds of thousands of people to pursue their chosen sport should not be in doubt. Hunting, shooting and fishing grow in popularity each year. It would be remarkable if even a successor government to that of Mrs Thatcher chose to legislate against field sports, unless the political mood of the nation is once more turned on its head.

Most of my generation grew up resigned to living in a society in permanent decline, in which the lot of the middle classes became relatively worse with each decade. Yet, today, the position has been transformed. The future for capitalism in Britain has not seemed so bright, arguably, since 1914. It is unlikely that any but a socialist government will legislate against field sports, *if these are seen to be sensibly conducted, in keeping with the demands and the spirit of conservation.* Only new abuses of field sports, I believe, can create the conditions now to imperil them, unless the country suffers a serious economic collapse, which revives the threat of a socialist government. I feel more confident than for many years, that hunting, shooting and fishing will continue.

A hundred years from now, a writer of another generation may pick up a tattered copy of this book in a second-hand shop, just as I have picked up so many Victorian and Edwardian sporting memoirs. I should like to imagine him going off to write another book like this one, about the hunting, shooting and fishing of his own century. I hope he will be as lucky in his happiness, as happy in his luck with them, as I have been.

INDEX